"Ms. Ferrarella...holds reader interest at fever pitch."

—Romantic Times Magazine

* * *

Any way Ben looked at it, the woman he'd just left behind didn't strike him as someone who would break the law even in a minor way, much less kidnap a child.

Yet she'd stolen someone else's name and created a fictitious life around it.

And then there was the boy, the boy who called her Mommy with no hesitation whatsoever, as if he'd always done so.

What was Ben supposed to believe?

Was he letting his feelings for Gina color his judgment or refine it? At this point, he wasn't sure of anything.

Except that he wanted to make love with her in the worst way....

Dear Reader,

Welcome to my latest installment of ChildFinders, Inc. Since I'm an overprotective mother, it's always been my recurring nightmare that I've "misplaced" my children who, when they were younger, enjoyed hiding in department store clothes racks and the like just long enough to give me a heart attack. Losing your kids is a very real fear that most mothers live with. The newspapers, sadly, are full of kidnapping stories that are not resolved happily. I thought it might be nice to create a safe haven where one could go and have potentially heinous situations brought to a happy ending. The people at ChildFinders, Inc. never met a case they couldn't solve.

Each time I finish writing a ChildFinders, Inc. book I think to myself, "That's it. I've exhausted all the possibilities for this kind of a case." And then, after a while, I get this itch to do one more, to find just another twist so that the story is interesting enough to demand its own space, its own book. And so it was with Ben's story. Ben Underwood appeared in the first ChildFinders, Inc. story as a policeman on the force, newly divorced and feeling his way around. He sparked my interest, and I threaded him through the second and third stories. By the time I was into my fourth story, dealing with Chad Andreini, Ben was part of the agency and comfortable with his single life. But he was a family man at heart, and I just had to find him a family worthy of the kind of caring man Ben actually was. I think I succeeded when I put him on this newest case. I hope you agree. Once again, I thank you for revisiting me, and from the bottom of my heart I wish you love.

Love,

Marie Ferrarella

AN UNCOMMON HERO

MARIE FERRARELLA

ChildFinders, Inc.

Silhouette® Books

Published by Silhouette Books
America's Publisher of Contemporary Romance

SILHOUETTE BOOKS

CHILDFINDERS, INC.: AN UNCOMMON HERO

ISBN 0-373-48424-0

This edition published by arrangement with Harlequin Books S.A.

Visit Silhouette at www.eHarlequin.com

Printed in U.S.A.

Also available from Silhouette Books
by Marie Ferrarella

CHILDFINDERS, INC.

Hero for Hire
Silhouette Intimate Moments #1042
November 2000

A Hero in Her Eyes
Silhouette Intimate Moments #1059
February 2001

Coming soon

Marie Ferrarella
celebrates her 100th Silhouette title.
Savor every romantic moment!

Rough Around the Edges
Silhouette Romance #1505
March 2001

Be sure to look for more Marie Ferrarella titles
in your local stores, or contact our
Silhouette Reader Service Center
U.S.A.: 3010 Walden Avenue,
P.O. Box 1325, Buffalo, NY 14269
Canada: P.O. Box 609,
Fort Erie, Ontario L2A 5X3.

To
S. Cloud Hsueh, Ph.D.
For guidance and warmth
over and above
the call of duty

Prologue

She wasn't going to cry, she wasn't.

There was no time to waste on tears. No time for anything. Only the hasty gathering of the very most important things. The things she couldn't leave behind along with everything else.

With the rest of her life.

She should have seen this coming, Gloria upbraided herself, tossing essentials into the suitcase that lay open on her bed. It wasn't as if this had suddenly materialized out of the blue. There had been signs. Signs she'd refused to acknowledge because things like this only happened in the movies. Or to people she read about in the newspaper. They didn't happen to people she knew. They didn't happen to her.

Except that now they were.

She glanced over at the small boy lying in the center of her bed, curled up right next to the suitcase. Poor baby, he'd dozed off and on the entire time she'd dressed him, waking just enough to ask her if he was having a dream. She'd told him yes.

It was better this way. She wouldn't have to field the tearful questions until later.

Maybe later, she could come up with answers that he could accept. Right now, she couldn't even come up with any that she could accept.

Regardless, she knew she had to hurry. If Stephen came looking for her here before she could get away, it would be too late.

She flipped the suitcase lid closed, pushing down on the locks. She prayed she knew what she was doing.

It was time to go.

Chapter 1

"You can name your own price, just find my son."

Ben Underwood studied the well-dressed man sitting in front of his desk. There was a time when the words *name your own price* would have been extremely tempting to him. A time, a little more than a decade ago, when he had stood at the crossroads of his life, wondering whether or not to take the easy road, the road his cousin and best friend, Vinnie, was taking. Or to take the road that, for the most part, followed a straight-and-narrow path.

It had been more of a mental wrestling match than he would have liked to admit now, but finally, Ben, in deference to his conscience and his mother and three sisters, had chosen the latter road. Only to "un-choose" it when he and the Bedford Police Department had come to a parting of the ways because of his untamable, independent methods. He'd gone from the department straight to ChildFinders, Inc. without so much as a breather and without looking back. He'd never regretted it.

It had been a very long time since money had had any sort of allure for him beyond providing for the basic creature comforts. Principles counted for so much more and were, in the end, longer-lasting.

Besides, Ben thought, he had a tendency to let money pass through his hands if he had it. He'd always been an easy touch.

He figured he'd better set this newest client, a man who seemed to fill up the room with his presence and who Megan Andreini, one of the agency's partners, would have undoubtedly referred to as a silver fox, straight.

"The fee depends on the length of time and expense it takes to locate your son, Mr. McNair." Ben smiled, comfortingly, he hoped. It wasn't that he didn't feel for these people who came into his office, quite the contrary. He just had never managed to master expressing his feelings satisfactorily. It was easier just tucking them away. "It's not determined by your net worth."

The last part wasn't strictly true, but not in any way that Stephen McNair could appreciate, Ben thought. On occasion, the agency took on cases pro bono. Cade Townsend, the original founder of the agency, didn't believe that lack of funds was any reason not to try to reunite a family with their missing child. Cade had been on the raw end of that situation, and knew the anguish of looking for a child who'd been kidnapped.

But there was no point in mentioning any of that to their newest client. McNair wasn't here to discuss the agency's policies, or its history. He had come here for the same reason everyone came to ChildFinders, Inc.—

to find his missing child. In McNair's case, it was a six-year-old blond-haired boy named Andrew.

Stephen McNair looked somewhat displeased at being lumped in with the general populace. Ben had a hunch the man had gotten accustomed to being able to buy anything he wanted, people and time included. If it were that easy, Ben mused, his son would have been back to him in minutes.

McNair's eyes narrowed a fraction. Ben felt himself being sized up. He couldn't say he liked it any. Given the circumstances, Ben decided McNair was entitled to some slack.

"Surely I'm permitted to throw a bonus into the agreement?"

"So we'll work a little faster?" Ben guessed, trying hard not to take offense.

McNair smiled triumphantly. "Exactly."

Ben shifted his lanky frame in his chair. He wasn't here to pass judgment. It was a given that the people who came into these offices were usually at their worst. It wasn't his place to like or dislike any of them. For the most part, he had to admit he felt for them and liked them. He didn't care for McNair. But that didn't matter one way or another. It was finding the boy that counted.

He couldn't help wondering if the boy would grow up to be like his father.

The man sitting before him in the six-hundred-dollar suit was about ten years older than Ben and gave new meaning to the word *polished.* The card McNair had made a point of presenting to him even before they had shaken hands identified him as Stephen W. McNair, president and CEO of IndieCorp, a fast-rising company that was, if he remembered correctly, on the cusp of a colossal merger with Mercury Electronics. The talk was that between the two giants, the semiconductor market was just about covered.

Ben rocked back in his chair, studying McNair in silence for a moment, questions occurring to him. A man like McNair could easily have a hundred agencies at his beck and call, including the FBI. Considering that kidnapping was every parent's nightmare and had become a reality for McNair, Ben couldn't help wondering what the man was doing here. Granted, ChildFinders had a heretofore unbelievable track record for solving kidnapping cases. For every closed case, there had been a happy ending. Not many places could boast a record like that. But the FBI had more manpower.

Ben leaned forward. "If you don't mind my asking, why haven't you gone to the police?"

There was a flash of annoyance in Stephen McNair's piercing blue eyes, but it was gone so quickly, Ben thought he might have imagined it. McNair looked the soul of cooperation as he answered, "Perhaps you're aware of the merger Indie is about to make with Mercury?"

Ben had found he learned a great deal when he pretended to be ignorant of things. "I don't keep up with the financial section of the newspaper, Mr. McNair. In my line of work, there's not much time for things that aren't directly relevant to the cases I'm working on."

A slight frown twitched McNair's lips before he proceeded to enlighten Ben. "Yes, well, my company is at a crucial stage of its development right now. We're to merge with Mercury Electronics. Any hint of scandal and the entire negotiations could be placed in jeopardy."

"I don't know the kind of people you're dealing

with, Mr. McNair, but I don't think they'd consider the kidnapping of a child as scandalous.''

In response, Stephen McNair merely shook his head. ''It's not the kidnapping they'd consider scandalous, it's the circumstances surrounding it.''

Now they were getting somewhere, Ben thought. He took out the tape recorder that was part of each office's furnishings and placed it on the desk beside him.

''Tell me about the circumstances.'' He pressed the red button down on the recorder and the tape began to whir softly.

McNair froze. He glared at the small rectangle on the desk as if it were an offending lower life-form. ''Turn that off.'' The three terse words were not a request. They were an order.

Despite his affable demeanor, Ben didn't respond well to being ordered around. That had been one of the reasons he and the Bedford Police Department hadn't remained on intimate terms. He made no move to comply with McNair's order. ''Sorry, company policy.''

''I said turn it off.'' Rather than wait, McNair leaned over and switched off the recorder himself. He met Ben's barely veiled annoyed look with a passionate verbal volley. ''I won't be recorded. I—'' He lowered his voice as he searched for the right words. ''This is very delicate, Mr. Underwood. Haven't you ever been in a delicate situation you didn't want broadcast?''

''This doesn't get broadcast, Mr. McNair.'' He indicated the tape recorder. ''The only reason the initial interview is taped is to help us go over the case. Sometimes things are said that are forgotten later. Other times, playing the tape back might inadvertently remind you of a detail or event you forgot to mention.''

McNair remained unmovable. ''I have a photographic

memory, Mr. Underwood. I assure you I do not forget anything.'' He paused, then added a bit more softly, ''Except, perhaps, discretion.'' His eyes met Ben's. ''But I am paying dearly for my error now.''

Ben made a judgment call. He left the tape recorder off. Curiosity had gotten the better of him. His mother had always warned him it would be his undoing.

''All right, we'll leave it off for the time being. Now, do you have any idea who might have kidnapped your son?''

''Any idea who kidnapped my son?'' McNair parroted the question incredulously. ''Of course I have an idea who kidnapped my son. I know exactly who's responsible. Gloria Prescott kidnapped my son.''

''Gloria Prescott,'' Ben repeated, and McNair nodded adamantly. It was a toss-up whether to ask first who the woman was or why she would abduct his son. Ben went with the more important of the two. ''And do you have any idea why she would kidnap your son?''

McNair passed his hand slowly over his face, a man struggling with his secrets, buying himself a tiny fragment of time in which to compose himself and frame his answer.

''She kidnapped Andrew to get back at me. She is—was,'' McNair said, correcting himself, ''Andrew's nanny.'' Just for an instant, his eyes grew soft, as if he were visualizing her. ''She's quite a stunning young woman.'' The laugh that followed was self-mocking. ''Too young for me, really.''

Mentally, Ben filled in the blanks. He had heard it often enough before. Older man, younger woman. The combination rarely yielded satisfactory results. According to his mother, that was why his own father had left. In pursuit of youth. In this case, youth had a name.

Claudia Gershon. Ben had a half brother named Jason who was half his age. For his father, things had worked out. Obviously, for McNair it hadn't.

"Go on," he encouraged when McNair continued to remain silent.

The older man shrugged. "You've heard it before, I'm sure. Older man trying to hang on to his youth, beautiful young woman bringing it to him in a gift-wrapped box." There was a faraway look in his eyes as he spoke.

The man had gotten it bad, Ben thought. He thought of his own mother. "And how did Mrs. McNair feel about you hanging on to your youth? Or Gloria's," he amended wryly.

McNair's eyes went flat as he regarded him. "She didn't feel anything."

"And why is that?" Ben was playing devil's advocate, but there was something a little too pat about the man sitting before him. He seemed a little too held together. Ben was used to people coming unraveled under the pressure of the crisis they were enduring. This man looked annoyed, nothing more. Fathers didn't look annoyed or inconvenienced when their sons were taken—they looked angry. Distraught, capable of mayhem themselves. On occasion, they looked lost. But not annoyed.

He wanted to get to the bottom of Stephen McNair.

"Because there is no Mrs. McNair." The annoyance deepened as McNair moved to the edge of his seat. "Look, I'm going to be perfectly frank with you. I'm rather new at this father business. Andrew is the result of a liaison I had with a young woman seven years ago. One of those flash-and-fire things. The whole thing lasted perhaps three weeks, perhaps less. I hadn't heard from her since. She died nine months ago, leaving me a letter and the boy. Both came to me via her lawyer. I had some lab tests done, DNA, that sort of thing, and the results were conclusive. Andrew was mine. Naturally, I saw him as my responsibility."

"Naturally."

McNair stopped, narrowing his eyes. "Are you mocking me?"

Ben straightened, all business. His remark had been a slip. "I'm not here to mock, Mr. McNair, or to sit in judgment. My only function is to help. I'm sorry if I gave you any other impression." He was going to have to work on his poker face, Ben thought.

"Look, I'm sorry if I don't live up to your expectations of the grieving father. It's not easy for me to show my emotions. But make no mistake about it, I am worried about my son and I want him back."

Ben nodded. "You were saying about Gloria..."

Scrubbing a well-manicured hand over his face, McNair sighed and continued. "I was completely besotted with her for several months."

Besotted. Now, there was a word he didn't run into every day, Ben thought. But somehow, coming from McNair, it seemed to fit the narrative. "What happened after several months?"

"I came to my senses. Realized that a man in my position—responsible for the livelihood of so many people—couldn't continue behaving like some smitten adolescent. I tried to let her down as gently as possible, make her see reason." McNair looked at Ben to see if he understood the awkward position he'd been in. "Unfortunately, Gloria didn't choose to be reasonable about it. I don't think she really cared about me as much as she did about the money. I think she thought I was going to marry her.''

''And you weren't.'' Ben waited for him to continue.

He shook his head. ''She wasn't wife material.'' His expression became superior. ''Gloria became very possessive, flying into jealous rages when she thought that I was seeing someone else.''

Ben was undecided whether the man thought himself to be a much-abused saint, or was only trying to present himself as one. ''And were you?''

''No.'' The response was indignant. ''And whether I was seeing someone or not is not the point.''

''No, but everything is a piece of this puzzle. In the interest of brevity, why don't you shorten the story for the time being. Why did Gloria suddenly kidnap your son? Why now, rather than last month or next week?''

''Because I officially broke off our relationship in no uncertain terms last Thursday.''

''Thursday,'' Ben echoed.

''I see why you might need a recorder,'' McNair commented impatiently. ''Yes, Thursday. I told her I couldn't have a woman stalking my every move no matter how beautiful she was.''

Ben toyed with the carved paperweight one of his sisters had made for him when she was twelve as he played with logistics in his head. ''What did she do with Andrew while she was stalking you?''

The question took McNair aback for a moment before he responded. ''She had him with her.'' He continued with his narrative, impatient to be done with it. ''Of course, I took total responsibility for the affair even though she was the one who seduced me, and I offered her quite a sizable severance package to tide her over until she found another position. After all, I wasn't heartless.''

Ben wondered if Stephen McNair actually saw himself as benevolent and blame-free. ''But that didn't fly with her.''

''No, it didn't 'fly.''' McNair wrapped his tongue around the word disdainfully. ''When I came home two nights ago from a business trip to Washington, D.C., I found that Gloria was gone and she'd taken Andrew with her.''

''Did she leave a note?''

The question caught McNair off guard. ''No.''

''Then you just assumed she'd kidnapped Andrew.''

''She was gone, he was gone, her clothes were gone. I came to the logical conclusion.'' He paused as if debating something, or hunting through the photographic memory he'd boasted of. ''And she'd threatened me earlier.''

''Threatened?'' Ben said, instantly alert. ''What kind of a threat?''

''She said she'd take Andrew away where I could never find him if I didn't marry her. That she was going to make me pay for what I 'did' to her.''

He supposed if the woman was being completely irrational, she might forget to write a note, although in his experience, writing a note would have added to the drama. Perhaps twisted the knife in a little harder. A woman making a dramatic statement wasn't apt to overlook writing a note.

But this woman hadn't. The minor point bothered Ben.

Something else was bothering him, too. Ben looked at the other man. ''And you waited almost five days before reporting this to anyone?''

It was an outright challenge and Ben half expected McNair to explode. Instead, the man looked contrite. "I was hoping that she was just angry. That she'd return him. I wanted to spare her being arrested if it was at all possible. I still do. You might have trouble understanding this because you're still young and not in my position, but I find I still have some residual feelings regarding Gloria."

For the first time, Stephen McNair seemed human to Ben. "Have you gotten in contact with her friends?"

The gesture was short, indicating a degree of helplessness that McNair looked unaccustomed to acknowledging.

"She's not from around here. As far as I know, she has no friends in the area. None that she ever went out with or even mentioned. For the most part, she stayed on the estate. She was very devoted to me and to Andrew."

Ben noted the order McNair had used. *To me and to Andrew.* But then, as the man said, he was new at being a father and hadn't had the luxury of experience to fall back on.

Sometimes all the experience and time in the world didn't help change the overall picture, Ben thought. His father had walked out on not only his mother, but on him, when he was thirteen. Being a father of four children hadn't made Jake Underwood any less the center of his own universe.

Still, whatever the order used, the word *devoted* had certain connotations. Ben was counting on them. "So you're pretty certain that she wouldn't hurt Andrew?"

There wasn't even a moment's hesitation. "Yes, I'm reasonably certain that she wouldn't do anything crazy like that. As I said, she's just doing this to get back at me."

"Are you sure there wasn't some sort of note?" Ben prodded. "Conditions she wanted met before she returned your son?"

Maybe, for his own reasons, McNair was lying about there not being a note. It did seem highly unlikely that, given the circumstances, Gloria Prescott would allow this opportunity to slip by. Kidnappings happened for a variety of reasons, the least of which was revenge. But if this was for revenge, it was running atypical to form.

"No." Exasperation peppered McNair's voice. "I suspect she was too angry to write anything. Besides, I already know her conditions. She'd want to take up where we'd left off. She wanted me to marry her."

In his experience, grasping people tended to want money, Ben thought. Or at least power. Silence was not the order of the day. He wondered again if there was something McNair was holding back. "And she hasn't attempted to get in contact with you?" Ben asked.

"No," McNair snapped. He took a deep breath, composing himself. With shaky fingers he dug into his pocket and took out a half-empty pack of cigarettes. "My one vice," he explained, holding the pack up. "Other than falling for beautiful women. Do you mind?"

Ben was surprised that the man even bothered to ask. McNair struck him as someone who did as he pleased. Ben inclined his head, taking out a small ceramic ashtray from his side drawer and placing it on the desk. He didn't smoke, but he understood the need.

"Thanks." McNair lit up and inhaled. His eyes closed for a moment, as if he were having a spiritual experience. When he opened them again, he looked calmer, more capable of continuing. "If Gloria had left a note, I would have been taking care of this myself." He glanced toward the closed door. "Is Townsend around? Maybe he...?"

It obviously rankled McNair to deal with anyone who wasn't the top man. "Cade's out of town on a case. The caseload is pretty heavy. Right now, I appear to be all you have at your disposal."

McNair wouldn't have been where he was if he wasn't good at damage control. A smile nothing short of charming creased his lips. "Sorry, didn't mean to fly off the handle that way earlier. I can usually keep my temper under wraps, it's just that this is all completely new to me. Being a father, being a kidnap victim..."

"Strictly speaking, Andrew's the kidnap victim, but don't feel bad, this kind of thing usually is new to everyone. Now, if you'll make yourself comfortable, I still have a few more questions to ask you." Ben saw the slight frown on McNair's face reemerge. "I'll try to make this as painless for you as possible."

McNair looked at his watch before answering. Ben saw the flash of a Rolex. Nothing but the best, he thought.

"All right," Stephen agreed. "But I have to be back at a meeting in an hour."

He'd never run into a kidnap victim's father who'd set a time limit before. Took all kinds, Ben supposed. "You'll be back sooner than that."

As Ben got out his pad, he wondered just when Stephen McNair had found the time to even father a child.

She frowned slightly as she settled in. She wasn't used to lying and this was certainly lying. Big time. It was going to take a great deal of practice and care on her part. One misstep and people were going to begin suspecting that something wasn't right.

And once suspicions were aroused…

She didn't want to go there. There was far too much at stake for her to dwell on the consequences. There was no point in thinking about losing everything, it would only paralyze her.

For a moment, she paused in the doorway, looking into the small room the little boy had taken as his own. It was remarkable how resilient he was. She could stand to learn a thing or two from him about rolling with the punches and bouncing back.

He'd thrown off the covers again. Quietly, she crept into the room, careful not to make any noise that might wake him.

Very softly, she draped the comforter around his small body. Pressing a kiss to her fingertips, she passed it ever so lightly against his cheek. He meant everything to her.

"Sweet dreams, sweet prince," she whispered before withdrawing.

She kept the door slightly ajar so she could hear him calling if he needed her. He was having those nightmares again.

She slipped into bed. It was early, but she was tired. Lately, she'd been so drained. But then, she had reason enough to be. Before she fell asleep, as she did every night now, she thanked God for a new chance. A new chance to finally, perhaps, find peace and make her life work.

Work for her and for the little boy she loved.

About to leave, Ben saw a pencil-thin ray of light slipping out from beneath the door of Eliza's office.

Savannah had mentioned that the woman had just wrapped up the case she'd been working on.

Rapping once on her door, Ben opened it and peeked in. Eliza was looking through one of the files that were spread out all over her desk and glanced in his direction. Her smile was warmth itself.

"I didn't think there'd be anyone still in the office. Don't you have a home to go to?" Ben asked.

"I could say the same to you," she replied.

He leaned against the doorjamb. "Caught a new case this afternoon." He peered at the agency's newest partner. "You feeling all right?"

"Not enough sleep lately," she confessed with a shrug. "I've been having dreams lately."

"Dreams, or *dreams?*" he asked.

They both knew what he meant by the emphasis. One of her "seeing" dreams. The ones that crept up out of the dark and wouldn't give her peace until she solved the puzzle they came from. The ones she'd been blessed, or plagued with, depending on the point of view, since she'd turned twelve. "The latter."

He looked at her with eyes that silently communicated his sympathy. "Know what it's about yet?"

She shook her head. All she knew was that there was a child somewhere who needed her. But where and who and why, she hadn't a clue and it was tormenting her.

"No, but I will. Eventually." Eliza changed the topic. "So, you didn't answer me. What are you still doing here?"

He noticed that she hadn't given him an answer, either, but he let it pass. "Gathering some background information. I'm going to be out of town for a couple of days. Let the others know when they come in tomorrow, will you?"

"Sure thing." She swung her chair around to face him. "Going somewhere good?"

He laughed. "Depends on what you think of Saratoga."

Interest highlighted her delicate face. She assumed he was talking about the tiny town up north from Bedford, California. "Why Saratoga?"

"Our main kidnapping suspect has a relative there. Only living one I can come up with at the moment. A widowed great-aunt named—" he grinned "—Sugarland Malone. Not sure if she knows where the suspect is, but it's worth a shot." Even if the great-aunt did know, she might not be willing to disclose the information, Ben thought. Blood was thicker than water and he was an outsider.

Eliza smiled. It didn't take a clairvoyant to guess what was on his mind. "If anyone can get the lady to loosen her tongue, you can."

He wondered how much of that was flattery and how much was intuition. Eliza was a genuine psychic, one whom the police had brought in on more than a few of their unsolvable cases. He'd been as skeptical of her as anyone when he'd first met Eliza, but she'd eventually made a believer out of him. "You give me too much credit."

Her smile deepened, the shy edge fading. "No, I don't."

Amused, he cocked his head. "Your psychic intuition, I take it?"

She shook her head. "More like female intuition. Some things are just self-evident." Like a man who could charm the feathers off a bird, she thought with a smile. She doubted if he knew just how persuasive those dark blue eyes of his really were. "I'll tell the others—and good hunting."

"Thanks."

That was the word for it, all right, he thought as he closed the door behind him. Hunting.

Chapter 2

The jarring noise pushed its way into his consciousness.

It was the phone, Ben realized as his brain surfaced out of a dreamless sleep. The phone was ringing. Groping for the receiver, he tried to locate and focus in on his clock.

Four-thirty.

In the morning?

He scrubbed his hand over his face, trying to pull himself together. "Hello, you'd better be an obscene phone call to make this worth my while."

"I've already offered to make it worth your while, Underwood."

The voice—cool and official—jarred loose a memory. "Mr. McNair?" Ben looked at the clock again. A hint of annoyance entered his voice. He'd come home and done further background work for his intended trip today. He'd slept for less than three hours and he liked his rest. "Do you have any idea what time it is?"

The voice on the other end of the phone grew cooler. "I always know what time it is. I'm on my way to a meeting in Seattle and will be back by this evening. What I don't know is if you've made any progress yet."

Ben sat up, annoyed now. Who the hell made phone calls at four-thirty in the morning? If he'd had any doubts about the man being a control freak, this cinched it.

"Some," Ben replied in answer to McNair's question.

"You've found her?" Excitement echoed in the receiver against Ben's ear.

Ben sighed, pulling up the comforter. Outside, the January rain was beating against his window. Telling him to go back to sleep. "No, but I might have located a relative."

"Where?"

The question echoed like a command for disclosure. Maybe it was because he was half asleep, but the tone rubbed him the wrong way. Instincts surfaced, making him just the slightest bit wary. McNair, polished CEO though he might be, was in this case a loose cannon. Loose cannons had a way of going off at precisely the worst time. Ben wasn't about to take the chance of having things blown apart by an overzealous parent.

"Let me check it out and I'll let you know."

The answer irritated McNair. "I'm not paying you to play games, Underwood."

Ben cut him yet a little more slack, though it galled him to do so. Stress did strange things to people, he reminded himself. Maybe, under ordinary circumstances, Stephen McNair was a completely likable person, although Ben sincerely doubted it.

In any event, rules had to be set and boundaries defined. "No, Mr. McNair, you're paying me to find your son and I intend to do that. But it'll have to be my way. Again, that's what you're paying me for."

He heard the man bite off a retort he couldn't make out, then say in a guarded voice, "You'll call as soon as you have anything?"

"I'll call," Ben promised, just as he had yesterday as McNair left the office. The man had tried to bully him into making reports at regular intervals. That might have been standard procedure at McNair's company, but that wasn't the way he operated and Ben had made his position perfectly clear. Or so he thought.

"Speaking of calling, how did you get my home number?" It was unlisted, and although he'd given out his number on occasion to more than one distraught parent, something had prevented Ben from offering it to McNair. Self-preservation, most likely.

"I have ways." There was a smug note in the other man's voice. And then he reiterated his earlier point. "I would appreciate you checking in with me regularly."

Maybe the agency should refine its screening process, Ben thought, growing closer to the end of his patience. At the moment, the agency took on all comers. Maybe it was time for Cade to rethink that when he got back from the case he was working on.

"There's nothing regular about my line of work. I'll call when there's something to call about. Goodbye, Mr. McNair."

Ben let the receiver fall back into the cradle, then slid back down on the bed. Less than five minutes of tossing and turning made him acknowledge that he was too irritated to go back to sleep.

Muttering under his breath, Ben got up to take a shower. The last time he'd been up on the wrong side of four-thirty, it'd been to get ready for his paper route before going to school. The nuns at St. Mary's, aware of his mother's financial situation, had said paying part of his own tuition at the parochial school would make a man out of him.

He didn't feel very manly right now. Just tired.

With a sigh, he turned on the hot water and stepped into the shower. There was no sense wasting time.

The drive up Interstate 5 from Bedford to Saratoga would have been scenic had it not been for the early morning fog that hung about the winding road. He was a careful driver by nature. It wasn't often, though, that he worried about the road and the hazards caused by careless drivers.

But a fog this thick made him aware of every inch of road. And the possibility of his own quickly snuffed-out mortality.

Ben slowed his vehicle down to a crawl.

He supposed he could have gone later, but the word itself held a foreboding threat within it. *Later* was too close to *never* when it came to kidnappings. It was always best to follow every lead as soon as it occurred. Later might be too late.

He didn't ever intend to be too late. So far, he'd been lucky. He'd never had to face a parent and say those gut-wrenching, eternally tormenting words that would forever cut them off from hope. He'd found every child he'd set out to locate. Which was what made his job at

ChildFinders so much more rewarding than the time he'd spent in the homicide division on the police force.

The coffee nestled in his cup holder had grown cold and stagnant by the time the fog had lifted, and he felt confident enough to risk taking one hand off the wheel to take a drink. By then, he was fifteen miles out of Saratoga.

The small town created an immediate impression the moment he entered it. Saratoga looked as if it should have been the subject of a fairy tale. Or, at the very least, a Frank Capra movie. There was a picturesque, storybook quality about it. The climate was cooler up here, and what had been rain in Bedford had transformed into light flurries in Saratoga.

The light layer of fresh snow on the trees and ground made Ben think of a Currier and Ives painting.

The woman he was looking for lived ten miles on the other side of Saratoga.

"I do so like getting visitors," the small, cherubic woman said, smiling at Ben. "Have another cookie." She pushed the near-full plate toward him. "I just wind up eating them myself half the time." Her eyes twinkled and she gave the illusion of lucidity as she smiled at her girth. "But I suspect you've already guessed that."

The wan afternoon sun had finally withdrawn from the parlor they were in, after losing a hopeless battle for space within a room crammed full of knickknacks and memorabilia. It was a room where an old woman sat, surrounded by things that reminded her that she had once been young, with the world at her feet. Too heavyset to be called elfin, she still had that way about her. She was charming, and maybe, at some other time, Ben wouldn't have minded spending an afternoon talking to her about nothing.

But he didn't have time. Because of McNair's admitted reticence, too much had already elapsed. The longer it took him to find Andrew McNair, the harder it would become.

"No." The lie came easily to him. It harmed nothing to pretend that she was not heavy. The woman's smile became wider. "No, I hadn't guessed." Picking up another one of the cookies she was pushing on him, he took a bite. The cookies, laced liberally with macadamia nuts, were quite possibly the best he'd ever had. Andrea would have killed for these, he thought, chocolate chip cookies being a particular weakness for his middle sister. "And much as I'd like to load up on these, Mrs. Malone—"

"Oh, please, everyone calls me Sugar. I forget exactly why. Sugarland isn't my given name, you know."

"I rather suspected that," he said, smiling. "But as to the reason I'm here—"

"Oh, yes, your reason." Her smile faded a little. "And once you tell me, you'll be gone, won't you?"

He'd met her less than twenty minutes ago. Knocking on her door, he'd been surprised when she'd ushered him in like a long-lost friend. Asking for his name had been an after-thought. It had left him wondering if there was anyone who looked in on the old woman from time to time to make sure she hadn't given up the deed to the old Victorian house, or its surrounding fields. He hoped that the foreman who managed her field hands was a decent sort.

"I'm afraid—"

Sugar waved away the excuse magnanimously. "That's all right, Gloria was the same way, flitting in and out before I could so much as blink twice. I expect it's the same with all young people."

"Gloria." He hadn't expected it to be this easy. Ben maintained a poker face as he asked, "Then she's been here?"

"Why, yes. Here and gone." Sugar brushed away the crumbs that had collected on her ample bosom. "But you were going to tell me something."

Was she really as vague as she let on, or was it all an elaborate act? She seemed genuine enough, but Ben kept his eyes on the woman's face, watching for a telltale shift in expression as he said, "As a matter of fact, I'm looking for your grand-niece."

"Why?" It wasn't a challenge. Curiosity filtered into her eyes.

He began to give Sugar the story he'd rehearsed on his way up here. "I represent Jacob Marley's estate—"

"Jacob Marley...." She closed her eyes, rolling the name over in her mind. Then, opening them again, she shook her head. "I don't believe I know the man."

"No, ma'am, probably not." Especially since he'd borrowed the name from Dickens' *A Christmas Carol*, Ben thought. "But he's left Gloria a sizable amount of money—"

Sugar clapped her hands together in simple, childish delight. "How wonderful. The poor dear could so use the money. I couldn't give her very much when she came. She promised to pay me back, but I told her I wouldn't hear of it. I'm the only family she has, you know."

"Yes, I do." Ben tried to press on before the woman became distracted again. "We have no forwarding address for her—"

Fluffy, cloudlike white hair bobbed up and down as Sugar nodded in agreement.

"That's because she's not where she used to be." She leaned forward, her voice dropping for a moment. "Can't be, you know. Too bad, it made her sad to leave."

This had to be what Alice felt like, trying to carry on a conversation with the creatures inhabiting Wonderland, Ben thought. Still, he was making some progress. "Do you know where she is now?"

"Not really." Sugar paused to nibble thoughtfully on one of her cookies. "But she said something about San Francisco. That's where she went to school, you know. Bright, bright girl." She sighed as that memory, too, slipped away from her. "Worked in a bookstore during those years. Practically ran the place. Don't know when she ever slept. The manager liked her, I could tell. Never acted on it, though." Suddenly realizing that her visitor was no longer chewing, she pushed the plate a little closer still. "Another cookie?" This time, the plate practically landed in his lap.

"Would you happen to know the name of the bookstore?" Gloria had to work, he thought. Maybe she'd touched base with the owner of the store, asking for a job. It was a long shot to say the least, but long shots had a way of paying off if you were persistent enough. Besides, it was a starting point. San Francisco was a big city to wander around in aimlessly.

"Why, as a matter of fact I do." Proudly, she recited the name of a popular chain that was currently sweeping the country, replacing older, independent stores. "It's located at Taylor and Turk. Or is it Turk and Taylor? I never know which way to say that." She looked pleased with herself for remembering the location. "I went there a few times myself. The bookstore,'' she clarified, almost more for her benefit than for his.

It was time to go, Ben thought. He could see she was about to push another cookie on him. ''One last question. Did Gloria have a little boy with her?''

Sugar blinked, staring at him as if he had just asked her if the sky was blue on a sunny day. ''Well, of course she did. Why wouldn't she? She was moving, you know.''

''Yes, so I gathered.'' On his feet, he extended his hand to her. ''Well, you've been a great help.''

Sugar took the compliment as her due. ''That's what Gloria said. But I couldn't help enough. Not her. Here.'' She slipped three large cookies into his pocket. ''For later. You might get hungry.''

He left feeling somewhat guilty about deceiving a woman who seemed bent on helping everyone who crossed her path.

The sun grazed off the window as she passed, catching her attention. Raising her eyes, surprise drenched her when she saw the reflection.

Idiot.

It still startled her, at unguarded moments, to see the different face looking back at her. To realize that the woman with the short, dark hair and blue eyes was not someone else, but her. In her mind's eye, she was still a blonde, still green-eyed. Yet now she was a woman with a life that held promise instead of one who had come full circle, returning to what she'd once felt was the beginning of the road.

Not the end, just a breather. She had to remember that.

With effort, she shook herself free of the morose

mood. It wasn't like her. No matter what, she'd always looked on the positive side. Stopping, she tucked a book back into place on the shelf.

There was more reason than ever to focus on the positive side. There wasn't just herself to think of. Her son needed her.

Her son.

She looked at her watch. The last customer she'd helped had taken more time than she'd judged. If she was going to be at the school in time to pick Andrew—no, Jesse, she upbraided herself. If she was going to be in time to pick Jesse up, she was going to have to get going. Now.

"I'm taking my break now, Jon," she called out to the burly man nursing a cup of espresso at the information counter.

The bald-headed man gave a half nod in acknowledgment to her announcement and went back to perusing a copy of one of the books UPS had dropped off this morning.

She smiled to herself. Some things never changed. Jon Peterson was lost to the world when he had his nose stuck in a good mystery. He'd been that way during the four years she'd worked here while she'd attended college. Heaven help anyone if they approached him with a question. Like as not, Jon was apt to send them into the self-help section even if they asked for a cookbook.

She blessed Jon for the umpteenth time since she'd arrived more than three weeks ago. If not for him and his calming influence, she could very well have come unglued that first night in San Francisco. If he had been away on one of his many minivacations that he'd always loved to take...well, she didn't want to think about it.

Trying to get to the front doors, she found her path blocked by a well-built man in his early twenties wearing a pricey sheepskin jacket and a cheap smile. He made no effort to move out of her way.

"Since you're free, why don't I buy you a cup of coffee to go along with that break?"

She'd been uncomfortably aware that the man had been sizing her up for at least the last fifteen minutes, meandering closely behind her as she stocked new books on the shelves. She'd caught him looking at her at least three times, attempting to make eye contact. She'd looked away each time. He gave her the shivers. Not the good kind.

Maybe it was her situation that made her so edgy, so suspect of every man who looked her way. Maybe she was being unduly sensitive and the man was just trying to strike up a conversation, nothing more.

But whatever he was attempting to do, she had no time for it. As it was, if she didn't hurry, she was going to be late.

Since he was a potential customer, she strove to remain polite. "No, thank you, I have an errand to run." Sidestepping him, she tried to get by.

One quick movement and he was in front of her again, blocking her path. He was not a man who was about to take no for an answer. "You work here, don't you?"

She glanced toward Jon, but his nose was buried in the book. None of the other people who worked in the store were within eye-contact range. She raised her head defiantly as she looked back at the man.

"Yes."

His eyes washing over her, he was obviously taken

with what he saw. "Well then, whatever happened to that old saying, the customer is always right?"

"That depends on what the customer wants."

A smile split his handsome face, failing to reach his eyes. "Guess."

If she called out to Jon, she'd cause a scene. The last thing she wanted was a scene. Just peaceful anonymity. "I'm afraid I don't have the time right now." She tried to move past him again, but the man swayed, blocking her every move. "I need to be somewhere else," she said.

He put up his hand against a shelf, cutting her off from making an exit. "Yes, with me."

Suddenly, he found himself being spun around and looking up at a stranger who was several inches taller than he was.

"The lady said no. What part of 'no' didn't you understand?" Ben asked.

Cold fury contorted the man's handsome features. It was evident he wasn't accustomed to being turned down, or opposed. "This doesn't concern you."

Ben's hand tightened around his arm. He gave the man no reason to doubt he meant business. "Lack of manners always concerns me. Now, apologize to the lady and let her pass."

She'd always loved westerns as a child. The rugged hero in the white hat coming to the aid of the wronged, put-upon but feisty heroine. Time and again, she'd eat up the stories even though they were always the same. Only the faces and names changed.

And now she had her very own cowboy riding to her rescue.

Annoyed but smart enough to know when he was

outmatched, the man glared sullenly at her. "I didn't mean anything by it."

Ben slowly nodded his head, as if evaluating the words. "A little lacking in poetry, but it'll do." Releasing his hold on the man's arm, Ben held his hand up. "You can go. Now."

Embarrassed, the man stalked out.

Ben shook his head, watching to make sure he left before turning back to the sultry-looking woman. He had no doubt she had more than her share of run-ins like that. Women with faces and figures as beautiful as hers generally did. "I apologize for my species. Just because we all walk upright doesn't make us all civilized."

The laugh that bubbled up in her throat was just a little nervous. "Thank you."

"My pleasure—" he glanced down at the small, square name tag "—Gina Wassel." He raised his eyes to hers. "And now, would you mind pointing me in the direction of the manager?"

She would have liked to stay and ask him if she could help, but the jerk who had tried to put the moves on her had eaten up her margin of time. She should have already been on her way.

"He's right over there." She pointed toward Jon. "Now, if you'll excuse me."

Ben nodded, stepping aside. "You have an errand to run."

"Emphasis on *run*," she said, tossing the words over her shoulder as she hurried out.

He allowed himself exactly half a second to take in the view. The woman looked just as good going as she did coming.

But he wasn't there to pass judgment on form. He was tracking a kidnapper.

With that in mind, Ben made his way over to the man the woman named Gina had pointed out to him.

Chapter 3

Jon Peterson slowly stroked his small goatee as he stared at the reprinted photograph of a woman with a little boy that Ben had handed him.

Longer than was necessary, in Ben's estimation. Gloria Prescott had either come in and applied for a job in the last few days, or she hadn't. Granted, the photograph wasn't a very good one, but it was the only one McNair had had of either Gloria, or his son. Ben could see not having photographs of the nanny, but it was difficult for him to understand why McNair had no available photographs of his son. He supposed that the man's excuse, that he wasn't the kind to take pictures, held some water. But he bet that McNair had plenty of photographs of himself around.

Blurred photograph or not, Peterson knew what Gloria looked like. According to her great-aunt, she'd worked here for four years. The man was either stalling for dramatic effect, or was debating something. Not knowing him made it next to impossible for Ben to tell.

When the bookstore manager finally raised his eyes to his, Ben had the impression that he was being scrutinized far more closely than the photograph had been.

"Nope, sorry, can't help you." Placing the photograph on the counter, Jon pushed it back toward him. He paused as if thinking. "Haven't seen Gloria in, what? I guess about four, five years now." The small, dark eyes gave no indication of what was going on in his mind as they looked at Ben. "Maybe even longer."

"Then she didn't come here looking for a job," Ben reiterated.

The meeting apparently over, Peterson drew his book back to him and lowered his head, effectively blocking out any noise and any unwanted inquiries.

"That would have meant I'd seen her, wouldn't it? Sorry, she's not here. Wish she was. Best damn employee I ever had here. She actually wanted to work, not like some of the others." He turned a page in his book. Because Ben wasn't leaving, Peterson raised his eyes to look at him again. This time, his displeasure was not that difficult to discern. "Anything else I can do for you?"

Ben had come across more sociable pit bulls. He slipped the photograph back into his pocket. "Would you happen to know where Gloria might have gone if she'd returned to San Francisco?"

"Nope. Never meddle." Peterson returned to his mystery, making it painfully obvious that he considered Ben an annoying obstacle to his reading pleasure. "Keeping your nose out of other people's lives is the secret to a long, healthy one of your own." Bent over his book, Peterson spared him one more pointed glance. "Know what I mean?"

"Yeah." He knew exactly what the older man meant. Get lost. Ben took one last look around the store. He'd already walked up and down the aisles methodically, not once but twice. That was how he'd happened to notice the college preppie putting the moves on the salesclerk. Not that he could actually blame him. The woman had been a looker in a classy sort of way. "Thanks for your help."

Engrossed in the book he was reading, the store manager grunted his acknowledgment.

There was nothing for Ben to do but retreat to his car.

Rather than drive off immediately, Ben put in a quick call to Savannah and came up empty there as well.

"If Gloria Prescott's in San Francisco, Ben, she's not using her charge cards," she told him.

"No paper trail of any kind?"

"Not unless she's leaving bread crumbs behind her on her way to the forest," Savannah quipped. "The canvassing down here's coming up dry, too. Rusty's been showing the photograph around in the area and he said to tell you that nobody's seen Gloria or the boy. I'm sorry, Ben."

"Not your fault," he murmured before hanging up.

Putting his cell phone back in his pocket, Ben stared at the bookstore across the street, not really seeing it. He doubted that driving back to Saratoga to ask Sugar any more questions would yield any further insight into finding Gloria.

That only left one other person to talk to.

The expression on Stephen McNair's face was far from welcoming when his secretary admitted Ben into his office. The man's countenance made Ben think of Zeus, presiding over Mount Olympus and bringing Mercury to task for failing to deliver the message he'd been anticipating. Ben had a hunch that even the man's furniture had been chosen with an eye toward intimidating anyone entering the office. Massive, opulent and expensive. The man certainly didn't assume his present position in life graciously.

Sitting as straight as a spear in his gray, imported leather office chair, McNair gripped the armrests as he scowled at him.

"Shut the door."

The tone rankled Ben, but he closed the door behind him. This was supposed to be private, anyway. The instant the door met the jamb, McNair was on his feet.

"Why are you coming to see me here?"

Definitely not a Mr. Congeniality candidate, Ben thought. In his book it would have had to have taken one hell of a greedy woman to have slept with this man for monetary gain. But then, it took all kinds, and he had yet to figure out just what "kind" his quarry was. Aside from cookies, her aunt had filled him in with stories of Gloria as well, all told with an abundance of affection and filial pride. Given the woman's state, though, he figured he had to take a great deal with a grain of salt.

"Because I didn't want to waste time making an appointment."

About to say something, McNair changed his tone. "Did you find her?"

Again, "her," not "him." "If you don't mind my saying so, Mr. McNair, you seem to be a great deal more interested in my finding Gloria Prescott than you are in my finding your son."

"Of course I'm interested in you finding Gloria. She has what belongs to me and no one, *no one* gets away with that. Now, did you find her or didn't you?"

"Not yet." Ben wanted to add that he wasn't a magician, but let the remark slide. It would only lead to an escalation of tempers.

"Then I repeat, what are you doing here in my office?"

Ben was beginning to feel really sorry for the little boy he was looking for. He had a feeling that McNair was probably just as cold and abrasive with the son he never actually wanted as he was with someone who was "displeasing" him. "I need more information."

Exasperation creased the remarkably unlined brow. "I already told you everything I could think of."

There had to be something, some tiny piece that would lead Ben to clues that would help him find the boy. He'd seen it happen often enough. The trick was finding that one scrap that eventually opened up everything. Maybe the answers he was looking for were in Gloria's recent past. "Where did Gloria work before she came to you?"

The annoyance on McNair's face deepened. "I don't remember."

He was being evasive, Ben thought, and wondered why. In any event, there was an easy-enough solution. "Check your references."

With an angry huff, McNair turned away. There was tension in the back Ben found himself looking at. "I don't know where they are."

He would have thought that McNair knew how to lay his hands on almost anything that remotely concerned him. "What about the agency that sent her? Can you remember its name?"

McNair swung around. "What does where she worked before have to do with finding her now?"

It was on the tip of Ben's tongue to say that he didn't appreciate having his methods questioned, but he thought better of it. He hadn't come here to argue, but to search for a lead. The sooner McNair gave him what he wanted, the sooner he could get going.

"There might be some sort of connection we've overlooked." McNair looked unconvinced. "No one we've questioned in the area has seen her, and her only relative sent me in the wrong direction."

"Relative?" He said the word as if he hadn't thought that Gloria had any, Ben noted. "Well, go back to him or her and get the truth."

"It's a her," Ben told him. "And I think the sky's a different color in her world than it is in the world the rest of us reside in."

"You mean she's crazy?" Surprise imprinted the distinguished features.

"No, just somewhat off. Eccentric." Ben had no idea why he suddenly felt protective of a woman he hardly knew. Maybe it was McNair's manner. He pressed on. "What I need right now is someone else who knew her, someone who might have a decent idea where Gloria might have gone with your son."

McNair blew out a breath as he scrubbed his hand over his face. Searching his memory. Or debating over something that he'd felt better about keeping obscure. Ben couldn't tell.

Finally, McNair said, "I think she used to work in a social security office."

Something to go on, Ben thought. "Locally?"

"I think so." The scowl returned. "Look, I'm doing all the work here."

Ben was already at the door, more than eager to leave. ''We'll arrange for a discount.'' He didn't bother sublimating the sarcasm.

It wasn't wasted on McNair. His expression bordered on malevolence. ''Damn straight you will. And don't forget, I want to be kept posted,'' he called after Ben.

''As soon as I find out anything, you'll be the first to know.''

No one was more eager than he was to wrap this all up, Ben thought.

There was only one social security building in the county. Even if Gloria hadn't worked in this particular one, Ben figured that with a little coaxing applied to the right people, he could find out which office she had worked in.

He didn't need to coax.

The section supervisor, Anna Philbert, a robustly built woman in her forties who had once been an Olympic shot-put alternate if he was to believe the certificate that hung on the cubicle wall directly behind her, instantly recognized the photograph he showed her.

''Oh, sure, Gloria worked here.'' She looked at the photograph again before handing it back to him. ''Is anything wrong?''

He didn't think the story he'd given Gloria's great-aunt sounded sufficiently credible in the government building, so he had created another one on his way over.

''She's missing and her fiancé's very worried about her.''

''Missing? You mean kidnapped?'' Anna asked, genuinely horrified. A beringed hand fluttered to her ample bosom. ''Gloria? You're kidding.'' She shook her head in pure disbelief even as she clearly reveled in the drama of the situation. "The poor thing. She was the sweetest person in the world."

Apparently Gloria's fan club was growing. Why would someone regarded as "the sweetest person in the world" kidnap a child no matter how upset and angry she was? It didn't make sense to him.

"It might not be a kidnapping," he said quickly. "It just might be a case of cold feet." He deliberately exchanged a conspiratorial look with the woman, drawing her further into his camp. "Tell me, if Gloria did want to get away, would you have any idea where she might go?"

As much as she looked as if she wanted to help him, Anna was forced to shake her head. "No, but I really wasn't very close to her." She thought a moment. "You might have better luck talking to Carla Wassel."

"Wassel?" An image of the woman at the bookstore came to him. If he closed his eyes, he could see the name tag she'd worn against her shapely breast. It wasn't all that common a name. He wondered if the women were somehow related. Maybe he'd finally stumbled onto a connection. "Is she in?"

Rising from behind her desk, Anna peered over the tops of the maze of cubicles.

"She's right over there." Anna pointed to the far end of the corridor, to a desk on the extreme right. "She and Gloria were pretty tight while Gloria was here."

"Thank you." He started to leave. "Oh, by the way, when did Gloria leave her job?"

"About nine months ago." Anna smiled affectionately. "She always called this her day job, though you wouldn't have known by the way she worked. I wished I had ten of her."

Day job. That meant she was trying to make a go of

something else. But what? It obviously wasn't being a nanny. Could she have plotted to kidnap Andrew all along in order to get a stake of some sort? It sounded like a shot in the dark, but he'd come across wilder theories that had turned out to be true.

He probed a little further into the woman's testimonial. "What do you mean? She put in a lot of overtime?"

"Oh, no, she never worked overtime. Couldn't. She kept regular hours, but she gave a hundred twenty-five percent when she was here. I tried to talk her into staying, but she was adamant. Now or never, she said."

Now or never. What was that supposed to mean? The nine-month time frame coincided with when she came to work for McNair. Had she seen the CEO as her ticket to better things?

He was holding two different puzzle pieces in his hand. So far, he'd gotten two unofficial testimonials. Both of which painted the image of a woman who believed in giving her employer everything she felt was due him or her. Giving, not taking. People like that didn't just wake up one morning and steal their employer's child.

Or did they?

Thanking Anna for her help, he made his way through the maze to Carla Wassel's cubicle. He could feel Anna's eyes following him.

Because there was no door, he rapped once on the side of the cubicle to get the woman's attention. "Ms. Wassel?"

A dark-haired woman with striking bright blue eyes turned from her computer screen to look up at him. The smile tinged in curiosity came a beat afterward.

Ben could see the resemblance instantly. Not so much

the hair, although both the woman he'd met in the bookstore and Carla Wassel were brunettes who wore their hair short, but in the eyes. A man didn't readily forget eyes like that. They had the exact same shade of blue. Like bits of cobalt.

"Yes?"

"I'm Ben Underwood." He indicated the chair within her cubicle. "Mind if I sit down?" Still curious, she gestured for him to take a seat. "I'm trying to locate a friend of yours. Gloria Prescott."

"Gloria?" Her eyes widened. "Why? Has something happened to her?"

Ben stopped before reaching for Gloria's photograph. He saw no reason for her to get as upset as she did. "What makes you ask that?"

Carla flushed, embarrassed. "I'm sorry, ever since my sister died, I'm afraid I overreact to things. The first thing I think of is..." Her voice trailed off as she let the end of her thought go. "Never mind." She waved away the rest of her sentence. "Why are you trying to find Gloria?"

For simplicity, and because there was a chance he might have to return for more information, Ben gave Carla the same story he'd given her supervisor.

"Her fiancé's trying to find her. They were supposed to go away together to Hawaii last week and Gloria never showed up. Personally," he said, leaning in a little closer, "I think it might be cold feet, but we have to investigate these things."

Caution entered her voice. "Are you a policeman?"

For a second he debated going that route. But the closer he remained to the truth, the easier it was to remember details. "A private one."

Carla took the information in stride. "I don't think I

can help you. I haven't been in touch with Gloria since shortly after she left the office.'' She raised her shoulder in a semihelpless movement. ''I meant to, but you know how that goes. I suppose I wasn't much fun to be around at the time. But I'm better now.''

''Nice to hear.'' He tried to sound sympathetic. Another dead end, he thought. But there was still the coincidence of the names. No stone unturned. ''How do you spell your last name?''

Carla's dark eyebrows drew together over a Roman nose. ''W-a-s-s-e-l, why?''

He jotted it down in the small notepad he carried. Tucking it back into his pocket, his fingers came in contact with the cookies Aunt Sugar had slipped in. He had to remember to take them out.

''Just for the record,'' he assured her. ''Do you have any relatives in San Francisco?''

The answer required no extensive deliberation. ''No, I don't think so. Why?''

It was probably a meaningless coincidence, but he'd learned never to ignore or omit anything that seemed the slightest bit unusual. He'd gone to the bookstore where Gloria had once worked only to run into a woman with her best friend's last name. There could be a connection. At the very least, the woman in San Francisco might know Gloria.

''I ran into someone with the exact same last name as yours just yesterday. You have to admit, it's not exactly in the same realm as Smith or Jones.''

Curious, Carla asked gamely, ''Maybe we are related. What was his name?''

''Her,'' he corrected the woman. ''Gina Wassel.''

Carla turned pale and grabbed the edge of her desk. Ben saw her eyes roll toward the back of her head, and for a second he thought he was going to have to catch her to keep her from sliding off her chair, onto the floor.

He grabbed her arms. "Take a deep breath," he ordered. "Again." He waited until she exhaled slowly. "Are you all right?"

When she looked at him, there was an accusation in her eyes. "Is this some kind of a cruel joke?"

He had no idea what she was talking about, but he'd obviously stumbled onto something. "Not that I'm aware of," he said slowly.

"Gina's my sister. Was my sister," she corrected herself. The pain was obvious. "She's been gone for ten months. Wait." Agitated, blinking back tears that were threatening to overwhelm her, Carla dug into the purse she kept under her desk. "Here, here's her picture." She shoved her wallet at him and showed him a photograph of herself and her sister standing in front of an old house. A beat later he realized that it was the Victorian-looking house he'd gone to yesterday. "That's Gina." She indicated the slender young woman on the right.

"Who took this picture?"

"Gloria. We went to visit her aunt on her seventieth birthday."

The resemblance between the woman in the photograph and the one he'd met yesterday was unmistakable. They could have been the same person. Folding the wallet closed, he handed it back to Carla.

"Ms. Wassel," he began as gently as he could, "I have to ask—"

Carla cut him off. She couldn't bear to hear the words. "I was driving the car when the camper sideswiped us. Gina was killed instantly." Her breathing was ragged as she spoke. "It was Gloria who helped me through that, who let me sleep on her sofa and kept me sane.'' Without looking, she dropped the wallet back into her purse. ''If she hadn't been around, I probably would have killed myself.'' Her eyes held his for a moment. ''If Gloria's in some sort of danger, you've got to find her.''

Ben had a feeling he already had.

There were huge, gaping holes in the puzzle he found himself working. ''You have access to all sorts of information here, don't you?''

Carla's expression told him she wasn't sure where he was going with this, or what she should answer. ''Depending on your level of clearance, yes.''

''Such as social security numbers.''

She laughed nervously, still uncertain. ''Well, of course. We're a social security office.''

''Does that mean social security numbers that are no longer in use?'' This would have been the perfect place for Gloria to forge a new identity.

''Yes.'' The single word emerged slowly.

He had a feeling he was on the right track. ''Ms. Wassel, I know this might sound rather strange to you, but would you be able to give me your sister's social security number?''

''Yes, but I already told you, Gina's dead.'' Carla began to access a program for him, then stopped and looked at him. ''You think Gloria's using Gina's social security number.''

''Yes.''

It didn't make any sense. ''But why?''

To hide from Stephen McNair until he agreed to her terms. But he couldn't tell the woman that. She wouldn't give him the social security number he needed, and right now, he didn't know if Savannah had access to inactive files.

"I won't be able to answer any questions until I have all the facts," he told her.

Confusion furrowed her brow as she looked at the keys, undecided. "If Gloria's in some sort of trouble, maybe I shouldn't be helping you."

His voice was quiet and authoritative. "If Gloria's in some sort of trouble, I might be the only one who *can* help her."

Carla sat looking at him for a long moment, then began typing.

The electronic doors opened and closed.

The chill that ran up her back was immediate, drenching her with an icy wave. Though she was in one of the aisles, her eyes darted toward the front.

How long before that reaction would leave her? Before she could hear the doors opening and not be compelled to look, holding her breath and praying. It wasn't natural to feel this way, as if she were doomed to cross and recross a tightrope stretched over a bottomless pit with slippery shoes.

He wouldn't track her here, she insisted silently. He didn't know enough about her to know about this place. And even if he did and was still looking for her, she wasn't really here. Not the way he knew her.

She was safe.

The breath she'd been holding escaped as recognition came. Gina's mouth curved. The man who had gotten between her and that pushy jerk the day before yesterday had returned.

What was he was doing back? When she'd left, he'd asked her to point Jon out, or rather, the store manager.

That meant Jon and the stranger didn't know each other, so it wasn't personal. Jon hadn't mentioned anything to her, but then, he'd been in a real rush to leave after taking that call from his brother.

He told her he had to take some time off and left her in charge, just like that.

Funny how you could work with someone for so long and not know anything about him. She'd spent all four college years working in the store, and in all that time, Jon had never mentioned even having a family. He'd been closemouthed as far as things like that went.

Pot calling the kettle black. She certainly wasn't in a position to throw rocks right now, she mused. Jon didn't know all that much about her, either. Nor had he asked anything, not even when she'd suddenly appeared out of the blue three weeks ago, asking for her old job back. All he'd said was sure, then added an addendum: If she needed him, he was around. To prove it, he'd gotten her in contact with a friend of his who was trying to sublet his condo. She had a job and a home within one day, thanks to Jon. He was one in a million.

He hadn't even made any comment about her changed appearance when she came in the first day. Just asked her what name she wanted to go under. Nothing more.

Gina suspected that World War Three could probably break out right in front of the bookstore and as long as it didn't intrude within the doors, Jon would remain oblivious to it.

Lucky for her.

Pushing the book she was holding back into its space, she walked up to the man who had just entered and smiled at him. "I see you're back. Come to see if I needed rescuing again?"

He'd taken measure of her as he'd walked in and still wondered if there was some sort of mistake. But it was too much of a coincidence for him to shrug off. What he needed was to find a way to find out her social security number. That might be more difficult than he'd anticipated if the store manager had agreed to pay her off the books.

"Oh, you strike me as someone who can take care of herself. If I hadn't intervened yesterday, you probably would have decked him."

He had a dimple, she realized. And a sense of humor. She found that an extremely sexy trait. "My boxing gloves are in the shop," she said wryly. "Jon's not here if you came to see him."

"Jon?"

"The store manager." Obviously the name meant nothing to him. "I'm sorry, I'm just taking a stab at why you're here."

He wondered what she would say if he answered her truthfully. If he told her that he was looking for Gloria Prescott and the little boy she'd abducted. Probably nothing. At close quarters, the woman looked cool enough to be able to pull it off. If she was Gloria.

"To do some research, actually."

Savannah had managed to access Gloria Prescott's transcript at the University of San Francisco for him. He'd discovered that while her degree was in the field of studio arts, specifically sculpting, she'd minored in American history. He'd guessed that the preponderance of courses on Native Americans meant her interest lay there. The drive up from Bedford had given him ample time to come up with a scenario.

He looked around. "Do you have a Native American

section? I'm working on a project and I'm kind of stuck. I need all the input I can get."

Ben saw interest enter her eyes. "Native American? What kind of a project is it?"

He pretended to hesitate. "You'd probably laugh."

That made her smile. "No, I wouldn't, try me."

He'd chosen his story carefully. "It's a screenplay—you probably hear that all the time. Everybody and his brother is writing one, or knows someone who's writing one."

Her smile was nothing short of encouraging. If this was Gloria, he could easily see why McNair had lost his head. Whether she was blonde or brunette, there was something about the woman's smile that got to a man, made him want to puff up his chest and do something extraordinary to make her take notice.

"I don't," she told him.

He caught her off guard by putting out his hand. "Ben Underwood. Now you know me, so you know someone who's writing one."

The smile turned into a soft laugh that wafted around him like the first breeze of spring, full of promise at what was to be.

"All right, Ben Underwood, what's your screenplay about?"

"The Battle of Wounded Knee." Other than Custer's last stand at Little Big Horn, it was the only Indian battle that he was vaguely aware of.

She caught her lower lip between her teeth, holding back a laugh.

"You're not going to believe this, but I minored in Native American studies at UCSF."

"You're kidding." He looked properly impressed.

"Damn, but this is my lucky day. Maybe you can help fill in the gaps for me."

"Maybe," she echoed, her mouth curving.

He did his best not to notice how inviting that looked.

Chapter 4

So far, so good, Ben thought, returning her smile. He'd managed to establish a beachhead, however small. But he was a long way from winning the battle yet.

What he needed was to gain her trust so he could get to the bottom of what was going on. As of right now, he still wasn't a hundred percent certain that he had the right woman. All he had to go on was the slightly out-of-focus photograph McNair had given him and a likeness of Gloria Prescott that Savannah had lifted from the DMV records she'd accessed. The only similarity between that and the woman he was looking at was they looked to be approximately the same age.

Ben summoned what latent acting talents he had and infused his voice with what he hoped was the right amount of enthusiasm. One of his best friends was a would-be screenwriter. Ben did his best to imitate the way he'd heard Nick talk when he was going on about his project of the moment.

"You know, this is almost like fate, meeting you."

He touched her shoulder lightly as he spoke, initiating contact, but making certain that it couldn't be misconstrued as anything remotely sexual. If the other day was any indication, she probably had more than her share of that, but he'd noted that the slightest bit of physical contact between people instantly brought them to a more familiar plane. He did his best to walk the fine line.

"Listen, I've got an idea." Ben dropped his hand, as if suddenly aware of what he was doing. He saw a hint of a smile on Gina's face and congratulated himself on his instincts. "I know you're working right now, but maybe we could grab a bite to eat later when you knock off and—"

Having displayed what he thought was just the right amount of eagerness, he stopped, as if realizing how his words had to sound to her.

"I know you're probably thinking that this is a come-on, but it's really not. I really do need your help. I want to be accurate about this and I'm willing to pay you for your time." He shoved his hands into his pockets. "Not much, I'm afraid—unless you're willing to take percentage points in my script."

Though she was trying to maintain her distance, Gina had to admit that this eager screenwriter did sound cute, stumbling over his words. She hoped he was better on paper. But she did appreciate that he realized she might be getting the wrong impression about his offer. Not many men would have picked up on that.

From the look of him, Ben Underwood seemed like the last word in manliness. Someone Aunt Sugar would have referred to as "a man's man—and a lady's heart-throb." Yet he was unapologetically sensitive to her feelings. After what she'd been through, he seemed more like a figment of her imagination than a real person.

Still, she had to turn him down.

"I can't tonight, I've got to close up." She was surprised at the regret she felt. Gina chalked it up to loneliness. "But I think I can manage tomorrow night after work, if that's all right." She could see he looked disappointed. "Unless you're in a hurry."

Ben noticed one of the other clerks looking their way and turned just slightly so that his body blocked her view of the other man. He didn't want her getting distracted while he made his pitch.

"I am—I'm getting close to my deadline." He paused, thinking that it was a lucky thing he'd decided to get a motel room close by. "But tomorrow night will be great," he added genially.

Intrigued, she cocked her head. "Deadline?"

The shrug was self-deprecating, with just enough boyishness thrown in to captivate her. Mischievous as a boy, he'd spent his childhood pleading his case to a tough audience. Looking sincere had become an art form. Dominican nuns ordinarily brooked no nonsense.

"I gave myself a deadline. If I didn't make it as a screenwriter within five years, I was going to stop fooling myself and go into the family business. I've got six months left."

She surprised him by whistling softly. His eyes lingered on her puckered lips.

"That's cutting it pretty close." She moved to the right, out of the way of a customer who was browsing through the section where they were standing. Perforce, she moved closer to Ben. "What's the family business?"

He silently apologized to Nick, whose life he was plagiarizing. "Furniture-making."

Gina studied him. She could definitely see this handsome stranger doing that. Wearing a leather apron over worn jeans and a checkered work shirt that was rolled up at the sleeves. Goggles perched atop his thick, black hair, the smell of freshly sawed wood about him. *You're getting carried away,* she warned herself. "Are you any good at it?"

Humor glinted in his eyes as he laughed, thinking of Nick. Every time Nick attempted to make something, it was inevitably reduced to a pile of splinters and wood chips. He had no idea why Nick's father was so adamant about his joining the business.

"I would be if the family had a sideline making and selling toothpicks. My creativity lies in other directions, but if I can't make a go of it, my father insists I come into the business. Maybe as a sales rep."

He made it sound like a life sentence with no possibility of parole. She found herself warming to him. "We'll see what we can do. I'm not free tonight," she repeated, "but I can point you toward an excellent book to get you started."

"Sounds great."

She led him to the American history section. One of the shelves was labeled Native American Studies. Eight years ago, it had been her personal baby, the one section she'd convinced Jon to set up. Now that she was back, she intended to keep on top of it religiously, making sure any new, relevant books were ordered while old standards were kept in stock.

She noticed two books were out of alphabetical order. Switching them to the right place, Gina selected one title and handed it to him. "This should be very helpful."

"Thanks." He nodded toward the small table that was off to the side. There were several throughout the store, besides the ones at the coffee shop in the center of the store. "Mind if I...?"

Reading sections of a book before you bought it had become an accepted custom. "Help yourself. That's why the tables and chairs are here."

Ben made himself comfortable and opened the book to the first page. This was going to be slower going than he would have liked, he thought, but he felt he had no option. He needed something more to go on than just a glaring coincidence before he brought McNair in or the police down on the bookstore clerk. What if, by some strange twist of fate, he was wrong? Truth had been known to be stranger than fiction.

And if he was right, if this woman was Gloria Prescott and she was impersonating a dead woman, he needed to find out where she was keeping Andrew. His proceeding cautiously could mean the difference between life or death.

Mixed into all this was the question that was beginning to hound him. How could someone whom everyone he'd spoken with so far thought was a saint, have done something so heinous as to kidnap a child, no matter what her motive? If this woman with the winning smile and the killer figure was Gloria Prescott, she was either a consummate actress who had managed to fool her co-workers, her friend and her aunt, or something just wasn't right.

Any way he looked at it, he had a puzzle whose pieces weren't fitting together.

With a sigh, Ben lowered his eyes to his book and returned to playing his role.

Darkness pressed its face against the bookstore's large bay windows, peering in forlornly. It was a few minutes shy of nine o'clock, and except for Gina, he was the last one in the store. He'd spent the last few hours watching her interact with people, trying to form an opinion. Trying, also, to be objective and not swayed by the fact that she moved with the grace of a spring breeze, or that when she smiled or laughed, everyone around her seemed to light up. Him included.

He'd also wound up reading the book she had recommended. Even though his mind wasn't really on it, he had to admit that parts of it had managed to catch his attention and seep in. Maybe he'd mention the subject matter to Nick when he got home. Most success stories began as accidents. Who knew, this might be Nick's long-awaited accident.

Glancing at his watch, he verified the time. Nine. That meant she'd be closing up and going home soon. Maybe he could change her mind about tonight. The sooner he gained her confidence, the sooner he could get to the bottom of this.

He rose to his feet, feeling stiff. He'd stayed in one position too long. The wound he had gotten when he was shot in the line of duty, protecting his partner, whispered its presence along his body. He rotated his shoulders, trying to work out the discomfort.

Gina was at the register. Ben made his way over to her and placed the book on the counter between them, then took out his wallet.

"You're right, it's an excellent book." Handing her a twenty, he watched her ring the sale up. The last of the day. ''Maybe we could go get that dinner now and discuss it.''

She was tempted, she realized in surprise. What's more, it felt good to be tempted. She'd thought that perhaps, all things considered, she would never entertain that sensation again. But tempted or not, there was no way she could say yes, not tonight. Betty, her teenage baby-sitter, could only stay until nine-thirty. Jesse was asleep and she wasn't about to wake him. Besides, she doubted that this would-be screenwriter, sensitive or not, would welcome a six-year-old's company at dinner.

Handing him his change, she slipped the book into a bag with the store's logo on it. ''I'm afraid I can't. There're...complications.''

He played it as if she wasn't the suspect he'd been sent to track. ''Husband?''

''No.'' She held up her left hand to substantiate her answer.

''Boyfriend?''

This time, Gina smiled as she shook her head, thinking him sweet and wondering if she was a fool for thinking it. ''No.''

Ben raised his brows in a supposed last-ditch, far-out guess. ''Strict parents?''

She laughed. ''No. Just...complications.''

Gina wondered how her son would take to being referred to as a complication. In reality, he was the most uncomplicated, most wonderful part of her life. But arranging her schedule around him, picking him up at school and making sure he was safe at all times, did lead to a great many complications.

''If you come by the store tomorrow,'' she told him, hoping that he would, ''I'll let you know about dinner.''

"Why don't you just give me your home phone number and I'll call you?" He made the suggestion as casually as he could.

He seemed like a nice person, but she'd made a costly error in judgment before. It was better to be safe than sorry. "Coming by the shop would be easier."

"Here, let me give you my cell phone number just in case you need to get in touch with me." He wrote it down on a slip of paper and handed it to her. Folding it, she slipped it into her pocket. "You've aroused my curiosity, you know." Ben realized his mistake the instant the teasing remark left his lips. A wary look had entered her eyes. He immediately went into damage control. "Will I have to guess anyone's name, climb up a ladder made of golden hair or slay a dragon before I earn the pleasure of your company and get access to your knowledge?"

Ben silently breathed a sigh of relief as he saw her smile again. "No, nothing like that, I promise." Taking out the day's cash, she put it into a metal strongbox, then slipped a cover over the cash register.

The cop in him had him glancing toward the front door. This wasn't known to be the most savory location in San Francisco. "Should you be here by yourself doing that?"

The note of concern caught her off guard. So did the warmth stirring in response. "I've done this before. The front door locks automatically at nine. I'm going to have to use a key to let you out."

"Why don't I wait until you're finished and walk you to your car?" He wasn't certain if it was the man he was pretending to be or the man he was who made the offer.

There was a part of her that yearned for just that. To

have someone walk her to her car, to offer her his protection by mutual agreement. But there was a part, a much larger part, that had become very leery of protectiveness because it could so easily turn into possessiveness. And that led to dark places.

So, very politely but firmly, she turned him down. "Thank you, but there's no need for that." Gina cut him off before he could offer a protest. "And Jon would be upset if I let someone remain in the store when I put the money into the safe." Slipping the strongbox beneath the counter, she came out from behind it and deliberately led the way to the front doors. Unlocking them, she pushed one open and held it for him. "I'll see you tomorrow, Ben."

"Count on it."

Walking to his car, he thought of following Gina when she left the bookstore. But it was harder tailing someone at night than in the light of day, and if for some reason she spotted him, it would definitely spook her. He didn't want to undo the groundwork he'd just spent the last few hours laying down. He was going to have to wait. Tomorrow night, he'd find a way to get himself invited back to her place. Once he knew where she lived, he could return and nose around while she was at work.

Chapter 5

Despite the fact that it had been busy ever since they'd opened their doors this morning, Gina's eyes darted toward the electronic doors when she head the tiny buzzer sound, announcing the entrance of a new customer. It was a woman in her late forties. The rise in adrenaline leveled off.

This was stupid.

She had a great many more important things on her mind than a good-looking man supposedly writing a screenplay about the massacre at Wounded Knee. A very good-looking man, her mind amended automatically and entirely against her will.

"Next, please," she called to the orderly line of people who stood behind the deep purple plush ropes strung up solely to keep them in their place.

A heavyset man with an armload of books walked up, depositing them on the counter. Tilted, the books scattered every which way, mostly sprawling out on her side of the counter, some falling beneath. Offering a vague, sympathetic smile at the flustered man, Gina gathered the books up.

For all she knew, Gina thought as she began ringing up the sale for the hapless customer, Ben's story about needing to do research for his screenplay could have all been just an elaborate pickup line. When she'd turned him down for dinner, not once but twice, that might have been the end of it.

Gina scanned two more books quickly, punching in the total, telling herself it was just as well that he hadn't returned.

No, it hadn't been just about a pickup, she thought, still carrying on the internal debate. He'd sounded sincere. She knew it. Besides, he'd come to her rescue the first time she'd met him and he hadn't tried to come on to her then. Sure he was sexy, but he didn't seem to be deceitful. Maybe he was exactly what he seemed, an earnest dreamer pursuing his dream. An earnest, sweet, good-looking dreamer.

Ben Underwood might be a dreamer, but she couldn't be, Gina reminded herself, slipping all the books she'd just rung up into a shopping bag and then handing it to the man with a vague smile.

"Have a nice day," she told him. She was in no position to daydream like normal people. She wasn't normal people. Not right now, at any rate. She was a woman on the run and she had to remember that.

Maybe not, a small voice whispered within her. Maybe the running was finally over. Maybe the man who'd robbed her of so many nights' sleep had decided she was too much trouble to pursue any further and had given up looking for her. Maybe she was finally safe.

Safe.

God, but she'd never realized how overwhelmingly seductive the four-letter word could be. Safe. Safe to go about her life doing everyday things, safe not to be constantly looking over her shoulder, wondering, worrying. Safe not to see shapes hidden in the shadows, afraid that she was being followed.

The front door buzzer sounded. She lost her place in counting out the next customer's change.

"Sorry," she murmured, beginning again.

The man buying the massive cookbook looked at her as if she were incapable of counting beyond five. "Maybe I should have given you a charge card."

The slightly condescending tone and tolerant expression on his patrician face made her want to whip out her college diploma to show him that she was quite capable of conducting monetary transactions of any amount.

A lot of good that would do, she realized ruefully. The name on the diploma didn't match the one on her name tag.

"Please come again," she murmured as cheerfully as she could muster.

The man mumbled something in response that was lost on her as she found herself looking up into eyes that were almost Wedgwood blue. Ben had come up on her blind side and was now leaning against the counter, blocking the next customer.

"Hi, are we still on?"

Was it possible for him to look better today than he had yesterday? Or was that just the self-imposed drought in her life that was making her suddenly thirsty? Thirsty for the companionship of a personable man who wanted nothing more from her than just her mind.

"On?" she echoed.

The customer took her books to the clerk at the next register, giving Gina an envious look. It wasn't lost on Gina.

"For tonight," Ben prompted. He didn't appear annoyed that she seemed to have momentarily forgotten. "You said that you couldn't go out after work last night, but that you probably could tonight." He looked at her hopefully. Or was that just her imagination?

She'd talked to Betty, who had checked with her mother last night. Since tonight was a Friday night and Betty hadn't hit the dating circuit yet—her mother referred to Betty as a late bloomer—Gina was assured of a sitter for Jesse.

Now all that remained was taking that final leap from self-proclaimed female hermit to socializing woman. Easier contemplated than done.

For most of her life, she'd loved company, loved going out. She'd always been a people person, until she'd had her trust betrayed at a college fraternity party. McNair had resurrected the leeriness that had come to define and delineate her life for months after her rape, making her hold all men suspect. Looking for ulterior motives.

She hated being that way, and yet…

"Oh, right." Gina beckoned forward the next customer who was about to bypass her. "I can take you here," she told the woman, then looked at Ben. "Um, I'm not so sure that I can, after all. There's the store, we don't lock up until ten tonight—" As she scanned the book, the numbers popped up on the register.

"Don't they let you go out for dinner?" Ben deadpanned.

"I'll lock up for you tonight, Gina," a deep voice on her other side rumbled.

She glanced toward the other register, not surprised to see the slightly superior look gracing the face of the tall, thin, prematurely balding young man. The man with the improbable name of Joe Valentine had regarded her as an interloper when Jon had given her responsibility of the store over him. Joe had been working at the bookstore a total of two and a half years and considered himself not just a clerk, but Jon's assistant. Gina had changed all that and he made no secret of the fact that he didn't care for it.

"After all, it's not like I haven't done it before," Joe said smugly.

There went her last excuse, she thought, secretly glad of it. She liked being divested of excuses, because part of her really wanted to see Ben again, under any pretext. Pretexts made her feel that it was all right. "Thanks, Joe, as long as you don't mind."

"Hey, where else am I going to go?"

"It looks like it's all settled, then," Ben said to her. "Unless you don't want to." He knew if he left it open like that, she wouldn't feel he was trying to pressure her into anything.

Oh, she wanted to, all right. Maybe a little too much. "It's not that—"

"Something else?"

The cop in him rose to the fore. He peered at her, keeping his voice casual, wondering if her resistance involved Andrew in some way. Was she keeping the boy someplace accessible? Was there someone else involved? Was this not just about revenge, the way McNair thought, but a child kidnapping ring with Andrew the latest victim?

It was a horrible thought, but one that was far from new. Ben knew that Cade's own son had been kidnapped for just that reason. It had taken Cade three years to find the boy again. Darin Townsend was the reason ChildFinders, Inc. existed.

She almost said something about Jesse and being reluctant to leave him, but at the last minute decided not to. She was undoubtedly being overly paranoid, but there was no harm in keeping her private life private. No harm and maybe a great deal of good.

"No, nothing else."

Score one for the home team. "Well then it looks like it's settled. How about Wellington's?" Ben asked.

She was familiar with the restaurant. It was a place she'd treated herself to once a month while she'd been attending college. The food was wonderful and the ambience even better. It was a place she could easily see him in, but not for the type of thing she'd thought he had in mind. Suspicions whispered in her ear again.

"Isn't that a little fancy? I thought you just wanted to grab a bite to eat and talk about research."

His smile disarmed her before he said a word.

"Who says the bite has to be in a fast-food place? Or that we have to chew fast?"

He saw the protest forming on her lips, saw the indecision in her eyes. He was winning her over, but he had to talk quickly to sustain his advantage. Getting her to a friendly, neutral place that might seduce her defenses was all part and parcel of his plan to get her comfortable enough to talk to him. The more she talked, the more likely she'd be to let something slip.

"Think of it as partial payment for your time," he told her.

She couldn't help smiling. "Script points and dinner?"

"Right. And anything else you can think of, too."

Her eyes narrowed. *Was* this just an elaborate come-on after all? She didn't want to believe it, yet... "Such as?"

"I'm very handy with my hands."

Her heart sank. It was a come-on. "I'm afraid I really don't—"

He stopped her before she said something he was going to regret. "That didn't come out right. What I mean is that I can fix things around the house. Cracking plaster, doors that stick, things like that."

The small condo she had sublet from Jon's friend could more than use a face-lift, but not from someone she didn't know. She knew the danger of opening her door and her life to someone.

"I don't need anything fixed," she assured him.

"All right," he replied philosophically, "then it'll just be dinner and research."

"Dinner and research," she echoed.

A line was beginning to form at the register again. Joe was looking toward them with a less than friendly expression on his face. Ben began to talk quickly before Gina saw the clerk and retreated to help him. "What time would you like me to pick you up?"

It would keep things simpler if he didn't know where she lived. "Since this is dinner and research, why don't I just meet you at the restaurant?"

He picked up on her reluctance to share her address. The scale tipped against her again. "You really are an independent woman, aren't you?"

The grin that curved her mouth nearly unraveled him. It was completely guileless and captivating. "Whenever possible.'' Hearing Joe clear his throat, she realized that she'd somehow managed to drift away from the register. She began moving back toward the registers. ''Now then, I'm afraid I've got to get back to work.''

He wasn't finished yet. There was one more thing he needed from her. Her prints. Ben glanced toward the section she had directed him toward yesterday. ''Um, I was wondering if you could recommend any other books for me from the store?''

She thought a moment, shaking her head. ''I think we covered that last time.'' Surprise flittered over her features. ''You didn't finish the one you bought yesterday already, did you?''

He nodded. ''Stayed up all night. I thought if there was something else—''

''All right, let's see.'' Because he seemed so eager, she went to check the books listed by subject on the computer. Going over the inventory, she stopped at a particular title. ''Well, there is one more that might help—''

All he needed was one. Because the books were accessible to the public, the idea of getting her prints from the one he'd already bought hadn't occurred to him until after he'd handled it extensively. He wasn't about to make the same mistake again. ''Take me to it.''

She couldn't help smiling. ''You really are eager about this, aren't you?''

He said what he knew she needed to hear, even though there was a part of him that was starting to feel uncomfortable with the duplicity. ''So eager I can taste it.''

Telling Joe she would be right back, she brought Ben over to the American history section and, after a moment, found the book she was looking for. It was out of place. "This one doesn't go into depth on the battle, but it does give you a pretty good background on the tribal life and the people." Turning from the shelf, she started to hand the book to him.

He made no effort to take it from her. Instead, he indicated the register. "Great. I'll take it."

"Don't you want to look through it first?"

"No, I trust your instincts." He began leading the way to the front counter. She had no choice but to follow. "Ring it up for me and I'll be out of your hair until tonight."

"All right." Joe spared her an annoyed look as she went to the second register and scanned in the book for Ben. "Twenty-three fifty-eight."

She took the two bills Ben handed her and made change, then tore off the receipt and slipped it, along with the book, into a bag.

He took the bag from her. "I'll see you tonight, then."

"All right." She said the words, banking down the excitement that popped up unexpectedly. A customer looked at her impatiently and she waved the woman forward.

"What time?" Ben asked.

"Excuse me?"

"You didn't tell me what time," he pointed out, then suggested one for her. "Seven all right?"

Gina hesitated for a moment. It would take a while for Jesse to settle in if he knew she was going out. "Eight would be better."

"Eight," he agreed. "I'll see you then."

A feeling of triumph mixed with something he couldn't quite identify flowed over him as he left the store.

His next stop was a stationery store he'd seen on the next block. He needed a padded manila envelope.

"Where's the nearest post office?" he asked the clerk who rang up his purchase.

The woman thought for a moment, then conferred with the woman at the next register before giving him a location. The branch was five blocks from his motel.

Back in his car again, Ben wrote out ChildFinders' address across the front of the manila envelope, marking it to Rusty's attention, then slipped the book, the receipt and the paper bag inside. The brief note he included asked Rusty to get all three items to the lab to be dusted for fingerprints. Since she'd been a government employee, Gloria Prescott's prints had to be on file somewhere. Between Rusty and Savannah, he figured it wouldn't be all that difficult to find the prints and get a match.

If there was one.

He tried not to dwell on his resistance to the idea. He wasn't getting paid to take sides, but to do a job. So far, the agency had solved every case of a missing child. He didn't intend to be the first one to fail.

Jesse scrutinized Gina with sharp green eyes. "Are we going out, Mommy?"

She'd been anticipating the inevitable barrage of questions all through dinner, especially since she hadn't eaten, just kept him company while he'd had his. "Not we, kiddo, me."

Uncertainty imprinted itself on his small face. "You're leaving me?"

She knew that ever since they'd uprooted from the only place he'd ever called home, he'd felt uneasy and threatened. She turned from the mirror that a number of earthquakes had managed to warp ever so slightly and looked down at him. "No, I'm not leaving you. I'm going out for a few hours. Like I used to, remember?"

He nodded, his small head bobbing up and down. "When we lived in Bedford?"

She stooped down to give him a quick hug meant to reassure him. And maybe herself, just a little. "Yes, baby, when we lived in Bedford."

He disentangled himself from her, giving her his most grown-up look. "I'm not a baby, Mommy. I'm six."

"Right, practically a man." She rose to her feet again. "Sorry, I keep forgetting." Slipping on her heels, she smoothed the sides of the dress, then looked down at her kindest critic. "So, do you like it?"

He cocked his head, doing his best to look as if he was scrutinizing her. "It's okay. Is it for somebody special?"

She wasn't taken in by the noncommittal tone. She knew what was on his mind.

"You're the only somebody special in my life, kiddo. And don't you forget it." Catching him by the shoulders, she tickled him. He dissolved in a fit of giggles. "How about me, am I the only somebody special in your life?"

He worked his bottom lip with baby teeth. "Maybe."

Pretending surprised indignity, she fisted her hands at her hips and gave him a penetrating look. "Oh, 'maybe' is it? Okay, spill it, kiddo, who's the hussy who stole your heart? Out with it. What's her name?"

He laughed, knowing she was only kidding. His mom was a great kidder. "Judy. Judy Camden."

"Judy, huh?" Even as she teased, she searched Jesse's eyes for signs of things she anticipated. He wasn't going to be hers exclusively forever. The shift had to start sometime. She knew she wasn't going to be ready for it no matter when it came, but for Jesse's sake, she was going to do her best to pretend she was. "So, what's this Judy Camden like?"

"Pretty," he said quickly, then added in a slightly lower voice, "and she's got candy."

Gina stifled a laugh. He was still her six-year-old. "Knew it, an ulterior motive."

Jesse's features drew together in concentration. "What's an ulterior motive?"

Picking up a comb, she did last-minute touch-ups to her hair. "A reason that you're doing something that isn't always obvious."

He was quiet for a moment. "Like why we moved away, Mommy?"

She was careful not to let him know how much she worried about the way all this was affecting him. At no time had she ever said anything to lead him to believe he was in any danger. "We moved away because I wanted to live in San Francisco for a while, and be not that far away from Aunt Sugar." Smiling brightly, she trusted herself to look at him. "You like Aunt Sugar, don't you?"

The grin was wide and infectious. "Yeah, she's nice. And she makes good cookies."

"That she does." Finished, she took his hand in hers. It felt so small, she thought, protectiveness welling up inside of her. "Now, it's off to bed with you, kiddo. Betty's coming, so you call her if you need anything and I'll be back before you know it."

He looked up at her as they walked into his bedroom. "Promise?"

She crossed her heart with her free hand. "Promise."

He beamed at her. "I love you, Mommy."

She picked him up in her arms, needing to hug him to her. "And I love you."

Jesse drew back his head so he could look at her. "Forever and ever?"

"Forever and ever," she repeated. "And a day longer than that."

Satisfied, he nodded. "Okay, you can go."

She laughed and scooted him into his bed, thinking herself to be the luckiest woman who ever lived. "Thank you, master."

"You're welcome."

He giggled at the face she made at him.

Chapter 6

Her perfume seductively preceded her as Gina approached his table. Just the lightest, stirring scent of honeysuckle teased his senses. The promise of spring within the heart of winter.

Ben got his mind back on his job and his role. He smiled at her as he rose in his seat. "I was beginning to think you weren't coming."

Slipping out of her coat, Gina slid into the seat the maître d' held out for her. She tried not to pay any attention to the strange, small quiver in the pit of her stomach. Ben's masculinity was just the slightest bit disconcerting.

His eyes were kind, but he wasn't a safe man. He was a man who could easily rattle a woman's foundation, who could make a woman stray from the clear-and-narrow path. A man who could have her forgetting her thoughts in midsentence. Like now.

"I was beginning to think I wasn't, either. Friday

night's not the easiest night to find—'' Gina caught herself, stopping abruptly. She met his quizzical expression with a soft one of her own as she continued. ''What I was looking for.''

That wasn't what she'd been about to say, Ben thought. ''Which was?''

''A new dress.'' She looked up at him brightly. ''Do you like it?''

His eyes slowly took inventory of what he could see. A simple high-necked turquoise dress that graced her curves as if it had been made with just her in mind.

And stirred a man's mind in directions that were best not traveled, he thought.

''Very much.'' He indicated the plate of stuffed mushrooms. ''I ordered appetizers for us, I hope you don't mind.''

The candle's flickering flame accented the pleased light that entered her eyes. ''No, I love stuffed mushrooms.'' She gingerly picked up one and popped it into her mouth. The familiar taste stirred memories. The last time she'd had stuffed mushrooms was at the art gallery show. When her life had changed forever.

He watched the small appetizer disappear between her lips and entertained the oddest sensation of being envious of a mushroom. And then he smiled.

''What?''

Instead of answering, he picked up his napkin. The tiniest scrap of cheese stuffing clung to the right corner of her mouth.

''Hold still.'' Capturing the point of her chin with his hand, Ben lightly wiped the telltale evidence away.

For just the slightest moment in time, he felt a current pass through him, tightening his belly. Ben dropped the napkin back down on his lap.

The look in her eyes told him she'd felt it as well.

God, but her eyes were blue.

Gina's mind turned to mush as the breath stopped in her lungs.

"You, um, had a little cheese on your mouth," he said.

"Thank you," she murmured, searching for something safe to talk about and trying not to think about the way her stomach had suddenly given birth to a squadron of butterflies just because a man she hardly knew had wiped away a dot of cheese at the corner of her mouth.

The waiter appeared to save her, ready to take their order.

"Would you like more time?" Ben asked. "You haven't had a chance to look at the menu yet."

"Allow me to tell you the specials of the day," the waiter offered, then subtly took a deep breath to launch into a recitation.

But Gina held her hand up, stopping the man before he could tell her the first item.

"That's all right, I know more or less what's on the menu and what I want. I used to come here all the time." It had been one of her favorite places to go. She'd taken Aunt Sugar here one of the few times the older woman had visited her in San Francisco.

"Used to? When?" Ben kept the question casual as he looked over his own menu.

"In another life," she murmured half to herself, then looked up at him, sensing he was looking at her. "I went to college around here."

"But it's not home."

"No, it's not home." Glancing at the menu to make sure the item was still being offered, she ordered shrimp with alfredo sauce and surrendered her menu to the young waiter.

"The same," Ben told him. The waiter nodded and withdrew. "He looked disappointed that he couldn't tell you the specials of the day." There was laughter in her eyes and he found himself momentarily mesmerized and lost. "What?"

She was being silly, she thought. Probably just giddy at the thought of getting out for the evening. She shook her head. "Nothing."

"You're trying not to laugh. Let me in on the joke," he coaxed. "What is it?"

"It's just that the waiter looks a little like Clark Kent." She nodded toward the departing food server. "Superman's alter ego," she prompted when Ben didn't say anything.

"I know who Clark Kent is." She'd given him an opening. He took it and ran with it. "I was just thinking about secrets."

"What about them?"

The shrug was purposely vague. "That everyone probably has one or two."

Gina looked away as she took another stuffed mushroom and eased it onto her small plate.

He was making her jittery. Good, that made two of them. Except that he wasn't supposed to be. He was supposed to be thinking about the case and not about the long legs that were beneath the table, next to his.

"How about you, Gina? Do you have any secrets?" He kept his tone light, teasing. Watching her eyes.

Gina raised them to his as the rest of the restaurant and its occupants seemed to recede. Despite the quavering in her stomach and its new winged occupants, she couldn't help wondering if Ben was fishing or flirting.

She was being paranoid again, she upbraided herself. Why would he be fishing? He had no connection with where she'd come from. No connection to why she'd left.

But looking over her shoulder was what kept her and Jesse free.

"Like you said, everyone has secrets, I think." With effort, she kept her voice as light as his. She looked at him pointedly.

"So, what's yours?" He topped off her glass of wine, though she'd only had a sip or two. "Better yet, what's your secret fantasy?"

A faraway look entered her eyes. That was easy. "Just to be happy."

Ben studied her, intrigued. "That's all? That doesn't sound like such an exotic fantasy."

The last thing she wanted was an exotic fantasy. She'd indulged in fantasy once and been slapped down just as it was about to become a reality.

"It's not. But don't kid yourself, it's harder to achieve than you might think." She'd sacrificed a great deal to that end. The look in his eyes told her he wasn't about to drop the subject. She turned the tables on him. "How about you? Any secrets up your sleeve? Any unfulfilled fantasies?"

He drained the rest of his drink. "Two very different questions," he pointed out.

"Then choose one." Finished with the mushroom, she wiped her fingertips on the edge of her napkin. "And answer it."

He thought a moment, then took his cue from her and embellished in a way he knew would draw her in. A way he actually believed in when cynicism didn't intrude, getting in the way. "I guess being happy sounds pretty good." He paused in just the right place. "And making the world a better place for being in it."

"Very noble." Was he just feeding her a line? She'd rather think that he wasn't, that he was being sincere. "Is that why you've decided to tell the story?"

He was getting lost in her eyes again, he realized. He'd hoped to use his charm on her to get her to open up, but it seemed that the reverse was proving true. And she didn't even seem to be trying. "Excuse me?"

"The massacre. At Wounded Knee. Your screenplay," she finally said when his expression remained ever so slightly bewildered.

"Oh, right." Annoyance at his own lapse rose up within him. He smiled engagingly. Covering. "Sorry, I got lost in your eyes for a second there. I don't think I've ever seen blue that intense before."

And he wasn't now, she thought. At least, not in the way he believed. She was wearing contact lenses. All part of the disguise. The pang of regret was unexpected and Gina blocked it, but not before it had made its presence known.

She struggled to clear her head and not lose her own way amid the lies that were tangled within the truth.

"So, any other fantasies?" she asked brightly. "Besides writing the great American screenplay?"

"No, that would about do it," he replied with a gentle smile. But if he were to indulge in a fantasy, he thought, it would have something to do with a woman who smelled of honeysuckle in the winter and had a waist that begged for a man's hand to slip around it. He reached for one of the breadsticks instead. "I guess I'm just your average, run-of-the-mill, boring guy."

The last thing this man was, was boring, she thought. There was a sexual vitality about him. Just being in the same room with him was enough to make that evident.

She liked the way he looked at her, as if she were the only one in the room instead of just one of many. There was a danger in liking it, but for a few hours, under the protective umbrella of a crowded restaurant, she'd allow herself to enjoy it. Just a little. What was the harm in pretending? As long as she remembered it was just pretend.

The waiter returned with their meals, murmuring something about hoping they enjoyed them before he retreated again.

"You're right," Ben acknowledged, lowering his voice as he leaned in toward her. "Clark Kent all the way." He grinned at her.

It was the kind of grin that went clear down to the bone, Gina caught herself thinking, as it took her hostage. She was going to have to watch herself. She was definitely still too vulnerable to be out with a man she didn't really know.

The evening passed far too quickly and he'd enjoyed it. Enjoyed talking to her, looking at her. The conversation hadn't brought him an inch closer to his investigation. Revolving around impersonal subjects as well as his supposed screenplay's subject matter, somehow it had still managed to give him an intimate image of the woman across the table.

Or maybe it was just a skillfully fashioned image he was meant to buy into. He wasn't certain. Instincts that had seen him through so much had suddenly proved useless. All he knew was that he found himself liking her. More and more.

Guilt ran through his conscience. You weren't supposed to like a kidnapper. If she was one.

When the check arrived, he paid it in cash rather than use a card, then rose to his feet to help her on with her coat. As he did, he palmed the scarf she'd worn tucked in at the neck, slipping it into his pocket. Then he leaned in close to distract her and keep her from noticing its absence.

"Sure I can't convince you to go dancing?"

Dancing. That would describe what the warm shiver that was traveling through her was doing. His breath touched her skin as he spoke, creating a longing that was almost overwhelming. A longing that reminded her she was a woman. Regret was abysmal but had to be obeyed.

"I'm afraid I'm sure."

He suddenly regretted that he wouldn't have an excuse to hold her in his arms, even if it was only for three- to five-minute increments. "Maybe some other time."

"Maybe."

The night wind was cold and brusque, as they left the shelter of the restaurant and stepped outside. He wasn't used to weather like this. Living in Southern California had made him soft. "So, can I drive you home?"

"I came in my own car, remember?" She pointed vaguely out into the parking lot.

He turned up his collar, thinking he should have worn something warmer. "How about if I follow you, just to make sure you get home safe?"

The offer amused her. And touched her. It'd been a long time since anyone had concerned himself about her safety.

"Thanks for the thought, but I'll be fine." She touched his face. "Really."

He didn't want to let her go yet. All he'd found out tonight was that he liked the sound of her laughter. But he already knew that. What he still didn't know was how to reconcile two very different Gloria Prescotts he'd been introduced to.

"Here's another thought," he said just as she began to turn away. She raised an eyebrow, silently questioning him. "How about a nightcap? Your place, my place, or somewhere in between. Take your choice."

She raised her eyes to his. They were completely unreadable. All he could read was his own thoughts, his own reactions. And a sudden surge of desire that was as out of place here as ice cubes at a bonfire.

Dammit, he wanted to take her into his arms and kiss her. He bit off an oath in his mind as he shoved his hands into his pockets.

Gina began to say no, he could see the word forming on her lips. "I really don't—"

He needed her confidence, needed to gain access to her house or apartment. "It doesn't have to be anything strong," he assured her. "Water would do." He was losing her. Ben went with the truth. Or part of it. "I just don't want the evening to end."

Gina hesitated, so tempted she ached. But there wasn't just her to think about. She came in a distant second, no matter what this man with the bedroom eyes did to her insides.

Suppressing a sigh, she shook her head. "No, I'd better not. I promised to be home early."

"Promised?" Something twisted inside of him as he repeated the word. "Promised who?"

"Someone," she said evasively.

"Does it have anything to do with those 'complications' you mentioned yesterday?" he guessed.

She smiled then, relieved that he was accepting the excuse. Touched that he could be so sensitive about it. If only…

There was no "only." What there was, she reminded herself, were lies. And safety. "That's very perceptive of you."

"I'm a perceptive kind of guy." Although that seemed to be getting further and further from the truth, he thought. "If I can't see you home—yours or mine—let me at least see you to your car."

That was safe. And nice. "All right."

That same itch he'd felt when she'd first walked in through the door and taken off her coat tonight began to take hold again. Complicating things. He reminded himself that he had his code.

He also had an itch.

As she turned toward him to say good-night, he had another strong, almost overwhelming urge to sweep her into his arms. The candlelit dinner they'd just shared hadn't helped keep his feelings impersonal. Neither did the full moon looking down on them. It made him think of romantic things.

Nothing romantic about looking at a kidnapper, he reminded himself. He was looking for proof, for a missing boy, not romance.

Gina put out her hand. "Good night, Ben. I had a lovely evening."

He slipped his hand over hers, thinking how delicate it felt. "Me, too. Thanks for coming." Reluctantly, he released her. "Tell him he's a very lucky guy, this 'complication' you're going home to."

She thought of Jesse, probably waiting up for her,

dressed in those pajamas with the feet on them. She'd left him in bed, but she knew he wouldn't be asleep. He was stubborn that way.

Gina shook her head. "I'm the lucky one in this case." Getting into her car, she shut the door, then looked up at him again. "I'll see you."

"You've got my number," he called to her. He told himself it was just a phrase as he backed up, watching as she drove off.

Things were just not adding up, Ben thought as he got a beer from the minirefrigerator in his motel room and sat down at the table where he'd set up his laptop and the paraphernalia Megan had talked him into bringing. He'd done some canvassing of McNair's area before he'd left Bedford. The man lived almost in isolation at the apex of a hill in an exclusive neighborhood. His neighbors hardly knew of his existence, much less of Gloria's. Certainly he hadn't found anyone who had seen her leave with the boy the day he disappeared. Rusty had been thorough in the report he'd e-mailed to him.

As pompous as McNair was, he certainly did like anonymity in his private life. Ben frowned, sipping his beer and trying not to think about the woman he'd just left.

Or who had just left him, he amended. Black hair or blond, he could see why McNair had lost his head over her. What he couldn't see was the grasping, ruthless woman McNair had made her out to be.

Maybe her true colors would come out later.

And maybe he should take the weekend to go back down to McNair's area and do some more canvassing.

Or prevail on Chad and whoever else was free to help do it for him.

Chad had to be back from his honeymoon by now, he mused. Who would have ever thought that Chad Andreini would ever fall in love, much less get married? Looked like once in a while, miracles actually did happen.

He was going to need one himself if he hoped to solve this, Ben thought.

This attempt to get close to Gina was leading him into areas he didn't want to go and really beginning to complicate things. He was having some definitely unprofessional thoughts about Ms. Gina Wassel and the sooner he got back on track, the better for everyone.

Especially a small kidnapped boy by the name of Andrew.

Ben glanced at the door he'd just shut, debating going out again. If he confronted her tonight...no, tomorrow morning would be better. He needed a night's sleep and a night's distance from what he'd almost done. Kissing a kidnapping suspect was definitely not in the rule book, not even under miscellaneous.

He leaned back in the chair, balancing himself on two of its legs and stretching. That was when he saw it. The answering machine he'd plugged in to replace the motel's telephone was sitting on the nightstand by the sagging bed. It was flashing.

Setting the barely touched can of beer back down on the table, he got up and crossed to the machine. He pressed the message button. A metallic voice told him that he had one message, then proceeded to let him hear it.

"Ben, it's Carrie. That man whose son you're looking for called three times in the last two days, wanting a progress report. I told him you were out in the field and would get back to him when you could. He's not very happy with that answer. Said you told him you'd keep him abreast of things. He's getting a little belligerent. Maybe you could get back to him?"

A little belligerent. That was his secretary Carrie's shorthand for pompous ass. He had a feeling that Stephen McNair's winning ways did not extend to people he viewed as underlings. Or the "hired help."

By rights, he knew he should have already told McNair where he was. But he had a hunch that the man might insist on joining him and possibly ruin everything. Until he found the boy, until he knew what was going on, Ben didn't want McNair showing up.

McNair hadn't exactly struck him as someone who was beside himself with grief over his son's kidnapping, anyway. The calls to the agency seemed almost out of character. Probably just McNair being a control freak, he decided.

Ben frowned, erasing the message. None of the pieces he was juggling seemed to fit in with the others, he thought. Not even when he examined them closely.

Was that because of Gina? Gloria, he corrected himself. It didn't matter what the woman's name was, she was definitely messing up his thought process and it had to stop.

With a sigh, Ben returned to the table, to his beer and to thoughts that were going nowhere.

Chapter 7

Like a small, intent shadow, the little boy followed her from the kitchen to the threshold of the small, crammed garage that was now too cluttered to hold a car, thanks to the condo owner's resistance toward never throwing anything out.

"But why can't you play with me?" He looked accusingly at his mother as she rummaged through first one area, then another. "You promised last night when you went away that you'd play with me today. It's today," he announced in case she'd missed that fact.

If dogged determination was the main requirement, this boy who was the light of her life was going to grow up to be a lawyer, there was absolutely no doubt in her mind.

"That was before the kitchen pipe decided to double as a colander."

Where *was* that toolbox? She was sure she'd seen one in here somewhere when she and Jesse had moved in. The condo belonged to a friend of Jon's who was out of the country and glad to be able to sublet it. Since the terms were reasonable, something she had a feeling Jon was responsible for, she felt the least she could do was make repairs when they came up.

Turning around, she looked at her son, still standing in the doorway. "Listen, kiddo, there's nothing I'd rather do than spend time with you, but right now, I need to try to fix the sink. Besides, you had a good time with Betty last night." She picked up a pile that represented laundry waiting to be washed and moved it. No toolbox. "I know you did. She read you all your favorite stories, didn't she?"

Jesse rocked back and forth on his sneakers. "Not all my favorites," he hedged.

She'd had time to talk to Betty while waiting for the baby-sitter's mother to come for her. Betty had given her a detailed account of the evening. "But most of them, right?" Finding a space between the washing machine and the dryer, she looked there. Victory.

"Most of them," he allowed casually, conceding defeat. He was bright enough to know what worked and what didn't when it came to evoking guilt and gaining favors.

"And she played games with you, don't bother denying it." She knew for a fact that Jesse had talked the sitter into letting him get up again after she'd left for the restaurant.

Using both hands, she dragged out the toolbox and carried it to the kitchen. What was in here, anyway? It felt as if it weighed a ton and had enough tools in it to reconstruct the Golden Gate Bridge.

"Not the good kind, Betty said. She likes video games."

Gina spared him a glance. This was an old, familiar tune.

She flipped the toolbox open and began rummaging inside for a torque wrench. "Too bad, we like board games, don't we, Jesse?" When she received no response, she looked up at him. Jesse had sucked in his lower lip pensively and was staring at her, the picture of petulance. "Don't we?" she repeated gently.

"I guess." Huge green eyes looked up at her from beneath wisps of wheat hair that were in the way. "Kyle has a really nice new video set, just like my old one. He's got Race Like the Wind and his mom lets him play it *all* the time."

She smiled sympathetically at him, ruffling the hair she'd so recently cut. She liked his hair longer, but for now, the close-cropped look would have to do. It was the only way she could change his appearance without alarming him. Luckily, Jesse thought he looked "cool."

"I'll get you a new video set when I can, kiddo. Until then, why don't you just enjoy the board games? Lots of kids grew up without video games, you know. They played board games instead."

He sighed dramatically. "Were they poor, too?"

Too. Was that how he felt? Aching for him, she gave Jesse a hug. "We're not poor, kiddo, we're just temporarily not well off."

"I know, Mommy."

He sounded so grown-up just then. Laughing softly, she shook her head. "I'll see what I can do."

Finally finding a torque wrench, she wriggled it out of the box.

Excited, Jesse clapped his hands. "Oh, boy!"

Gina pretended to look at him sternly and failed miserably. "That doesn't mean we're getting one right away," she warned.

"Yes, it does." Because she was on her knees, he could reach her. Jesse threw his arms around her neck and squeezed hard. "You're the best, Mommy."

The words, the embrace, was what it was all about to her. There was nothing more precious to her than this little boy. The single being who made everything worthwhile and bearable. How could she say no to him?

"Yeah, the best pushover." Bracing herself, she got down as far as she could and angled herself beneath the kitchen sink. That the doorbell should pick this time to ring only seemed fitting somehow. Murphy's Law. "Now what?" she muttered irritably. She had half a mind to let it ring.

"The doorbell's ringing," Jesse sang out gleefully. An open, loving child, he loved company. It made no difference if the company was an adult or a kid his own age, he welcomed everyone.

"I hear it, kiddo, but I'm busy right now." Whoever it was would come back if it was important.

"That's okay, Mommy. I'll get it for you," Jesse volunteered.

Crammed into an uncomfortable position underneath the sink, Gina didn't hear what Jesse said at first. But when she called out to him to repeat himself and received no answer, a vague semblance of his words echoed back to her.

He was answering the door.

"Jesse, no!"

But even as she called out, she knew that it was already too late. Time and again she'd instructed Jesse not to talk to strangers or to open the door to anyone, but it was like trying to take wheels off a wagon. Somehow, magically, the wheels always reappeared and the wagon would go merrily on its way. Jesse was the last word in friendliness. Part of her hated to squelch that innocence, especially so early in Jesse's young life, but it was exactly his life that she worried about.

Scrambling up quickly, Gina smacked the top of her head against the cabinet. The impact went right through her, rattling not only her head but jarring the pit of her stomach before traveling clear down to her toes. That one really hurt.

Wobbly, she got to her feet and hurried to the front of the house.

The door was standing open.

"No!" she shouted, launching herself at it. She was about to push back the man she was certain was standing on the other side.

But it wasn't who she thought it was.

It was Ben.

Wavering, she stared at him, confused. Fear began to trickle in. She hadn't told him where she lived. What was he doing here?

Had he followed her last night?

The single question flashed through her mind, dragging up all the dark implications that went along with it.

Gina felt her throat begin to close up.

"What are you doing here?" she demanded.

Ben had had less than half a second for the image of the little boy answering the door to register. Intent on seeing Gina, he hadn't expected to be looking down at a little boy. A little boy who, with longer hair, would look a great deal like the little boy he'd been sent to find.

She had Andrew.

He had to get in touch with McNair.

The thought telegraphed across his mind, then faded. Instead of saying anything to her, he stood there, trying to come up with some sort of explanation for what he was so obviously seeing.

There wasn't one. He didn't have enough input to form one, yet he couldn't quite make himself believe that he was seeing what he thought he was seeing.

Her insides shaking suddenly, still wobbly from the blow to her head, Gina got in front of Jesse. She pushed the small boy behind her protectively, his resistance to the act vaguely registering.

"I said, what are you doing here?"

Putting his hand into his pocket, Ben pulled out the scarf he'd purloined from her last night.

"I came to give you this. The waiter came out with it just as I was getting into my car."

Gina spared the scarf a glance. She hadn't even realized it was missing. "That still doesn't explain how you knew where I lived."

"Simple. I stopped by the bookstore. Some guy named Miles said you weren't coming in, and then he volunteered to give me your address."

Miles. That explained it. She thought of the slightly developmentally challenged young man who Jon kept around to do menial work. Beneath Jon's brusque exterior beat the heart of a kind man. He just didn't like people knowing about it. Miles was always eager to be helpful. She was sure that he'd been more than happy to volunteer where Ben could find the information he wanted.

Ben made eye contact with the boy she was attempting to hide behind her and smiled at him. He was rewarded with a huge grin. The boy looked none the worse for the ordeal. As a matter of fact, he looked as if he was thriving. Any way Ben tried to look at the situation, it just didn't make sense to him.

Gina raised her chin in what could only be taken as a challenge. He blocked the image of nibbling on that chin that suddenly flashed through his mind.

"You went through all that trouble to return my scarf?"

"Seemed like the thing to do." He nodded toward the wrench she held at her side. "Is something wrong?"

Jesse peered out from behind his mother's hip, volunteering to field the question. "Mommy's a pushover and she's fixing our sink because it's a calendar."

The boy called her "Mommy." Had she brainwashed him? Ben knew it wasn't out of the question for kidnappers to force children to answer to different names, to scrub their memories of the lives they'd led before their kidnapping in order to reshape their identities. Those children were taken with the intention of never being returned to their homes.

Was that what she had in mind? Was Andrew filling some hole left in Gloria's life, replacing a child she'd lost? Or was there something else going on here, something he was being kept in the dark about?

Instincts warred with common sense. He needed more input.

"Hush, Jesse." She kept her hand against the boy. Exasperated, she slanted a look toward Ben. "He's telling you things out of context."

Jesse. She called the boy Jesse and he responded to the name. Could it be possible that he'd made a mistake after all? Ben wasn't really certain one way or another. But one thing at least seemed to ring true. Especially since she was holding a torque wrench in her other hand, and now that he looked, he noticed that the edge of her shirt was damp.

"What's wrong with your sink?"

"It's leaking." She fought to keep her voice from taking on a nervous edge. "Now, if you'll excuse me, I was in the middle of trying to fix it."

Rather than leave, Ben moved around her and into the house. "Let me have a look at it. I'm pretty good at fixing things, remember?"

She recalled his offer to trade handyman services for her help. "So am I. Usually." Although, she had to admit that at the moment, she was out of her depth.

The feisty spark in her eyes got to him. He liked women who could hold their own. "I'm sure you are, but do you mind if I take a look? It's this macho gene in me. I try to squelch it, but it seems to rise to the surface whenever I'm around any tools."

"Tools?"

He reached for the wrench she was holding, his hand meeting hers. "Wrenches, hammers, screwdrivers, things like that."

Drawing her hand away, Gina blew out a breath. After an incredibly short internal debate, she relented. Temporarily. "Are you really any good?"

The boy was regarding him with unabashed interest. One of the straps of his overalls was sinking down his shoulder. Ben pushed it back into place, then ruffled the boy's hair. A wide smile met him.

"Worked summers for a general contractor while I was in college. My uncle," he added, hoping that would sway her. He'd been pretty good at it, too, but working with his hands had never been more than a means to an end for him.

Gina wavered. She really didn't have the money to

pay for a regular plumber. That was why she was trying to fix the leak herself in the first place. Beyond applying plumber's putty to strategic places and running an auger down a plugged pipe, she was pretty much in the dark when it came to plumbing problems.

"Okay, I guess you can't do any harm." At least, she hoped not. With Jesse running on ahead, she started to lead the way to the kitchen, then stopped just short of the threshold and looked over her shoulder. "Can you?"

"Never lost a sink yet," he told her cheerfully. He edged around her again, deliberately moving her aside. "Let's see what you've got here."

Crouching down, he surveyed the offending pipe. He was aware that he'd been joined by a pint-size shadow who was mimicking his every move. The kid was definitely none the worse for whatever had happened to him. That was a good sign.

Ben sat back on his heels. "It's leaking, all right."

Gina crossed her arms in front of her. Macho gene, huh? "That much I could figure out for myself."

"The next thing we have to see is if it's leaking from a hole or a fitting that's come loose." As she watched, Ben lay down on his back and snaked his way under the sink. "Got a flashlight?"

"Right here!" Jesse announced. Grabbing it from the drawer where he'd seen it being put away the other day, he shoved it into Ben's outstretched hand.

"Thanks." Ben managed to cock his head slightly, just enough to look at his undersize assistant. "My name's Ben."

"Pleased to meet you, Ben," Jesse said, just the way he'd been taught. "My name's Jesse."

The boy said his name as if he believed it. He needed

time to sort this out, Ben thought. He figured fixing the leaking pipe might just buy him a little.

"Yes, I know." Moving from side to side, Ben snaked his way out again. He sat up, looking at Gina. "Well, the pipes haven't come loose. There's a hole in one of them. You need to have it replaced."

So much for hoping that it was just a matter of having to tighten something or slapping on a liberal application of plumber's putty. She peered at the guilty pipe, though from her angle she couldn't detect anything. "Is it expensive to replace?"

"Shouldn't be, unless you want to use a pipe made out of gold." He got up a scant few inches away from her, brushing himself off. He couldn't help noticing that she'd done a quick survey of his body, even though she was trying not to be obvious about it. Ben tried not to dwell on the fact that it pleased him. He wondered if she knew just how close she'd come to being kissed last night. "If you tell me where the hardware store is, I can have you leakless in about an hour or so."

She couldn't overcome the suspicion that kept scratching away at her. She longed for the days when she could just accept a favor without wondering what the price tag, or ulterior motive, was. Very deliberately, she placed her hands on Jesse's shoulders to keep him from gravitating to Ben's side.

"Why would you fix my sink?"

"Because it's broken," he replied simply. And then he flashed a grin at her. "Besides, you're helping me with research, the least I can do is return the favor."

Ben Underwood was simply too good to be true. Handsome, friendly, helpful and, from the looks of it, handy with his hands, and basically good with kids. That made him every woman's dream come true. But she'd learned the hard way that when things seemed too good to be true, they usually were.

And even if he was as altruistic as he was trying to come across, she didn't want to be in debt to him. "I'd have to pay you."

"You can pay for the pipe," he agreed, tucking in his shirttail, which had come out as he'd gotten under the sink. "The rest we can negotiate." He could swear that he saw fear flash briefly through her eyes. Why? What had he said? It was just a joking, offhand comment. "You could feed me lunch," he added, just in case the pale color of her cheeks was an indication of some sort of fear that he might attempt to take advantage of her.

"Lunch?" she echoed.

"Yeah." He slipped his jacket back on. "That thing between breakfast and dinner. A sandwich will do if you have it."

Jesse tugged on the bottom of his jacket. "I like sandwiches," he told him. "Ham and cheese are my favorite."

This was one adorable kid. He shuddered to think how many people would pay a great deal to have a son like Jesse. Was that it? Was this some sort of black-market stolen-child ring he'd stumbled across?

Glancing at Gina, he just couldn't reconcile his thoughts with his instincts.

"Sounds good to me, Jesse." He fixed his collar and then turned to Gina. "So, where's the hardware store around here?"

She thought a minute, trying to remember the location of the one she'd passed the other day. "There's Harold's Emporium at Sequoia and Main. I don't know the exact address, but the building looks like a big red barn. You can't miss it."

"I know where it is, I know," Jesse told her excitedly.

There were times that nothing Jesse said surprised her. She humored him. "How do you know?"

"I saw it when we were coming home from the movies last week."

Last week. But McNair said the boy had been taken only a few days ago. More discrepancies, Ben thought. *Was* he barking up the wrong tree after all? In which case, Andrew's trail had become exceptionally cold. But somehow, he didn't think he was that far off.

Jesse was moving from foot to foot, his excitement building. "I can show him where it is. Can I go with Ben, please, Mom?"

"No!" The word had come out too emphatically. But there was no way she was about to let him out of her sight with a man who was essentially a stranger. Gina pressed her lips together, trying to sound calmer. "I need you here, Jesse. You can help me make lunch for Ben."

Jesse clearly would have rather accompanied his new friend on the field trip, but he nodded his blond head, forlorn and crestfallen as he looked at Ben. "I guess I'd better stay with Mom and help."

The boy's command of the language impressed him. McNair had told him that his son was six. Most six-year-olds, at least those he had come in contact with, were a rowdy bunch who barely had a nodding acquaintance with manners unless they were force-fed down their protesting throats. McNair hadn't mentioned that the boy was bright, or lively. The man's description of his son had been just the bare minimum. Without the photograph to go on, Ben would have said that the description could have fit any number of boys.

He bent down to the boy's level. "I'd like mustard on mine," he told him. "And I'd like you to watch that pipe for me while I'm gone. Let me know if the leak gets worse. And don't let your mom," or whoever she was, Ben added silently, "use the sink while I'm gone."

Jesse nodded as if he'd just been entrusted with a solemn duty. "Okay," he promised.

"I'll be back as quick as I can," he told Gina, rising to his feet again.

"You really don't have to put yourself out this way, you know," she said, walking with him to the door. She noted that rather than go with them, Jesse remained behind, watching the pipe intently. Ben had found a way to temporarily cap Jesse's exuberance.

"There's nothing in my refrigerator. Call it working for my lunch."

She watched him leave, wondering if she was being overly trusting.

Chapter 8

Frowning, Gina picked up the cloth and wiped the bits of clay from her hands. She couldn't give the bust she was working on her full, undivided attention. Not with Ben Underwood lying flat on his back just a few feet away in the kitchen, fiddling with pipes beneath the sink that had seen better days.

Giving up, she threw down the towel and walked into the kitchen to see just how he was doing. He'd returned from the hardware store approximately half an hour after he'd left, armed with enough things, in her opinion, to replace all the pipes not only beneath the kitchen sink, but the ones in the two bathrooms as well.

The man had the air of an overachiever about him, she thought with a smile.

She'd be the one to know about that, she thought ruefully. When she'd graduated from school, she'd been all set to conquer the world. Instead, it had conquered her.

Not yet, she thought fiercely. *Not yet.* She'd deal with those thoughts later, when she felt they actually were safely in her past.

She looked at Jesse, crouching on the floor beside Ben's outstretched legs, ready to jump in and help at the slightest sign from his newly adopted mentor. In an incredibly short amount of time, Jesse had taken to Ben as if he'd been waiting for a man like him to come along all of his young life.

Maybe he had.

This, she had to admit to herself as she slanted a look in Ben's direction, was the kind of man she would have chosen to be Jesse's father. If she could have chosen. She thought of Jesse as the most fortunate accident of her life. He'd been conceived in the worst of all possible circumstances, but despite his beginning, Jesse had turned out far better than even her wildest dreams.

His father had been a smart man, at least as far as book intelligence went. But genes only went so far, even erudite, sophisticated ones, she thought wryly. Environment counted for something. She'd tried desperately to provide everything that a sensitive, impressionable child like Jesse might need, but in her heart, she'd always known that it wasn't enough. What Jesse truly needed was a man by his side he could look up to.

Didn't they all, she added silently.

She was trying very hard not to notice that the would-be screenwriter had a body that had been fashioned in someone's sculpture class on a good day. Firm and rippled. Certainly better than any of the male models that had been recruited to pose in her art classes all those years ago. But then, those were boys, this was a man with a capital *M*.

Although looks had never really been that important

to her, they certainly didn't hurt, either. And this man had his share. Any way you cut it, from the top or the bottom, Ben was very easy on the eye.

As long as that didn't lead to a softening of the brain, Gina reminded herself. She'd been that route once, and though she had Jesse to show for it, once was definitely enough.

Gina glanced at the clock on the stove. Ben had been at this for more than an hour. Her eyes rested on Jesse's crouched form. Of course, he'd had help and she would be the first one to agree that small helping hands had a tendency to lengthen the time it took to do a project rather than shortening it.

"How's it going down there?" Not that she could actually see for herself, but Gina bent her head down to look in, anyway.

The flashlight Ben was using managed to also illuminate his chest and the T-shirt that was draped tightly over it. Even lying down, the man had pectorals to spare.

God, but she would love to capture that in clay. She could almost feel his chest forming beneath her fingers, the clay falling back to allow that firm, muscular body to emerge.

Her fingers itched.

She was romanticizing again, she upbraided herself.

Turning his head slightly away from what he was doing, Ben saw a long, curvy silhouette encased in well-fitting jeans that underscored the shapely legs beneath. Her breasts were straining against her blue sweater as she leaned in toward him.

He had the sudden urge to tangle his fingers in her short, dark hair, to bring her face down to his and find out if her lips really did taste of wild strawberries, or if they only looked that way.

He was going to need a shower after he finished here for more than one reason, he thought. A particularly cold one, even if it was chilly this time of year up here.

"Almost done," he told her, retreating back under the sink.

It would be safer all around, he told himself, if he just looked at the pipes and concentrated on what he was doing. He had to stop letting himself be distracted.

She looked at the clock again. "I guess I'm lucky you don't charge by the hour."

"But I do." His voice floated out from under the sink. "A sandwich an hour." Ben looked out to the left where Jesse squatted by his feet, eagerly awaiting his next request. "How about you? Does a sandwich an hour sound fair to you?"

Jesse shook his head up and down with vigor. "Very fair."

He probably meant that, too, Ben thought, grinning as he tightened the pipe seal slowly, careful not to crack it. The kid looked as if he actually had a handle on what he was being told.

Cute, smart and helpful. What more could a parent want?

The return of their child, that's what, he reminded himself sternly, thinking of McNair. But in the last couple of hours, it had become so natural to think of this towheaded boy as belonging to Gina, not McNair. They had this easy relationship, this give-and-take that he would have thought would have taken time to develop.

Gloria had been Andrew's nanny, he reminded himself. That was time enough to develop a rapport. As for calling her Mommy and responding to being called

Jesse, for all he knew that was a game she'd told the boy they were playing. A pretend game. Kids were good at games. Especially smart kids.

There were a thousand possibilities within the framework of what was going on. A thousand ways to fit the jagged pieces together.

Until he had some more facts he could work with, facts he could make sense out of, he was going to have to keep up this charade, and if that meant fooling around with corroded pipes in order to get the information, so be it. He'd certainly been called on to do worse.

For the time being, however, he'd dragged out this particular fix-it project as far as it could go. With little effort he could have had the sink back together in half the time. Ben couldn't remember ever working so slowly in his life.

But he'd done what he'd set out to do. Created a rapport with Jesse. The boy had talked a blue streak. Unfortunately, none of it was actually helpful in piecing together what had happened. He hadn't even mentioned his father, but that could have been due to his feeling like an outsider in McNair's home. The man had told him he'd had trouble adjusting to his role as father. Andrew, or Jesse, had probably picked up on that. Asking the boy any direct questions about his father was out of the question. Gina was too close and would hear everything. For now, he had to keep a low profile.

Relieved to finally be out from under the sink, Ben scooted out and retired the wrench that Jesse had given him a few minutes ago, putting it on the floor beside him.

"I think we're done, partner."

He watched as Jesse picked up the tool and placed it back into the toolbox. Glancing to the side, he noticed that the boy had also replaced the lid on the plumber's putty the way he'd asked him to. Hell, the kid was neater than he was.

Rising to his feet, Ben dusted off his hands. His shoulder, the one he'd been wounded in, ached a little. He rotated it automatically, then looked at Jesse. "Okay, ready to see if she flies?"

Jesse's brows came together in a puzzled blond line. "It's supposed to fly, too?"

"That's just an expression, kiddo," Gina told him, coming up behind Jesse. Looking at Ben, she draped her arms on either side of the boy. The gesture wasn't lost on Ben. She was silently establishing boundaries. Silently saying that the boy was under her protection.

"Oh. An expression." Jesse nodded his head sagely, as if committing another thing to the vast catalog of his memory.

Damn cute, Ben affirmed. He gestured toward the faucet. "You want to do the honors? You turn it on and I'll watch to see if it leaks."

"Okay." But even standing on his tiptoes, Jesse still couldn't reach the faucet to turn it. Frustration creased the concentration on his face.

Gina moved to pick him up so that he was closer to the faucet, but Ben stopped her. "Tell you what, let's switch jobs. You watch, I'll turn."

The reversal brought out a broad smile. "Sure." Holding the side of the sink just the way Ben had a moment ago, Jesse squatted down. His eyes were trained on the new pipes.

Ben had the water running full blast. "See anything?" he asked the boy.

"Just pipes," Jesse replied solemnly, his gaze never wandering.

Ben bent down to inspect his handiwork for himself. He shone the flashlight from one end of the new pipes to the other. No telltale leaks, squeezing themselves out of almost invisible spaces, appeared.

"How about that, you're right. Just pipes. Looks like we fixed ourselves a sink, pal." He rose to his feet again, Jesse popping up like golden toast beside him. "Put 'er there." Ben stuck out his hand.

Surprised and pleased, Jesse slipped his hand into Ben's, shaking it as if he were Ben's equal. Only his dancing eyes gave away the combination of pride and joy he was feeling at being treated this way.

"Now it's time for you to do your part." Ben turned to look at Gina. "Got those sandwiches ready for a couple of hungry men?"

"Yeah, hungry men," Jesse echoed, standing close to Ben.

Jesse was having the time of his life, Gina thought. She'd taken him to Disneyland last summer and she could swear he was having more fun now than he had then. Had she known, she thought wryly, she could have just bought Jesse a toy sink to fix and saved herself a lot of time and money.

She knew it wasn't just playing with tools that had brought that wide smile to Jesse's lips, it was feeling that he'd been helpful and treated like an adult by an adult.

He was a good kid. And maybe, just maybe, Gina thought, Ben Underwood was a good man. A really good man.

There had to be at least one around, didn't there? It wasn't just a fairy tale she'd been buying into all of her life, was it? Somewhere, men who were kind and good really did exist. She still believed that, needed to believe that. And maybe one had gotten loose and found his way to her doorstep.

Her mouth curved with just a touch of self-mocking. She was going to have to stop buying into those bedtime stories she read to Jesse.

"Already taken care of. The sandwiches are waiting for you right there."

Gina pointed to the tiny breakfast nook where she and Jesse took all of their meals. The table in the dining room had been taken over by a computer on one side and the bust she was currently working on when she found the time on the other.

From where he was standing, Ben thought he caught a glimpse of something that looked like a mountain of clay. He edged over just a little, still looking, trying to get a better view.

Gina saw where he was looking. Self-consciousness slipped over her. "Your sandwich is over here, on this table." She thought of moving and blocking his view, but he was faster than she was.

"Just a sec."

He realized that she could take it as a clear invasion of privacy, but curiosity had him walking into the other room to get a better look at the unfinished work.

It was a bust of the little boy. As he studied it, Ben saw that even though Gina hadn't finished it, she had somehow managed to capture the essence of the boy, the lively spark in his eyes. He didn't think that was possible with clay.

Impressed, he looked at her as she came in after him. "You do this?"

She sculpted to let out feelings, to work through emotions. In part, she considered it to be like therapy. But, until it was finished, it was a private thing she didn't want viewed by strangers. Elbowing Ben out of the way, she picked up the towel she'd used earlier and draped it over the bust.

Ben looked at her. It wasn't so much a desire for privacy, he thought, scrutinizing her expression, as intense embarrassment that had prompted her covering the bust.

"It's not very good," she murmured. Not yet. But it would be, she promised herself. When it was finished.

"Not good?" How could she say that? Even unfinished, it looked remarkable, and he wasn't one impressed by works of art. "It's fantastic." Something from his childhood nudged itself forward. "All I ever managed to do with clay was make those thin, long snakes. You know, the kind you get by taking a hunk of clay and rolling it between the palms of your hands over and over again." One eye on her face to see if he had her silent permission, he removed the cloth again and then dropped it to the side. Subtle nuances, like the dimple in the corner of the boy's mouth, rose to meet him. She had real talent. "This sure beats that."

"Lunch" was her only response as she turned on her heel to lead him back to the kitchen. But he thought he detected the hint of a pleased smile flirting with her lips.

He thought of flirting with her lips himself, then banked down the intruding urge.

Again, he wondered what a woman like Gina was doing, mixed up in something like this. She was not only beautiful, but talented. Why jeopardize all that? Though his first allegiance was to his client, Ben felt he had to get to the bottom of this before he made any calls. Otherwise, it might go badly for her, and he didn't want that happening unless it was absolutely unavoidable.

Once they were brought in, the police department was not going to go out of its way and take mitigating circumstances under consideration. That was for the courts to deal with.

And even then it might not go well for her. He'd seen too many trials won by the sharpest lawyer, the one who played tricks and pulled rabbits out of a hat. Truth got lost somewhere along the way. But while the case was still his, he intended to take on the parts of both law enforcement and judicial system until he got some answers that at least partially satisfied him.

Jesse pushed his chair over, bringing it closer to Ben before scrambling up on it. The huge grin on the boy's face when he looked at him was infectious. "You were a great help today, partner," Ben said.

"After lunch, can we fix something else?" Jesse asked.

Ben popped the top of the can of soda Gina had put out and raised his eyes to hers. "I don't know, what needs fixing around here?"

The thing that needed fixing most, Ben couldn't do anything about, Gina thought. She gave Jesse a slight reproving look. He knew better than to pester. "Mr. Underwood has better things to do than to hang around here fixing things, Jesse."

"Actually, I don't," Ben contradicted. He saw that his response seemed to throw Gina off a little, but sticking around here for the rest of the afternoon was better than he could have hoped for.

She didn't want Jesse making too big a deal out of this. If Ben stayed, if he just hung around as if he belonged, Jesse might get the wrong idea. He might get used to this and she didn't want him to. Not when he was going to be disappointed in the end.

"No scenes to write?" she asked Ben pointedly.

"I thought I'd take the day off, let things just simmer in the back of my head for a while." He paused to take a drink.

Out of the corner of his eye, he saw Jesse do the same. When he bit into his sandwich, chewing slowly, Jesse aped his every movement. Ben couldn't help being amused. He also couldn't help seeing that Gina noticed Jesse's actions as well.

"Jesse, Mr. Underwood doesn't need you to ape everything he's doing."

He smiled, then winked at Jesse who, pleased, fluttered an eye shut in response.

"That's okay, Gina. I don't mind. It's kind of flattering, I think." It was, he realized. He'd never been anyone's hero before. "I think you've got yourself a real winner here."

Unable to resist, Ben ruffled the boy's hair again. It felt incredibly soft to the touch. Ben couldn't help wondering if Gina's hair felt the same. He pulled himself up short. For a minute, he'd forgotten that the boy wasn't actually her son.

"I don't think I've ever met a kid who's better behaved or more willing to help. You've done a great job raising him." He watched her face for any sign of some sort of discomfort at the praise.

There was none. Either she was one hell of an actress, he thought, or…

Or what?

"Jesse's just a naturally good kid," she told him. "When he wants to be," she added affectionately, thinking of times when he'd been less than angelic. But for the most part, he was the joy that kept her life centered. Very deliberately, she shifted the focus away from her and her son to Ben. "So, how long have you been a writer?"

The question caught him off guard. He'd been getting lost in her eyes again, in the soft, supple curve of her neck, in watching the way the ends of her hair brushed along the outline of her face.

Ben cleared his throat, rousing himself. "All my life, really. I just decided to get serious about it a few years ago."

"And you've just been working on this one screenplay all this time?" Was he a procrastinator, she wondered, or had there been some day job to sap his time, the way there had been with her.

Ben looked appropriately embarrassed. "No, there've been others, but nothing that seemed sellable."

"But this will be." It was half a question, half a general assumption.

"I think so. I think the story of Wounded Knee is a story whose time has come. If I get it right," he added with a touch of modesty he knew would go over well. "Which is where you come in."

The thought was not without its merits. It also produced a smile that seemed to form deep within her. If she wasn't careful, he was going to charm her just like he'd managed to charm Jesse.

Going to? Hell, he'd already done it. All she needed was to be stuffed into a box and tied up with a big, plump pink ribbon.

"I'll do my best."

"Me, too," Jesse chimed in, a dab of mustard smeared on his chin. "I'll do my best."

Ben lifted the boy's chin with his hand and wiped away the mustard with the tip of his thumb. "It does a man's heart good to know he's got a good team behind him,'' he said solemnly.

Gina both loved and worried about the way the boy's eyes lit up when he looked up at Ben.

Chapter 9

She had to admit she was impressed.

Ben had helped her clear the dishes away and then dried while she washed. And when Jesse asked him to watch a videotape with him, the one he'd almost worn clean through in the last few weeks about a celebrated mouse and his duck friend, Ben hadn't begged off with some spur-of-the-moment excuse. Instead, he'd sat down with the boy and actually watched the tape. Twice.

When it ended the second time, Gina walked over to the television set and switched it off. Jesse looked up at her in surprise. "Mom."

"Twice is enough for now, Jesse. You've already watched that tape so many times, we both know the dialogue by heart." She looked at Ben on the floor beside her son. It was a scene she could too easily let herself get used to. And so could Jesse. She needed to nip this in the bud before it went too far. "It's not fair to make Ben watch it a third time."

Playing peacemaker, Ben asked Jesse, "Got anything else you'd like to watch?"

"Yes." Jesse began to run to his room for his other prized videotape.

"No," Gina said firmly. Jesse stopped in midstep and looked at her. "I think we've detained Ben here long enough."

Which was his cue to leave. Ben rose to his feet inches away from her, wondering what had caused her to suddenly do a one-eighty. He kept his expression and remark amiable. "You know, if I didn't know any better, I'd say you were trying to get rid of me."

Relieved that he wasn't going to try to talk his way into staying longer, Gina was already leading the way to the front door. It was one thing to spend a little time with him at the bookstore, or even over dinner, but having him in her home was a whole different ball game. She'd allowed his engaging manner and the leaking sink to mitigate her resolve. Watching him with Jesse had almost made her forget it entirely. But it was because of Jesse that she couldn't afford to let her guard down. She'd already established that she could never tell where the next threat was coming from, and though it seemed unlikely, it might be from him. For Jesse's sake, she had to be cautious.

"I'm not trying to get rid of you but, um, I've got some things to do and I'm afraid that I don't have the time to entertain a guest."

Though she'd started to open the door, he lingered just a moment. He needed to be invited back. To make her trust him enough to be willing to open up. There was this feeling in his gut he had to work through and he couldn't do it without concrete evidence to refute it.

"Gina, I've held your corroded pipes and plugged up your leak. I'd think that puts me beyond the realm of a guest. Maybe somewhere in the area of student and teacher, seeing how you're helping me get my story straight. Or maybe," he added more softly, "with a little luck, we could be friends." He looked into her eyes, seeing her soften. Trouble was, he was feeling the same way himself. And that wasn't good. Especially since he was fighting off the very real, very intense urge to kiss her. "Friends don't need to be entertained. I can hang out with Jesse."

For a second, she wavered. It took effort to remind herself that she'd heard that before. Pretending to enjoy her son's company when it was all a ruse just to get to her.

At a loss, that same nervous feeling slipping over her, the one that warned her something was out of kilter, Gina put her hands on her hips and looked Ben squarely in the eye.

Could you tell if a person was lying to you just by looking into his eyes? She'd never been very good when it came to uncovering the truth. Until it was too late.

For Jesse's sake, she had to make herself sound distant. "Why are you so intent on staying here?"

There it was again, he thought. That look. The one that telegraphed fear. What was she afraid of? It couldn't be him. He was deliberately being his most harmless, most charming. And yet, he could swear there was a leeriness in her eyes, as if she thought perhaps he was the devil himself, or one of his minions.

"Not intent," he said, beginning to correct her, then

deciding to play it more simply. He looked at her with concern. "What is it, Gina?"

She stiffened, raising her chin, her body language warning him off. "What's what?"

"You look like an inexperienced soldier who just sighted the enemy and you don't know whether to shoot or retreat." She began to protest, but he added gently, "I'm not the enemy, Gina. Why would you think I was?"

For just a second, when he looked at her like that, she felt her mouth go dry. She couldn't let him get to her. But he was. So quickly she could hardly draw a breath. It wasn't even anything he said, it was just the way he looked at her. The way he smelled. It had been a very long time since she'd been with a man, and up until Ben came along, it hadn't really bothered her.

But it did now. That made her nervous, too. Because she didn't want primitive yearnings coloring her judgment or making her drop her guard.

"I don't think of you as the enemy. You're letting your imagination run away with you," she told him shortly. Gina opened the door, her message clear. "Now, I don't want to be rude, but I'd really appreciate it if you left."

Hands raised, he stepped outside. "I never overstay my welcome. Well, hardly ever," he amended just before she closed the door in his face.

Definitely more going on here than met the eye, he thought, walking back to his car. One minute she was friendly, the next, it was as if her own actions surprised her and she became distant and formal.

Guilt did funny things to people, he thought. But if she felt guilty about taking the boy, why didn't she attempt to contact McNair and return him? For that matter, why hadn't she contacted McNair at all, at least to torment him? That had been the man's implication, and he knew that if McNair had received any word from Gina—no Gloria—Ben corrected himself, McNair would have been on the phone immediately, reporting this latest event to the office, which in turn would notify him.

No one was notifying anyone, which meant she hadn't called. Why not? What was her game? *Did* he have the right woman, or was there some sort of colossal blunder going on?

The only blunder, he told himself, would be if he allowed himself to get sidetracked by this woman. He was already feeling far too kindly toward her.

One way or another, he intended to get to the bottom of this. He hoped that the bug he'd planted in her kitchen phone while she'd been busy in the other room would tell him what he wanted to know. Maybe she wasn't in on this alone, and whoever her silent partner was, he or she would get in contact with her in the next few days. It was something to hope for. He was grateful now that Megan had insisted they all keep surveillance equipment with them, just in case. At the time he'd thought carrying it around was rather melodramatic.

Live and learn, he mused, watching the condo in the middle of the block become smaller and smaller in his rearview mirror.

That had been his real reason for showing up on her doorstep with the scarf he'd taken last night—to plant the bug. When Jesse had become his miniature shadow, he'd been afraid that he wouldn't get the opportunity, and as long as Jesse was with him, Gina was never far away. But he'd finally managed to plant the bug when Jesse had gone to the bathroom and Gina was out of the kitchen. The few minutes he'd been alone in the kitchen had been all the time he needed.

He just hoped it would bear some fruit.

"I want to apologize."

Ben had been uncertain how to proceed given the way things had ended on Saturday. The day and a half he'd spent waiting for any incoming or outgoing calls on Gina's line had amounted to an exercise in futility. The only call out she'd made was to a theater that played children's movies. That had been early Sunday morning. There had been no incoming calls. The woman was a nun. It should have frustrated him, and it did, a little. But it also pleased him. More than a little. That in itself worried him, because he felt it was getting harder and harder to hang on to his objectivity.

But here it was, Monday, and he needed to find a way to get himself back into her good graces and remain there until at least he had positive confirmation from the prints he'd sent in to be analyzed. So he'd walked into the bookstore a little after noon, prepared to do any damage control necessary to get to his goal.

She was glad he'd come into the store. She hadn't thought he would, after the way she'd brushed him off. She'd tried to talk herself out of regretting it later, but hadn't quite managed to get there. Seeing him here now brought with it an elation she hadn't been prepared for.

There was almost no one in the store. Mondays were notoriously slow. The browsers tended to come in the latter half of the week, as did the college students who suddenly needed books for weekend assignments they'd put off to the last minute. Monday saw only diehard book lovers and people who had nowhere else to go for half an hour.

She motioned Ben over to the side, away from Joe, who wasn't even trying not to look as if he was listening.

"Apologize?" she asked, curious. "For what?"

"For making you uncomfortable," he began, feeling his way around slowly. But Gina cut him off before he got his footing on the path he was searching for.

"I'm the one who should apologize." This wasn't easy for her, but just because she'd taken a few wrong turns in her life and had paid the consequences for it was no excuse to be rude to someone whose only fault was being nice. "For being so abrupt on Saturday. I mean, you did go out of your way to fix the sink and you saved me more than a few dollars. I know what plumbers cost these days. It's easier to marry one than to pay one." She was digressing. Gina forced herself back to her apology. "I shouldn't have pushed you out like that."

She was wearing it again, that vague stirring scent that made him think of long, cool spring evenings under the stars. Of stretching out on bright green shoots of grass made velvety by the night and holding a woman in his arms. "I don't recall any pushing."

"Not physically." A rueful flush washed over her cheeks. "But you know what I mean."

Gallantry was the best inside track and he knew it. Women appreciated a man who was willing to forgive quickly. "Consider it forgotten."

"Good."

That over with, Gina was about to get back to work. Except that she couldn't. She'd behaved in a manner she would have taken Jesse to task for if she'd caught him at it. Ben was being incredibly gallant about it. The least she could do was give him some sort of explanation. She knew it shouldn't matter one way or another, and that after he was finished with his research, she would probably never see him again, but she didn't want him thinking of her as some moody, mercurial woman.

Gina forced herself to turn around. He was still looking at her. She pushed the words out before she stopped herself. "It's just that...when you showed up on my doorstep like that...I guess in a way it really freaked me out. I..."

She trailed off, feeling helpless and hating the feeling. Helplessness was something that was new to her. It'd become her jailer in the last few months. She didn't like what the twists and turns of her life had made her become. She wanted to be free to be open again. To not look for hidden meanings in words and hidden agendas in people. To stop looking over her shoulder all the time and just enjoy her life for a change instead of being forced to guard it zealously.

He saw her struggle. Something beyond practicality had him saying, "That's all right, you don't have to explain if you don't want to."

Because he didn't press, she told him. Told him what she hadn't shared with anyone. Because no one would have probably believed her. The deck had been stacked against her right from the start, she'd just been too naive to realize it at the time.

Even so, she tempered her story so that Ben couldn't piece it all together. She had to be careful. Even with the truth.

"I was stalked once. It lasted several months. When you showed up like that on Saturday, it sort of brought everything back. I'm sorry if I took off your head."

The would explain her initial behavior, but not why

she'd suddenly all but asked him to leave. For the time being, he figured it best not to point the fact out.

"I'm very resilient. Head's still attached," he told her, moving it from side to side to illustrate. And then, slowly, his smile faded on the off chance that she was telling him the truth. "I'm really sorry. I didn't mean to drag up any bad memories. I had no idea."

Having him apologize made her feel worse. "Of course you didn't, how could you?" She shrugged, looking around the bookstore. And then her eyes came back to his. Was she making another mistake, letting him know about this? She hadn't even told Jon or Aunt Sugar about this. Neither one of them had pressed for an explanation, either. So why was she sharing this with Ben? Why was there this feeling that this almost-stranger could actually be someone to her, if things were just a little different?

"A lot of people think you bring it on yourself, being stalked," she heard herself saying. "Or that you're just imagining it, turning harmless attention into something sinister."

She wasn't making this up, Ben thought. The look on her face when she spoke was real. Unless she was a better actress than he'd ever come across. He restrained the urge he had to put his arm around her shoulders and comfort her. "Did they ever catch the guy?"

Her expression changed right before his eyes. Growing distant again. "I'd rather not talk about it. I just wanted you to know it wasn't you, it was me."

This time, as she began to leave again, it was his words that stopped her. "My sister had the same problem."

Gina looked at him. Was he just fabricating something to put her at ease? "Really?"

"Really." It had been his youngest sister and he could still remember the fury that had gripped him when she'd finally told him about it. "She was in college at the time. Guy wouldn't leave her alone. Followed her around, memorized her schedule. Would constantly pop up, chase away any guy she would start seeing."

It took effort for Gina not to shiver. Except for the college part, he could have been talking about her. It had gotten to the point that she'd been certain her every movement was being monitored. And then the final threat had come, sending her hurrying with Jesse into the night.

"What did she do?"

"Cindy went to the police and they took care of it for her." He didn't add that he was the police Cindy had gone to and that he had taken the stalker aside to describe, at length, in great detail, exactly what would happen to each of his body parts if he didn't stop bothering Cindy. That had been the last Cindy had ever seen or heard from the guy.

Gina laughed shortly. He noticed that her mouth remained set firm. "I guess she had a more sympathetic police department where she lived."

"Maybe," he allowed offhandedly. "Did you try going to the police at the time? Get a restraining order?"

Gina shook her head. She hadn't bothered. She knew what the results would have been. "It was just my word against his."

"So?" In his experience, the police tended to be more sympathetic toward women in these cases. Unless she was lying simply to take him in for reasons that were unclear to him.

"So he was someone with clout. I wasn't. End of story." She heard the electronic doors opening as the buzzer went off. Customers. It was time to get back to work.

But she hadn't ended it, he thought. "He just stopped stalking one day?"

"Let's just say...." But saying anything would be giving away too much. Giving away information she didn't want him to have. "Yes," she finally said. "He did. Now I've got to get back to work."

"I still have some questions." While monitoring her phone, he'd spent the time reading the other book he'd bought. And making notes so that his conversation on the subject wouldn't sound uninformed. "Could we try dinner again tonight? I could have you back and in bed by ten. Your bed. Alone," he emphasized, knowing she'd turn him down if she thought he was hitting on her. He laughed ruefully and not completely for effect. "I guess I've got a long way to go before I get to be smooth."

"Not such a long way," she contradicted. And he knew it, she thought. Still, maybe he was trying to put her at ease. She appreciated it.

"I'm afraid tonight's not a good night." Betty, she knew for a fact, was busy. The girl had told her all about the sweet sixteen party one of her friends was having, even though it was a weeknight.

"Going out?"

She knew she was within her rights to tell him that was none of his business, but she didn't want to. Instead, now that he knew about Jesse, she told him the truth. "I don't have a sitter."

"That's all right, I'll bring dinner to you. Enough for all three of us," he added to forestall any protest. "How does pizza sound?"

He'd hit upon Jesse's favorite meal. And one of hers, too, if she were being honest.

"You don't take no for an answer, do you?"

"Not unless no's the answer I want to hear." His smile was engaging, seductive. Gina felt herself weakening. "So, is that a yes?"

She gave in and felt herself smiling. From the inside out. "It's a yes. I know Jesse certainly wouldn't mind seeing you."

"Great." *Score one for the home team.* "Pizza it is."

"Not so fast," she interjected. "There's one condition."

He tried not to look wary. "And that is?"

"That you bring some of your screenplay with you." Maybe she was taking too much of an interest in him, but she found herself wanting to know things about him. Small, intimate things. The way he wrote was definitely a major part of that. "I want to read the kind of work you do."

We've got trouble, right here in River City, he thought to himself, feeling like the famous huckster in *The Music Man* once the jig was up. "I haven't polished it yet."

His sudden shyness struck her as sweet. "I'll keep that in mind."

There wasn't a single word on paper to offer her. His mind scrambled for viable excuses to give her in place of the screenplay. "The truth of it is, I don't really feel comfortable about letting someone see the unfinished product...."

The more he resisted, the sweeter he seemed. Gina grinned. "I'll keep that in mind, too. Unless this whole thing is a hoax," she teased.

There was a smile on her lips, but he had the feeling

that she might be more than a little serious. He had to produce something in order to keep this charade alive a little while longer, at least until he received word about the fingerprints one way or another. If he pulled the plug now, without the final proof he was waiting for, without getting to the bottom of what he felt was a problem, she might just take the boy and disappear on him. She'd already done it once; there was nothing to prevent her from doing it again.

Which meant he had to come up with something on paper between now and tonight.

"All right," he agreed reluctantly, hoping magic would strike somehow, "I'll bring a few pages—but don't say I didn't warn you."

She grinned. The buzzer sounded again and there was someone at the register. Joe was nowhere to be seen. "Don't worry, I'm sure it's wonderful. You're probably a lot better than you think."

Great.

Feeling less than triumphant, Ben was already striding toward the door. He had work to do.

Ms. Parsons had once told him he had potential, if only he learned how to apply himself. Ms. Parsons had been his eleventh-grade English teacher, strict in her own way but extremely supportive if she felt there was a reason to be. She'd found that reason in him, or so she'd said, except that he'd never done anything to justify that faith. And he'd never quite figured out what she'd meant by saying he should "apply" himself.

The most he wrote these days were the reports that Cade insisted on at the end of each case. And even that was like pulling teeth.

He just wasn't the literary sort.

But Ms. Parsons had thought he could be.

Ben sat at the computer, scowling at the void that comprised the blank screen. God had taken a void and created an entire world in six days. All he had to do was create a few pages in six hours. How hard could it be?

Very, he discovered after an hour had elapsed.

Disgusted, Ben surrendered and got on the telephone, tapping out the number to ChildFinders. He was big enough to admit he needed help. Fast.

"ChildFinders, Inc."

"Carrie, this is Ben. Give me Savannah."

"She's out of the office, Ben," the secretary told him. "She said something about needing to take a few hours' personal time."

Murphy's Law, he thought. "Damn."

"Will Eliza do?"

"Maybe. Wait a minute, how are you at writing?"

There was a pregnant pause. "Writing what, checks?"

He had a feeling this was leading to another dead end. "No, creative writing."

Ben heard a groan on the other end of the line, followed by a laugh. "I took English pass-fail in college. Does that answer your question?"

He was right, another dead end. Mentally, he crossed his fingers. "Give me Eliza."

"Good choice."

Eliza listened patiently to his problem, then regretfully informed him she wouldn't be of any help to him. "Not on this kind of short notice, at any rate. I'm afraid I don't know anything about the subject of your screenplay."

He was pacing now, trying to think as he talked.

"Got any suggestions? She's expecting to see at least a few pages."

"Level with her. Tell her the dog ate it."

It took no effort on his part to visualize the smile on Eliza's face. He could hear it in her voice. "Very funny. Nice to know psychics have a sense of humor."

"I'm sorry, but—hold it, didn't you once tell me one of your friends was a screenwriter?"

"Would-be screenwriter," he corrected her. "Yeah, Nick Paraskevas."

"All the better, that means he probably won't be busy. Maybe he could help you out."

"Yeah, maybe."

At least it was worth a shot.

Chapter 10

He couldn't reach Nick.

In the end, he had no choice but to write the handful of pages himself. It was either that or show up at Gina's house tonight without them. That would be difficult to explain, not to mention awkward, especially since she had made a point of mentioning it.

Finished, Ben got up from the crammed desk and dropped onto the sofa, then bit back a curse. The rain was bothering his shoulder. He thought back to all the times he'd teased his grandfather whenever the latter complained about the weather affecting his aches and pains.

"Wish you were around, Granddad, so I could tell you I was sorry. I know how you must have felt now." Grabbing a throw pillow, Ben tucked it under his back and tried to get comfortable for a minute.

His brain felt as if it were in the middle of a fog. What he needed, he thought, was to go out for a good jog. Jogging always cleared his head and got him back on track.

No chance of that happening right now, he thought, glancing out the window. It was coming down in sheets outside.

Ben reached for the telephone. He needed to talk to Savannah before she left the office for the day. Time had slipped away from him as he sat at the computer, agonizing over the pages.

"You just missed her," Megan told him when she answered the phone on the fourth ring. "She went home to take care of one of the girls. Some kind of post-Christmas flu going around. I'm the only one here."

"Where's Carrie?"

"Dental appointment, she left early. Why, what's the matter, don't want to talk to me?" He heard her laugh softly. "Might be your only chance. I'm going out of town tonight."

"New case?"

"Nope. Long overdue honeymoon. Garrett and I finally got our schedules to coincide."

From what he'd heard, it'd only taken over a year. Megan and her man from the DEA had been married before Ben ever came to the agency. "What do you need a honeymoon for? By now the two of you should have it down pat."

"Ever hear the saying practice makes perfect?" Her laugh was low, husky, anticipating things to come. "So, what can I do for you?"

"Do you know if Rusty and Chad had any luck showing Andrew McNair's photograph around?"

They were aware of each other's cases, always on the alert for any crossover. It wasn't as uncommon as it might seem. He heard her shuffling paper.

"Adorable face," she commented. "Chad mentioned earlier that so far, there hasn't even been so much as a nibble. Same goes for this Gloria person's photograph. Savannah posted Andrew's photograph and description on the Internet site as soon as we got the case," she reminded him, "but you know that's just a shot in the dark."

He knew. There was a disheartening wealth of photographs on the nonprofit site. It was one of two. Both sites attempting to locate children who had either been kidnapped, or were simply runaways. ChildFinders had only one success story tied to the site, and that had come about sheerly by accident.

Most cases were solved that way, he thought. Hard work, long hours, skill, at times none of that seemed to matter. Luck played the biggest hand. He could use a healthy dose of it himself right now.

That, and maybe a larger helping of common sense. Whether or not he admitted it, he was playing with fire.

Sitting up, he felt the pillow slip down behind him. He had to get going. "All right, well, tell them I appreciate the help. I was just checking in—"

"I'm glad you did. McNair's been calling, harassing Carrie."

The man didn't give up, did he? "Harassing her? Why?"

"Because she won't give him your number up there. Carrie can hold her own with the best of them, but she said McNair is threatening to sue the agency for some sort of breach of promise if you don't get in contact with him immediately."

Ben grimaced in disgust. "Damn him, there's no breach of promise. I told him that I'd call when I had something."

There was a pregnant pause. "Well, don't you?"

It was curiosity, not judgment he heard in Megan's voice. There was a time, when he was on the police force, and she was with the firm, that they had gone head to head. But those days were behind them. He realized now what she'd had to contend with, working the cases she did.

"What I have right now is a situation. I want answers."

Reading between the lines was a habit of longstanding for someone who'd once been with the FBI the way Megan had. "We're not supposed to rehabilitate anyone, Ben, we're supposed to just bring kids together with their families."

"Yeah, I know. But there's something more going on here, Meg. I can feel it. But if I press too hard, I'm not going to get anything. It's like the Golden Goose story you read as a kid. Striking at the source might kill it, while coaxing it can get you everything."

Megan laughed. "Well, if anyone can coax things along, I guess you can." And then her tone shifted. "Listen, I hate to ask, but will you give McNair a call? Carrie said he sounded serious and I don't want to worry Cade with this."

He picked up on the note of concern. This was more than just one partner looking out for another. "Why, what's up with Cade?"

"His wife's having a tough time with the last stages of her pregnancy, and he's got enough on his mind without having to deal with a pompous jerk like Stephen McNair, no matter how important the man thinks he is."

It looked as if McNair had no fans at the agency, despite his being the parent of a kidnapped child. "Consider it done. Oh, and give Cade and McKayla my best when you talk to them.''

"Thanks, Ben. One of us'll give you a call if anything crops up about the case on our end.''

''Appreciate it. And try not to wear Garrett out on your honeymoon.'' He laughed when she told him what she thought of his comment, then hung up.

The smile faded the moment he thought of McNair. Ben had never liked being forced to do anything. He'd planned to call his client in his own good time. He didn't appreciate being kept on a short leash.

Ben glanced at his watch. He wasn't due at Gina's for another hour. He blew out a long breath. Might as well get this over with.

Taking McNair's phone number out of his pocket, he tapped out the numbers on the keyboard. The phone on the other end rang several times. Ben was about to hang up, glad of the temporary reprieve, when he heard the crackle of static and then McNair's voice.

''McNair here.''

So much for the reprieve. ''Mr. McNair, this is Ben Underwood.''

McNair's tone shifted from assertive to angry. ''Well it's about damn time you checked in with me, Underwood. Where the hell have you been?''

Ben had always considered himself relatively easygoing, but that didn't mean he was anyone's lackey. Mentally counting to ten, Ben waited before answering. Telling the client where to go wasn't considered to be in the agency's best interest.

''Working, Mr. McNair.''

McNair gave his opinion of that by using an expletive. ''If you are working, and I'm assuming you mean working for me, why haven't you called?''

Edges of his temper began to unravel. Ben struggled to remain civil as he answered, "I said I'd call you if there was anything to report."

"And I said I wanted you to check in periodically. I'm not paying you to be coy with me, Underwood. Where is she?"

Ben felt his jaw clench in response to the demand. "She? You mean 'he,' don't you?"

"Don't tell me what I mean. I said she and I mean she," McNair snarled. "*She* has my son, remember? Now, where the hell is she?"

If it wouldn't have reflected badly on Cade and Megan, Ben would have gladly told McNair to go to hell in no uncertain terms. But though he'd been made a partner, the agency was Cade's baby and he had to respect that. Even if the man he was talking to was an absolute jerk. "I don't know yet."

"Don't know yet? I thought you people guaranteed results. What the hell have you been doing these last few days?"

Allegiance to Cade notwithstanding, Ben was just inches away from telling McNair what he could do with his case. There was just so much a man could be expected to put up with.

"Sometimes these cases take more time than others," he told him through clenched teeth.

"I'm not interested in excuses, Underwood, I'm interested in results."

Ben had a feeling the CEO addressed stockholders, employees and boards of the directors in the same manner he was using now. As if he was entitled to absolute obedience and demanded nothing less. Well, it might work with everyone else, but the abrasive, condescending manner didn't cut it with Ben.

"Now, have you located that woman or haven't you?"

"I said not yet," Ben repeated. "Listen, Mr. McNair, if you're not satisfied with the quality of service you're getting from ChildFinders, specifically from me, you're welcome to go anywhere else you think might do a better job. Or the police, for that matter."

It still bothered him that the only reason McNair hadn't gone to the police was because he didn't want the notoriety it would bring. What did notoriety matter when his son's life hung in the balance? Maybe the boy had wanted to run away from his self-centered, despotic father and Gina had helped him get away because she'd seen abusive behavior on McNair's part.

He kept thinking of her as Gina, not Gloria. He had to stop that and remember to keep not only his distance but a healthy perspective in this.

There was silence on the other end of the line. It lasted so long that Ben thought McNair had hung up and the line had gone dead.

But McNair was still there. Ben heard his voice just as he started to hang up. The voice he heard was subdued. "I'm sorry, I didn't mean to fly off the handle that way. It's just that I'm worried about the boy. There's no telling what she might do to get even."

"I thought you said you weren't worried about Gloria harming Andrew."

A hint of McNair's annoyance returned. He obviously didn't like having his mistakes pointed out. "I was basing my response on past performance. But a woman who would steal a child right out of his own home is liable to do anything if she's desperate enough."

Personally, Ben didn't buy into that. He'd always believed there was a basic core within everyone. They were either decent, or they weren't. Some people were incapable of the final act of murder no matter what. Others…

He let the thought go, wondering only which category Gloria Prescott fell into. According to McNair, she was a coldhearted witch capable of anything, while everyone else had presented Ben with the opposite picture. Which was the real Gloria? He knew which he believed it to be. What he'd witnessed hadn't jibed with McNair's characterization.

Is that your head you're thinking with, or some other part? an inner voice mocked him.

"Look," McNair was saying, "accept my apologies. Just let me know if you find anything. Anything at all," he emphasized. "I might not be the best father and I am new at it, but the boy is still my blood and my one claim to immortality."

"Right. I'll let you know," he said, then dropped the receiver into the cradle. "One claim to immortality." It was still all about McNair, wasn't it? Ben thought.

The hot water felt better than good as it ran down in steamy rivulets along Gina's body.

Because she was alone in the house, she allowed herself to savor the moment. Jesse was playing three doors down with his new best friend, Kyle. She'd taken him there less than half an hour ago. It had been a spur-of-the moment invitation from Kyle, backed by Grace, Kyle's mother. Gina's first inclination had been to say no because Jesse hadn't finished his homework.

But Jesse had been persistent. He'd promised to do it at Kyle's and Grace had told her that she would see that both boys completed their assignments.

She'd given in, the way she knew she would. It wasn't in her to say no to him. But she hadn't told Jesse that Ben was coming over for dinner. That would have put him in the position of having to choose. She'd chosen for him. It was better this way.

She'd already detected a touch of hero worship in Jesse's eyes when he looked at Ben. The boy was so hungry for male companionship, it broke her heart. With Jesse here, Ben might not leave when she wanted him to.

And she didn't want him staying too long.

Gina turned the hot water up a little higher. She felt the tension leaving her, felt herself relaxing. Her eyes drifted shut. A myriad of rivulets ran along her body, zigzag patterns caressing every part of her. Like exploring fingers of a man's hand.

She missed that. Missed the feel of a man's hand touching her.

It had been so long, so very long since she'd loved and let herself be loved.

Yearnings rose to the surface again, reminding her that she was something more than just a mother, something more than just a person who worked in a bookstore. She was a woman, with needs that she had been valiantly struggling to ignore.

How much longer did she have to continue pretending they weren't there? How much longer before she would feel safe enough to let herself care about someone again?

She couldn't think about that. There was no point. She had her son to think about. His safety to worry about. If she allowed herself to get sidetracked, to feel responses when a man looked at her…

With a sigh, she shut off the hot water.

There was no use in torturing herself like this. Someday, she could be herself again. But not yet. Not today. Not until she was sure that Jesse and she were both safe.

She stepped out of the shower and began to quickly towel her hair dry, deliberately making her mind a complete blank. Otherwise, she might begin to visualize Ben in the role of the man who was missing from her life.

The thought brought her head up with a jolt.

Ben? That was almost as ridiculous as having a fantasy lover. Yes, he was good-looking and personable, but he was just someone passing through San Francisco. Someone passing through her life. He could be gone by next week.

Unless he decided to stay…

Why should he? He'd told her that he lived in Southern California, not here. She wasn't even sure where in Southern California. He'd mentioned Bedford, but he hadn't actually said he lived there.

Wouldn't that have been a coincidence…?

Gina tossed aside the towel. Still naked, she reached for a comb and began pulling it through her short, wet hair. What kind of a possible relationship could she have with any man, given her present circumstances? Her whole existence was a cobweb of lies.

Leaning forward, she examined her hair. Were those blond roots beginning to show? She frowned. Maybe it was the light in here, playing tricks on her eyes. She would have thought that hair dye would last longer than just two weeks. Even so, she made a mental note to color her hair the first opportunity she got.

The jarring noise had her heart slamming against her rib cage automatically. The doorbell.

That couldn't be Ben. It was too early.

She took a deep breath to steady nerves that had gotten dangerously frayed over the last few months and hurried into her clothes. There was no time to dry herself off. If she had to flee, she didn't want to make a run for it in a towel.

Sliding her hand along the banister, she rushed down the stairs and reached the front door in a matter of seconds. She held her breath as she stood on her toes, peering through the peephole.

The air left her in a huff, ushering in a surge of relief in its place. Gina pulled open the door. "You're early."

Ben walked in. "I was taught it was impolite to be late. Where can I put this?"

"This" was the umbrella he'd leaned against his neck and his shoulder as he'd hurried from the car to her front step, carrying the pizza box. Waiting for an answer, Ben turned around to face her as she closed the door.

The overhead light fixture was illuminating the drops of water that still clung to her neck and hair. He saw small, dark stains where her cotton shirt made contact with skin that was far from dry. She'd missed a button while putting on her blouse and she wasn't wearing a bra. Her nipples were pushing against the fabric with every breath she took. And with each breath, the material beneath the buttonholes spread apart just enough to tantalize him with a glimpse of firm, moist skin. Maybe an inch, maybe less. Just enough to arouse him.

Ben slowly realized that if he held on to the pizza box any more tightly, his fingers were going to go through the cardboard.

With effort, he forced himself to pull back mentally. He was here to get information from the woman, to pull the pieces of the puzzle into some sort of order, not indulge in erotic fantasies about her.

The fantasies did not go gently into the dark night.

Turning away, he pretended to look around. "Where's Jesse?" There was safety in numbers, and right now, he figured they both needed that safety.

Leading the way to the kitchen, Gina pulled out the edge of her hair from the collar of her shirt, brushing her fingers against her neck at the same time. She should have taken the time to dry off, she upbraided herself. But she'd been afraid, afraid of using up precious time. Of being caught unaware.

Struggling with her thoughts, she banked down vivid memories of a break-in and a face so contorted with anger, it haunted her nightmares. McNair had thought she was with another man and had broken down the door when she hadn't come to answer it quickly enough. Afraid, angry, she'd sent him away. McNair had managed to not only violate her home, but her mind as well.

"He's at Kyle's house." She saw the look of surprise on his face.

"Who's Kyle?"

"Kyle Abernathy. Jesse's new best friend. He called around four o'clock, asking if Jesse could come over and play. I didn't have the heart to say no." Why was she explaining herself to him? There was no reason why he needed to know her thought process. She felt nerves beginning to shuttle forward again. "I know he'll be sad he missed you."

Ben placed the pizza down on the table. He couldn't shake the feeling that she'd sent the boy away on purpose. But why? Was she afraid he'd find a way to be alone with the boy and that Jesse would say things she didn't want him to?

That had to be it. Nothing else made sense. "Why, what time is he getting back?"

"After you leave."

Rather than take offense, humor curved his mouth. "Would it make you feel better if we get an egg timer and clock my visit? I can leave when the timer buzzes."

Gina blew out a breath, then laughed herself. "I'm sorry if that came out wrong, Ben. It's just that—"

"You don't trust me."

"It's not that." At least, not exactly. It was far more complex than that.

Opening up the pizza box, he slanted a look in her direction. "Well, it's certainly not that you don't trust yourself, because from what I can see, you're a pretty together lady who doesn't let life just sweep her along."

A smile curved her lips. "Are you trying to flatter me?"

Experience had taught her to hold flattery from good-looking men suspect. Yet there was a tiny part of her that warmed to the words like a kitten coming in out of the rain and lying down in front of a fireplace.

Could flattery turn her head? He had his doubts about that. She seemed much too down-to-earth to be the type to hang on to a man's word. Besides, the picture McNair had painted in his interview had been that of a cold, calculating woman who knew how to use her body to get what she wanted.

Ben tried to remember that, but it wasn't easy. Other thoughts kept crowding in the way. Thoughts he kept telling himself he could handle.

"I'm trying to do whatever it takes to make you feel comfortable with me," he said.

Suspicion, never far away, rose up as the first line of defense. Was there some ulterior motive at work here after all? Her eyes narrowed as she looked at him. ''Why?''

There were napkins on her table at the nook. He took several and brought them over to the counter where the pizza was.

''Because you're an attractive lady, Gina, and I'd like to spend some time with you. And it'll make my picking your brain easier. Things always flow more smoothly if people are comfortable with each other.''

He saw the momentary struggle in her eyes, saw the instant her guard went down. For the time being, he knew he'd won.

There should have been a sense of triumph. But there wasn't.

Chapter 11

"More likely than not, you'll be going back to Los Angeles soon."

Gina said the words as much for herself as to put him in his place. Maybe more.

She wasn't immune to this man and therein lay the problem.

No, she argued with herself, the problem was that she'd been alone too long, and emotionally, that made her a prime target. If she let herself feel anything for this man, she was bound to be disappointed. He was just passing through.

"Yes," he agreed, trying to keep it light. "But not *too* soon. I like it here. There's an energy in San Francisco that helps me create." His eyes met hers. The words seemed to come out of nowhere. They certainly weren't anything he'd considered on his own. "And even if I was leaving soon, that doesn't mean we can't enjoy each other's company." The smile he offered her was engaging and he knew it. ''People usually find me pretty nonthreatening.''

Gina took a deep breath before answering. ''I don't find you threatening.''

Yeah, she did, he thought. And that was exactly what he had to try to get her over, if he was going to get any information out of her.

A part of him was liking this assignment less and less, even though his intentions were for the right reasons.

''Then why do you look as if you're about to shrink back?'' He studied her for a moment, trying to get into her head. Not for the first time, he wished he had Eliza's knack of reading people. And then it came to him. ''Just when did this stalker thing happen?''

''A while ago.'' The answer was evasive, her tone dismissive.

For a moment Ben wondered if she could be making the whole thing up, using it as a convenient cover to throw him off, but she looked so sincere, he couldn't seem to help himself. He believed her. More than that, he wanted to protect her.

He had to remember to keep things in perspective.

''Excuse me.'' Physically moving her aside, Ben reached into the cabinet behind her where he remembered she kept the dishes. Stretching, he purposely brushed his body against hers.

What he hadn't counted on was his own reaction to the calculated movement. He felt his gut tightening in a response that was far more pronounced than what he'd expected.

Startled by the brief contact, Gina moved even farther out of the way. She felt heat rising up her torso, like fire eating its way through dry leaves. What was the matter with her? This was less than nothing. Strangers brushed against one another while passing on a busy street all the time.

But they were something other than strangers.

She cleared her throat, looking at him. "What are you doing?"

Ben was the soul of innocence as he answered, "Getting plates." He took two dinner dishes down and looked at her. "I thought we could eat and talk at the same time. That way you can be rid of me faster."

He made her feel guilty. She hadn't really meant to make him feel unwelcome, it was just that...

Just that suspicion seemed to govern every moment of her life, she acknowledged, and she hated it. Ben was just being open and friendly and she was acting as if he was the enemy. What was wrong with her?

She watched him as he brought plates and silverware over to the small table. If she was in the market to reenter the world of dating and intimate relationships for even a short length of time, he would be a perfect candidate for her to begin with. There would be no consequences to face, no need for any real explanations, because there would be no future. Just two people enjoying themselves in the present, in the moment.

Right, she laughed at herself. Since when was she such a free spirit? Fleeting relationships had never been her style. She needed more. She needed commitment, a future, the promise of tomorrow.

In her present frame of mind, having been through what she had, Gina knew she could never trust anyone long enough to lay the foundation for that. At least, not yet.

And you had to walk before you could run.

Run.

She suppressed a sigh. She was so tired of running. Of fleeing mentally if not physically. Was it ever going to be any different?

Time, she told herself, *give it time.*

"I don't mean to sound as if I'm trying to get rid of you, it's just that it's hard for me to trust anyone on a personal level."

His eyes held hers for a long moment. "The stalker."

She felt as if he was looking into her soul. "The stalker," she agreed.

He slid a napkin on the right side of each plate. "Why don't you tell me about him? Like I said, I'm a good listener."

Not a good idea, no matter how much part of her wanted to unburden herself. She just couldn't afford to be too trusting.

As politely as she could, Gina shrugged away his offer. "But I'm not a good talker, not when it comes to this."

"All right." Moving the pizza box to a better position, Ben took out a slice and placed it on her plate, then took one for himself before sitting down. "So let's dig in and then get to work—if you don't mind."

"No," she said quietly. "I don't mind." She looked at him for a moment, trying to picture him as a writer, as someone who bet his future on what he put down on paper. She couldn't exactly explain why, but it seemed like far too iffy a proposition for someone like him. "No offense, but do you really think you'll be able to sell this screenplay once you finish?" It occurred to her that he hadn't even told her what his "day job" actually was, or how he managed to put food on the table and keep a roof over his head. He'd told her very little about himself and she found herself wondering and wanting to know.

He grinned at her. ''Absolutely,'' he said. And then he winked. ''You have to have faith, Gina.''

Faith. There'd been a time when she'd had faith, when she'd believed that the world was a warm, wonderful place. Even after her parents had died when she was thirteen. Aunt Sugar had swooped down, enveloping her in love and taking her back to live with her. It had taken her time, but thanks to Aunt Sugar, she'd gotten there. Her feeling had been that, all right, she was a single mother, but she'd had her career and a future that was finally beginning to look up.

Until she had to leave everything behind.

''Maybe you do, but I don't,'' she murmured, taking two cans of soda out of the refrigerator. Collecting two glasses, she set them all down in the center of the small table.

He raised his eyes to hers, waiting until she took her seat opposite him. The table was so small, her knees brushed against his. He felt the same response, the same electricity he had minutes ago, and forced himself to concentrate on the situation at hand.

''Why, Gina, I would have never pegged you as a pessimist.''

She smiled at that. ''Funny, neither would I.'' But things had a way of changing. Through no fault of her own. Or maybe, it had been. Maybe if she hadn't been so trusting, so blind… ''But that was before.''

''Before…?'' Ben deliberately let his voice trail off, waiting for her to fill an event in.

''Before,'' she repeated with finality, firmly closing the door on the subject. ''And this is now.'' She glanced out the window. The darkness was underscored by

BOOKS FREE!

Hurry!

Return this card promptly to GET 2 FREE BOOKS & A FREE GIFT!

The Best of the Best™

Affix peel-off MIRA sticker here

YES! Please send me the 2 FREE "The Best of the Best" novels and FREE gift for which I qualify. I understand that I am under no obligation to purchase anything further, as explained on the opposite page.

(P-BB3-01)

385 MDL C6PQ **185 MDL C6PP**

NAME (PLEASE PRINT CLEARLY)

ADDRESS

APT.# CITY

STATE/PROV. ZIP/POSTAL CODE

Offer limited to one per household and not valid to current subscribers of "The Best of the Best." All orders subject to approval. Books received may vary.

▶ DETACH AND MAIL CARD TODAY! ▶

The Best of the Best™ — Here's How it Works:

Accepting your 2 free books and gift places you under no obligation to buy anything. You may keep the books and gift and return the shipping statement marked "cancel." If you do not cancel, about a month later we will send you 4 additional novels and bill you just $4.24 each in the U.S., or $4.74 each in Canada, plus 25¢ shipping & handling per book and applicable taxes if any.* That's the complete price and — compared to cover prices of $5.50 or more each in the U.S. and $6.50 or more each in Canada — it's quite a bargain! You may cancel at any time, but if you choose to continue, every month we'll send you 4 more books, which you may either purchase at the discount price or return to us and cancel your subscription.

*Terms and prices subject to change without notice. Sales tax applicable in N.Y. Canadian residents will be charged applicable provincial taxes and GST.

If offer card is missing write to: The Best of the Best, 3010 Walden Ave., P.O. Box 1867, Buffalo, NY 14240-1867

BUSINESS REPLY MAIL

FIRST-CLASS MAIL PERMIT NO. 717 BUFFALO, NY

POSTAGE WILL BE PAID BY ADDRESSEE

THE BEST OF THE BEST
3010 WALDEN AVE
PO BOX 1867
BUFFALO NY 14240-9952

NO POSTAGE NECESSARY IF MAILED IN THE UNITED STATES

sheets of rain. It gave no indication of letting up any time soon. It made her feel lonely. She struggled to shut out the feeling. "So, you're planning on being a big-time screenwriter."

Ben inclined his head. "Something like that."

How many dreamers were there out there? she wondered. But some of them wrote screenplays that were produced, why shouldn't Ben be among their number? "What are you going to do with all the money you make?"

He shrugged. "I hadn't really thought about that part of it. Getting the story told is the main thing."

For her, perforce, it was all about the money right now. She thought of her great-aunt and the money she'd borrowed just to come here. Though it wasn't easy, she'd started setting a tiny bit aside each week, to pay Aunt Sugar back. The kind of money Ben was talking about would have definitely set her on her feet, debt free. The way she'd once anticipated her career as a sculptor would do.

"And the money doesn't tempt you at all." Money represented security to her, but for most people, she'd come to realize, it was the end-all, be-all. Even Stephen had always wanted more, and he had enough money to buy his own small country if he wanted to.

But not enough to buy her, she thought.

"Oh, don't get me wrong, money's great. But I just don't believe it's its own reward. Money just buys you peace of mind. But if you don't know what that is..." She was smiling at him and he congratulated himself on picking the right path to embellish. He just wished her smile didn't sink straight into him so deeply. Made it hard for a man to think. Hard for a man to remember his lies.

"You're so different," she said.

Finished with his slice, he wiped his fingers on his napkin and cocked his head, looking at her. He tried not to wonder what it would be like to kiss her. He wondered, anyway. "Different from what?"

"From what I would have expected, looking at you."

Ben rested his chin on his fisted hand. "And what would you have expected, looking at me?"

She laughed then, looking down, a little embarrassed. She shouldn't have said anything. "Someone who knows how to enjoy himself," she allowed. "And would spend money like water, given half a chance."

He wondered if she was just making idle conversation, or if that was really the impression she had of him. And why any opinion she had should matter. He was just gathering information to help him unravel what was going on and, ultimately, to reunite McNair with his son. He ignored what the consequences of that would mean to Gina.

"I guess you can't always tell a book by its cover."

"I guess not," she agreed. Something was stirring inside her. A yearning she didn't want. Digging into her pocket, she took out a list. She glanced at it, though she knew every book there, before she handed it to him. "I used the computer at the bookstore and made up a basic list of books you might find useful in your background research. I'm not sure just how deeply you want to go into the material, or how much you know, for that matter. So don't get insulted if some of these strike you as elementary."

He glanced over the list quickly and noted her handwriting. It was very precise. Every "i" dotted, every "t" crossed, not a thing like his.

"I'll hold on to my temper," he promised, his mouth

curving. He nodded at the list. "This looks pretty extensive."

"It is. Some of the books might be hard to find, but, like I said, if you want to be thorough—" He hadn't really told her the basic focus of the story, other than bandying the word *epic* around. It might have been just to catch her attention. "Do you?"

He was flying by the seat of his pants here. "As thorough as possible without putting the audience to sleep."

She had no idea why that tickled her as much as it did. "That would depend on your protagonist—I take it it's a he."

He grinned, spreading his hands. "Write about what you know, right? At least to some extent, although the guy's an orphan, so right there, we have a parting of the ways." He was deliberately baiting her, waiting for her to launch into a story about her "sister"—the woman he'd met at social services.

Instead, he saw her eyes cloud over just a little. "I might be able to help you with that, too."

Was this a lie or the truth? He didn't know what to believe. He had no choice but to continue playing along. "You're an orphan?"

"Not to begin with, but I lost my parents pretty early in life. Too early." Even the simple words brought a hitch to her throat. She could never think about her parents without experiencing a mixed bag of emotions.

He took another slice of pizza, but his eyes held hers. "What happened to them—if you don't mind my asking?"

Gina wasn't sure what had come over her. Maybe it was the weather. Rain always made her sad. It'd been raining the day she lost her parents. Normally, she kept it all bottled up inside, but this evening, for some reason, she needed to talk.

"They died in a car accident." A sigh at the loss, at the grief she would always feel, escaped. "I was raised by my late grandmother's sister." She smiled affectionately to herself. Where would she have been, then and now, without Aunt Sugar? "Her name's Sugarland."

"Sounds like there's a story behind that." His smile was kind and coaxed her to continue.

"A very short one. There was an old song she liked to sing as a little girl. One of the lyrics mentioned a place called Sugarland. The nickname stuck. I don't think I actually know what her real name is."

"Maybe she doesn't, either, anymore." The comment had just slipped out in the ease of the conversation they were having. She looked at him, her brows narrowing, and he realized his mistake. "Just a creative guess."

"Good one. She doesn't." The one time she'd actually asked Aunt Sugar, the woman hadn't been able to tell her, promising to look it up in a family bible "soon." That had been several years ago.

"What was it like, growing up without your parents?"

That was the writer in him asking, she told herself, trying not to take the question personally. Trying not to see it as a sign that he was interested in the answer in any other way than intellectually—even though right now, she wanted him to be.

"For the most part, I managed. Aunt Sugar did everything she could to make it up to me. But there were times I still felt disconnected. I guess I was just trying to find my place in the world after they died."

"And did you?"

She thought for a moment. If there had been somewhere she was finally coming together, it would have been the house back in Bedford. The place she'd had to leave so quickly. But that was in her past. She had to think ahead.

Gina smiled with a half shrug just before she took a bite of her slice. "I'm still working on it."

Picking up his napkin, he leaned forward. "Hold still."

"What?" She did as he instructed, wondering if there was a spider crawling on her. It took effort not to shiver. "Why?"

To her surprise, he took her chin in one hand. "Never met a woman yet who liked to wear tomato sauce on her cheek."

This was the second time. "I guess you bring out the messy part of me."

He smiled. "I guess so." Ben wiped away the small, telltale red streak that had smeared on her cheek with the corner of the napkin. "I kind of like you messy. Makes you human."

"At times, I'm all too human," she replied quietly.

His strokes were deliberately slow, deliberately meant to arouse her. But he realized too late that he was getting tangled up in his own trap.

He was trying to get to her, he reminded himself, not the other way around.

It didn't help.

She raised her eyes to his and he felt the last of his footing go.

One moment he was wiping her cheek, the next, he was bringing his mouth in closer to hers. Hardly daring to breathe, he kissed her. Lightly. Just enough to excite her.

And himself in the bargain.

Ben leaned back, the napkin slipping from his lax fingers. Very slowly, he ran just the tip of his tongue along his lips. "Never had pizza served quite that way before."

"I find that very difficult to believe." Good, she could still talk. For a second, she'd thought that she'd completely lost the ability to form coherent words. Other than wow.

"Would you mind if I kissed you again?"

"Yes," she whispered, using the last thimbleful of air that had been left in her lungs.

The smile that she watched slip over his lips was slow, sexy. She couldn't draw her eyes away from his mouth.

"Yes, you mind, or yes, I can?"

Her mind went blank. "I—"

"Never mind," he said softly, taking the decision out of her hands. "Forget I asked."

Asking wasn't his style. It took control of a situation out of his hands, and right now he wanted to be in control. He wanted to hold her. To kiss her. She was the chief suspect in this kidnapping case, but somehow, the fine line between good and evil, black and white, had gotten blurred for him. He'd gotten himself lost in her eyes, in her smile. He wanted to kiss her before he found out things that might make moments like this impossible.

His mouth came down on hers.

Rising to his feet, his lips still sealed to hers, Ben held on to her shoulders and brought her up with him until they were both standing.

Ben could feel her heart pounding hard and he knew his was doing the same, beating double time.

Damn, but she tasted tangy and sweet, with the promise of things he couldn't even begin to fathom. He could feel his body responding in ways he couldn't allow it to.

But for a moment longer, he savored. Drawing her into his arms, he drew her further into the kiss and followed willingly himself.

Why did it have to feel this good?

And why couldn't she have just been someone he'd met by chance on an evening when he was free to think of nothing else but making love with her?

She couldn't breathe. She didn't care. Threading her arms around his waist, all she could do as she kissed him was hang on to this man who was making the room tilt at a forty-five-degree angle.

Her head was spinning.

Gina knew she should draw away while she still had a prayer of being able to think, but she couldn't make herself do that. More than anything, she wanted this feeling, this wild, heady feeling that she hadn't felt for longer than she could remember. Certainly since before her son had been conceived.

For two cents she'd...

For two cents, she'd what? She'd make love with him? Wasn't that where this was heading? To a few stolen moments of mindless ecstasy?

The thought startled her, making her pull back from him in stunned wonder. What was she thinking? She hardly knew the man.

Shaken, she tried to get her bearings. "What just happened here?"

She looked afraid, he thought, the realization bothering him. He ran the back of his hand slowly against her cheek. Blocking out everything else except the way her skin felt. Soft. Like newly fallen snowflakes.

"I'm not sure." He refrained from kissing her again, not particularly pleased that it was harder than he'd anticipated. "I think we might have discovered a new natural phenomenon."

Her eyes crinkled at the corners in response.

He wanted to share her amusement. "What?"

"You're good. Oh, you are very good," she said.

She was smiling at him, but he couldn't help wondering if that was some sort of a put-down. "I have a funny feeling you're not talking about what just happened here."

That was part of it, but she tried not to focus on it. "I'm talking about your gift of turning a phrase—and a woman's head."

"I wasn't trying to turn your head." It was a lie, but he managed it well. That was part of the job. However he didn't have to like it. "If the earth had moved, I wouldn't have been surprised."

Her smile widened. "Neither would I, this is San Francisco. Every doomsday prophet keeps warning us we're about due for another major quake."

He wasn't ready to let her sit down just yet. Instead, he tucked his arms around her waist and held her with just a space between them. If he had his way, there wouldn't have been any space between them, but he knew he had to go slow here. "That notwithstanding, you had to have felt that jolt between us."

There was no point in lying. He'd sensed her reaction. "Yes, I felt it."

"I'd like to see you. Socially. Without a pizza or an unfinished screenplay between us."

And probably any clothes, too, she'd be willing to

bet. And that, she knew, was much too dangerous a scenario to leave herself opened to. Especially since she wanted it herself so much.

She shook her head. "Sorry, you're going to have to settle for this." She disengaged herself from him. "For the research and the pizza and the screenplay. You're just passing through and I'm not."

"Maybe I could stay." He was as surprised to hear the words coming out of his mouth as she was.

It was just part of his cover, he reminded himself.

But if he were being honest with himself, he knew that there was a part of him that would have been willing to give it a try without the case looming over him.

Even if she wasn't guilty, if, by some stroke of luck, she wasn't who he thought she was, what chance did he have with her once she knew of the deception he'd perpetrated? Once she knew he was here to trap her?

She turned the words around to her benefit. "And maybe you could go. This wasn't a good idea."

He didn't want to leave yet, even if he wasn't playing by the rules. "Gina, what are you afraid of?"

She drew her hands away from his. "More things than you could possibly begin to imagine."

She said it so earnestly, he believed her. But it seemed unlikely that she was telling him the truth. After all, McNair had ultimately discovered that Gloria had lied about her references, and when Ben had checked them out himself, he had discovered that Gloria Prescott had never been anyone's nanny. It had been a calculated maneuver to get close to McNair and his money.

Maybe Gina or Gloria or whatever name she chose to go by was lying to him now, too.

Chapter 12

For a fleeting moment, Ben thought of pressing his advantage. Instinct told him he definitely had one and that he could.

All he had to do was reach for her again.

Somewhere in his mind, the phrase about discretion being the better part of valor surfaced.

With a smile, Ben lightly touched her cheek with the back of his hand again. "All right, I'll go. Thanks for the list." He touched his shirt pocket. "Tell Jesse I'm sorry I missed him."

She was getting a reprieve. From what, she wasn't sure, but the feeling was there nonetheless. Pulling herself together, Gina nodded as she accompanied him to the front door.

"He'll be sorry he missed you, too." Maybe because she still hadn't gotten her complete bearings, she admitted a little more to him than she ordinarily would have. "He's always been a friendly kid, but I've never seen him take to anyone as quickly as he has to you."

That goes for Jesse's mother, too, she thought, except that in her case, she was doing her best to block out her response to Ben.

He flashed a grin. "He's a great kid."

She touched his cheek, tempted, yearning, then let her hand drop. "Thank you, I think so."

A gust of wind assaulted her, ushering in rain the second she opened the door for him. Reflexes had her pulling the door shut.

Gina blew out a breath in surprise, then looked at Ben. "Wow, they didn't say it was going to turn into a storm. Maybe you'd better wait it out." She didn't want to send him out when it was coming down like this. It was close to flash-flood conditions. "It can't last this way all night."

Temptation reared its head. Temptation that had nothing to do with furthering the case. Ben hesitated, then made a decision that was based on nothing that remotely had to do with common sense or his work ethic. Just his sense of decency.

"That's all right, I think maybe it's better if I do go now." He looked out the narrow window next to the front door. "Does look pretty bad out there, though. Want me to go pick up Jesse for you?"

"No." The answer was immediate. She knew it had come out too emphatic, too loud. The next moment, she tempered her tone. "That's very nice of you to offer, but I'd really prefer to get him myself." She added a coda to make it sound more believable. "I have something I need to drop off with Kyle's mother."

Maybe it was just his nature, making him suspicious, but he had a feeling she was making the last part up. Something had her nervous and it wasn't just him.

"Thanks, anyway," Gina said.

"Well if I can't be of any use, I might as well leave." He turned up his collar, then picked up the umbrella he'd left standing in the corner, a small pool of water gathered at its tip where the rain had dripped down.

Ben paused just before opening the door. "Would you mind if I dropped in at the bookstore sometime? To work out the knots? In the screenplay," he added after a beat.

She couldn't believe that he was actually asking permission. No one had ever treated her with such care before, such consideration. Gina couldn't help the smile that rose to her lips, coaxed there by the feeling that she didn't want to begin to identify. It was better if it remained without a name. Things without names stood a better chance of being ignored.

As if.

"No, I don't mind." She bit back the urge to tell him to come tomorrow. "We'll play it by ear."

He nodded. "Should be exciting." With that, he opened the door. The gust that came in ruffled his hair and sent drops of rain all through it. The umbrella would be useless against the wind. He'd waste his energy fighting the wind for possession of it and get wet, anyway. Leaving it closed, he hunched his shoulders forward and made his way into the darkness.

Her cheeks were stinging, but she didn't retreat immediately. "Drive carefully," she called out after him. Ben raised his hand over his head to indicate he heard her, but didn't risk turning around again. If he did, he just might rescind the noble act he was presently trying to pull off.

And if he rescinded, if he turned around and walked back into her house, he knew he was going to cross that invisible line he'd set down for himself. The one that separated his professional life from his personal one. And while being with Gina might not exactly be classified as sleeping with the enemy, it wouldn't be entirely ethical, either.

Drenched, he laughed shortly to himself as he got in behind the wheel of his car. Entirely? Who was he kidding? It wouldn't be ethical at all—even if it did bring her to the point where she could trust him enough to tell him what was really going on.

He jabbed his key into the ignition.

Any way he looked at it, the woman he'd just left behind just didn't strike him as someone who would break the law even in a minor way, much less kidnap a child. Yet she'd stolen someone else's name and created a fictitious life around it.

And then there was the boy, the boy who called her Mommy with no hesitation whatsoever, as if he'd always done so.

What was Ben supposed to believe?

Was he letting his feelings color his judgment or refine it? At this point, he wasn't sure of anything.

Except that he liked the taste of pizza when it was enhanced by her lips. And that he wanted to make love with her in the worst way.

Emphasis, he told himself, on "worst." Unless there were extreme extenuating circumstances, he'd never believed that the ends justified the means.

He allowed himself one last look at her condo. Maybe the rain and the streetlights were playing tricks on his eyes, but he thought he saw Gina standing in the window, watching.

Probably just shadows melding with wishful thinking. Ben stepped on the accelerator and drove to his motel.

* * *

The wind fought him for the door when he unlocked it. He slammed it shut behind him, exerting more force than he'd anticipated. Peeling off his jacket, he tossed it aside on the floor and began unbuttoning his shirt. Both had gotten soaked in the short distance from Gina's house to his car. Shedding the shirt, he shivered.

The room felt cold. As he made his way to the thermostat, he took out his cell phone and looked at the number still visible on the screen. The phone had rung while he was driving, but the rain and wind had made keeping his car within the lane a challenge, requiring both his hands on the wheel and his full concentration. He'd let the call go unanswered.

The number belonged to Erika, his next-to-youngest sister.

He hit the fifth number on his automatic dialer, then dragged one hand through his drenched hair. Raindrops scattered in all directions. The weatherman on the radio had boasted that it'd rained more in the last twenty-four hours than it had the entire rainy season. He didn't doubt it.

He heard the phone being picked up on the other end. "Hello, Erika?"

"Benji!" A myriad of excitement and joy vibrated in the single salutation. That was Erika. Enthusiasm was her credo. "I wanted you to be the first to know. Well," she amended almost faster than he could process her words, "the second, really. I told Mom first. You know how she gets when she doesn't know things immediately—"

If he didn't stop her now, he knew he'd be trampled in the onslaught of words. "Slow down, E. The second to know what?"

"I'm getting married. Justin just asked me. Isn't that

the greatest news you ever heard? Tell me that's the greatest news you ever heard.''

With Erika's exuberance filling his ear and his head, Ben made his way to the small refrigerator in the corner and looked inside. A lonely bottle of beer, only half full, sat forlornly on the shelf, its only company the eerie light from the bulb above.

Why should there have been anything else? He hadn't gone shopping and the last he'd heard, the food elves didn't make house calls this far north. If he'd been home, there would have been a fifty-fifty chance his mother might have made a pit stop, filling his refrigerator with food he'd reimburse her for the next time he saw her, over her loud protests that he was robbing her of one of her few remaining joys.

He had to get better organized. With a sigh, he reached in and took the bottle, letting the door close again.

''Greatest news I ever heard,'' he said, echoing her words back to her.

''You don't sound happy for me.''

With no effort at all, he could close his eyes and visualize the pouty lower lip making a fleeting appearance before another wave of exuberance kicked in. He had years of experience to fall back on.

''I'm happy. Happy for you, happy for Justin and most of all, happy for Mom. She loves to cry at weddings.'' And divorces, he recalled. She'd taken his hard. It hadn't stopped her from launching into a campaign to try to find him a wife before his divorce decree was cold. ''But I'm also wet and clammy.''

There was a beat of silence on the other end, as if his words were registering belatedly. ''Are you getting sick, Benji?''

He looked down. His shoes were probably ruined, thanks to the small lake that had formed next to his car when he got in.

"No, just don't have enough sense to come in out of the rain." He had to get out of these clothes and into something dry. "Look, can I call you back in a few minutes?"

"Sorry, Justin and I are going out to celebrate. I can call you later. Oh-oh-oh, wait, don't hang up," she cried, anticipating his next move. "Justin wants you to be best man."

It struck him as odd. He'd spoken to the man maybe three times and hadn't been all that impressed any of those times. "Why, doesn't he have any better men in his life than me?"

"Nobody's better than my big brother," Erika declared playfully.

This was a far cry from the little girl who had periodically shouted that she hated him. If Erika sounded any happier, he had a feeling it would probably have been ruled illegal.

"You're only saying that 'cause it's true. Look, E, I'm really thrilled for you, but if I don't get out of these clothes soon—"

"Got it." Again he heard noise, as if she was suddenly yanking the receiver back from meeting the cradle. "If you get sick, I'll have Mom send you up a huge bowl of chicken soup."

He stifled a groan. "Not a word to Mom," he warned. "Not even a hint." They both knew what their mother was like. Maureen Underwood was probably the prototype for earth mother. She counted it an incomplete day if she hadn't mothered at least one person and made their world a better place for them.

"She won't hear it from me," Erika promised. "I love you!" she crowed.

He was happy for her. He just wished she had slightly better taste in men. But who knew, maybe it would work out. God knew Erika would give it her best.

"Love you, too, E."

The connection was gone before he had a chance to hang up.

Ben dropped the receiver into the cradle. Well, at least someone was happy, he thought, walking into the bedroom.

There was a shower waiting with his name on it.

He heard the low, soothing sound of her voice as he walked into the bookstore the next day. Feeling oddly like one of the sailors who'd been lured to their demise on the rocks by the sound of a mythical siren's song, he followed Gina's voice to the small alcove that comprised the children's section.

She'd taken a chair at the small table, her knees tucked temptingly against her chest, a large book in her hands. Surrounding her on both sides were ten small children who looked to be between the ages of three and eight. All seemed to be held spellbound by the misadventures of a cat named Scrappy and his best friend, a nearsighted, loyal dog named Hawkeye.

Ben paused, leaning against a bookcase, listening not so much to the story as to the animated cadence of her voice. He found it soothing, yet oddly arousing at the same time, which he knew was far from her intention. But then, he figured he was reading a great deal more into it than the kids were.

She was enjoying herself, he thought. He could see it in her face. How could someone like this be a kidnapper? Every instinct he'd ever developed told him she wasn't. But he didn't know if he could trust his instincts anymore, not when it came to her.

Turning a page, she happened to look up in his direction. He saw surprise in her eyes. Surprise that turned to pleasure. It pleased him and he wished it wouldn't, but he savored the feeling for just a moment.

The rollicking tale was suddenly interrupted as she started to cough. Holding up her hand, Gina set the book down.

"I'll be right back," she said before she got up and went into the back office for a glass of water.

Ten small faces turned to look at Ben, the only other adult in the immediate vicinity.

"Is she going to come back?" a petite strawberry-blonde in forest-green overalls asked.

"I'm sure she'll be right back," he assured her.

A little boy tugged on his pant leg. "What's going to happen to Hawkeye?"

"Well, I don't know—" he began.

Another child thrust the book into his hands. "Mister, can you read to us until Gina gets back? It's almost time for my mommy to come for me and I want to know what happens next."

"Please?"

Several other voices joined the chorus.

Which was how Ben suddenly found himself sitting on a bright green chair that was far too small for him, reading to a pint-size audience. He figured with any luck Gina would return before he got to the bottom of the page.

It took three pages before she made her appearance. When she did, she kept her distance.

His mouth dry from reading, he was quick to offer her the book. "Here."

But Gina made no move to take it from him. Instead, she smiled encouragingly. "No, you're doing fine. Why don't you finish the page?" She pointed to the bottom. "It's the end of the chapter."

He had no choice but to go along with it. Feeling self-conscious for perhaps the first time in his life, Ben read to the end of the page.

"What happens next?" the strawberry-blonde asked. She clearly seemed like the self-appointed leader of the group.

"You'll have to come back next week for that," Gina told her.

The girl sighed dramatically and rose to her feet. She was all smiles when she looked at Ben. "Will you be here next week to read to us?"

He wanted to say "Not if you're lucky," but knew the response would be lost on someone so young. So he took the coward's way out. "Maybe."

"I'll be here too." The little girl beamed at him and then joined her friend as they both went to where their mothers were waiting for them.

As the children shuffled away, Gina began to gather up the books that they left behind and leaned her head close to his. Perfume, sweet and tempting, began to fill his senses before he could block it.

"I think you're about to be on the receiving end of a gigantic crush," she whispered.

He stared at her. "From whom?"

In response, she shook her head, doing her best not to laugh.

"It's true what they say about men. They are all

dense.'' She moved a little closer to him so that her voice wouldn't carry. ''From Emily.''

Bewildered, he looked around. ''Who's Emily?''

''The strawberry-blonde who all but made a date with you for next week.''

Ben looked toward the front of the store. Several of the children he'd just been reading to were clustered there. He picked Emily out by her strawberry hair that seemed to be in perpetual, independent motion, even when she had been sitting down. She was blatantly staring at him. When she saw that he was looking, she covered her face with her hands and giggled.

Ben looked back at Gina. ''You're kidding.''

Men *were* dense, even the good-looking ones. ''Takes very little for a girl that age to give her heart away to an older man.''

''But I just read a few pages of a short story—not even a complete one,'' he protested.

''And you paid attention to her.'' The main point was that he was kind, sensitive and good-looking, not necessarily in that order. Gina could see that it just didn't compute. ''What's the matter, didn't you ever have a crush on anyone older in your life when you were a kid? Maybe a teacher?''

Ben almost laughed out loud at the thought. ''All my teachers were Dominican nuns. I was lucky to make out eyebrows on them.''

''Well, most kids get crushes on someone older in their lives.'' She thought back to her major one. ''I had a fierce crush on Mr. Novak.'' She saw him look at her with interest. ''Tall, blond, blue-eyed, with the soul of a poet.'' In retrospect, he didn't, however, hold a candle to the man standing next to her. ''He was my tenth-grade English teacher and I would have run off with him in a heartbeat.'' Her smile widened.

He looked at Gina. The sun, finally out in full force, filled the reading area, shimmering all around her. ''I guess I'd better watch my step, then, seeing as how I like older women.''

She cocked her head. ''Older women?''

''Older than seven.'' He paused, his eyes sliding along her skin. ''A lot older than seven.''

A sudden fluttery feeling entered unannounced and took up residence in her stomach. She was beginning to like the feeling, she decided. And gave herself permission, guardedly, to like the man who was the cause of it as well.

''Well, since you came to my rescue just now, the least I can do is offer you dinner.''

''A working dinner?'' he asked. ''A real one this time. We didn't really get all that much done last night.''

She caught her lower lip between her teeth. ''No, I guess we didn't. Did you have a chance to look at any of those books on the list I gave you?''

''Not yet, that's why I'm here. I wanted to see how many of these you had in stock and buy them.''

She didn't want him to think she was pushing the books here. That wasn't why she'd made up the list. ''You could go to the library—''

He shook his head. ''No card.''

She found herself fighting back a smile. ''They can issue you a temporary one—''

''My permanent address is in L.A. I don't think a San Francisco library would be eager to issue me a card, temporary or otherwise.''

''No, but I could—''

God, but he wanted to hold her. To draw her against him and just drink in the feel of her. He was grateful they were standing in a public place. "Are you deliberately trying to get me not to buy books?"

"I'm trying to get you to save your money."

She was, too, he realized. "Thanks, but I like underlining and dog-earing. Can't do that with someone else's property."

Rules, he went by rules. She liked that. "Okay, let's see what we've got."

Trouble was, he thought he already knew and it didn't work itself into the framework of an investigation, at least, not in its present ramifications.

"When would you like me to come over?"

Gina thought a second. "Make it six. I've got to stop at the store on my way home."

He didn't want her to go to any trouble. "I could just as easily take you out to dinner."

She shook her head. "No, this is my treat and I can't afford a restaurant. Besides, I promised Jesse I'd help him with a school project." It was a lie, but one she knew she could be forgiven for. She didn't want to give away too much because it might make things seem other than they were. "Six," she repeated.

"Six," he echoed, and tried to tell himself he wasn't looking forward to it.

Chapter 13

He was early.

She was late.

Or at least not as on schedule as she would have liked to have been, she thought as she went to answer the doorbell. She'd barely finished changing, hurrying into her clothes just as she'd heard the doorbell.

But at least Jesse was ready. He'd gone over the things in his backpack a total of three times to make sure he had everything he needed for the anticipated night ahead—a spectacular sleepover that had very little sleep worked into the actual game plan.

As Gina opened the door to admit Ben, the first thing she saw was the grocery bag he was holding in front of him.

"I told you I was taking care of dinner. What did you bring?"

She hadn't answered the door the first time he rang

the bell and he'd begun to think that maybe he'd gotten his evenings confused.

Seeing her wearing a simple black dress that nonetheless flattered every single curve he wanted to get acquainted with temporarily fogged up his brain. It took him a second to reclaim his orientation.

He looked down at the bag, as if to check before answering. "Well, I wasn't sure what you were serving, so to be on the safe side, I brought a bottle of white wine and a bottle of red."

The last time she'd had wine had been at the fundraiser that had wound up changing her life. "You didn't have to—"

He wasn't finished. "Plus something to keep Jesse from feeling left out."

To illustrate, Ben reached into the bag and produced a bottle of sparkling cider that had only bubbles mixed into the apple concoction.

If Ben had bought her diamonds, he couldn't have warmed her heart any more than he had just now. Gina stopped midprotest and just looked at him, her mouth shutting as an afterthought. And then she just shook her head, more to herself than to him. Where had men like this been when she'd been ready to give her heart away? Before she'd built up her arsenal of suspicions?

"Maybe he'll have a quick 'drink' with us before he goes," she remarked.

"Goes?" Ben followed behind her as she walked back into the kitchen. He'd thought it was going to be the three of them tonight. "I thought you were helping him with a project. Jesse's not going to be here for dinner?"

"Project got postponed," she told him vaguely.

Her son, lured by the sound of Ben's voice and lugging his stuffed backpack down the narrow stairs, made his appearance in the kitchen. Coming up behind him, Gina placed her hands around the boy's neck and held him to her. To his credit, Jesse squirmed only marginally.

"My son is about to embark on his first sleepover tonight."

And Jesse had no idea what allowing him to go was costing her, she added silently. But that was for her to know and wrestle with, not Jesse. No matter what was going on in her life, she was determined that her son was going to grow up a normal, well-adjusted boy.

That meant, among other things, slowly allowing him a measure of his own independence to discover his identity—no matter how much she wanted to keep him tied to her for her own peace of mind.

"This true, partner?" Ben asked solemnly as he made eye contact with the boy.

The blond head bobbed up and down with enthusiasm. "It's Kyle's birthday."

"Wow, are you going to have fun. I can remember my first sleepover." Ben glanced up to look at Gina. "It was at my best friend Nick's house. I don't think I closed my eyes all night."

Gina's sympathies immediately aligned themselves with Nick's mother. Ben looked as if he'd been quite a handful at Jesse's age.

He looked as if he'd be quite a handful now.

Jesse's high voice broke into the moment. "I've gotta be at Kyle's house in ten minutes."

Just before he was actually supposed to arrive, Ben thought. He wondered if Gina was clearing the way for them to be alone tonight, or if he was reading too much into this. Maybe it was nothing more than just a coincidence.

Not for the first time, Ben wished the case wasn't getting in the way of things. But it was the case, not his attraction to Gina, that was supposed to be getting center stage, he reminded himself for the umpteenth time. He couldn't lose sight of that. The safe delivery of a small boy depended on his keeping that foremost in his mind.

"Ten minutes, huh?" Walking past Jesse, Ben placed the grocery bag on the table and took out the cider. "Okay, so what do you say we make a toast and then we'll take you over to Kyle's house?"

Not waiting for an answer, Ben began taking down three glasses from the cupboard.

He was making himself at home, Gina thought. As if he'd always been coming here to visit them.

As if…

Everything was just transitory, she reminded herself. She couldn't get carried away. There would be nothing but disappointment if she followed that route—disappointment and perhaps something far worse. She'd had her guard down once and barely gotten out alive. It wasn't going to happen again. This time, she was keeping her eyes wide open, her instincts on alert.

Jesse accepted his glass, now filled with a golden liquid that fizzed and had bubbles rising in it, and looked at Ben with solemn eyes. "What are we going to toast?"

Thinking a minute, Ben raised his own glass of cider. "How about to the future?" His eyes swept over Gina's face before coming to rest on Jesse's. "May it be everything we want it to be."

That sounded wonderful to her.

If only.

Gina raised her glass up, clinking it against the side of Jesse's and then Ben's. "To the future." For a moment, her eyes locked with Ben's before she lowered them.

"The future," Jesse echoed. He took a sip of his drink and then giggled when the bubbles came up to greet his nose. "It tickles," he explained.

Ben pretended to nod solemnly. "Just like champagne," he confided.

Jesse's eyes grew larger and he looked into the contents of his glass with new reverence. "*Is* this champagne?"

Ben fought hard not to smile. "Sure. The G-rated version."

Delighted, Jesse drained the rest of his glass, then set it down on the counter with a contented sigh. "Wow, wait until I tell Kyle."

Anticipating problems, Gina warned, "Make sure you tell him it was cider." That was all she needed, repercussions from Kyle's mother that she was giving alcoholic beverages to her six-year-old son.

"Okay, Mom," Jesse promised.

Ben set his own glass, still half full, down. "You about ready, Tiger?"

With barely harnessed enthusiasm, Jesse looked over toward his backpack. "Sure."

About to usher Jesse out, Ben heard the bell go off behind them. He turned around, looking at the stove. "Is that the end of round one?"

"No, that's dinner announcing itself." For a second, looking at Ben and toasting the future, she'd almost forgotten all about the chicken in the oven. "Just give me a minute, sweetie, and I'll be ready,'' she promised Jesse.

Jesse looked uncomfortable at the nickname as he slanted a glance in Ben's direction. Antsy, the boy shifted from foot to foot, anxious to get to the new adventure waiting for him at his friend's house.

Ben didn't need to be an expert in child psychology for him to read between the lines. He caught Gina by the arm before she could open the oven.

''Look, I came early and threw you off. The least I can do is take Jesse over to Kyle's. No need for you to rush.''

The protest that rose to her lips was automatic, but she swallowed it. Ben was only trying to be helpful. There was no earthly, tangible reason to feel uneasy at his offer. Look how well he fared with the children at the bookstore today. If she couldn't get herself to trust him, she really was a hopeless paranoid.

But the final call was Jesse's. She looked at the boy. ''How do you feel about that, Jesse?''

''Cool!'' he crowed.

''Well, no margin for confusion here.'' She shook her head, pretending to be mystified. ''I had no idea I was so uncool and cramping your style.''

''Oh, no, Mom, it's just that Ben—''

Laughing, Gina touched her son's nose with the tip of her forefinger, reminiscent of a game she'd once played with him.

''That's all right, kiddo. I understand. You've got wings, you want to try them. You're free to go.'' She waved him off. ''Just remember to thank Kyle's mother for having you—and behave.''

''Yes, ma'am.''

Excited, Jesse was nearly to the doorway before he

remembered. Doubling back, he stood on his toes, pulled Gina down to his level and then gave her a huge hug, adding a little more feeling to it because he knew it had to last her all night.

But when she went to kiss him, he whispered "Not in front of Ben" out of the side of his small mouth.

Ben could remember those days, trying hard to look macho for the immediate world. It had taken ten years to outgrow. He was still apologizing to his mother. "I still kiss my mom."

"Really?" Jesse asked.

Gina could have kissed Ben when, very solemnly, he drew an X over his heart. "Cross my heart and hope to die."

"Wow. Okay." And with that, Jesse gave his mother a good-sized, loud smack on the cheek before retreating to the doorway where he had left his backpack. "I'm ready," he needlessly announced.

"Don't forget your coat," she warned, and was rewarded with an "Aw, gee, Mom."

"Not negotiable," she informed her happy wanderer.

Jesse sighed mightily, taking the coat he had helped pick out off the hook where he'd hung it up earlier.

Ben slipped on his own windbreaker, then picked up Jesse's backpack. It was heavier than he'd anticipated and he groaned for Jesse's benefit. "Gee, what do you have in here?"

"Stuff," Jesse informed him, stifling another fit of giggles.

Ben hooked one strap over his arm, his other hand around the boy's shoulders. "How long are you planning on staying over? A month?"

Gina heard Jesse giggling as the two went out the front door.

For a fleeting second, she allowed herself to pretend that this was a typical scene in her life. The life she'd always wanted. With a child and a husband sharing a moment while she looked on with a warm heart.

If only.

Suddenly remembering their chicken dinner was still in the oven, she quickly donned oven mitts and removed the pan from the rack.

Her daydreams, she thought, banishing them, were only that. Daydreams.

Ben was back before she had a chance to finish setting the table.

The sound of the front door opening and then closing again softly had her freezing in place, listening. Busy, she hadn't stopped to turn the lock on the door when Ben and Jesse had left. Now, her fingers icy, she wondered if that had been a mistake.

She raised her voice. "Ben?"

"Right here."

And he was. Right there. Standing in the doorway between the living room and the small dining room.

She couldn't stop the pleasure from filling her. Surprised by her reaction, she didn't even bother to try to block it. Going with the moment, she simply allowed herself to enjoy it. What was the harm in pretending, just for an evening…?

"So, how did it go?"

He crossed to the cabinet. "Great. The boys were off and running up the stairs before I had a chance to say goodbye." Reaching into the cupboard, he took out two glasses and carried them into the next room. "Does Kyle's mother have X-ray vision?"

He just did things without waiting to be asked. Gina

liked that and couldn't help wondering if he'd grown up with a houseful of women. Men weren't usually that intuitively helpful.

"No." She laughed at the question as she placed the large bowl of mashed potatoes on the tablecloth she'd ironed less than an hour ago. "Why?"

"Well, she was looking at me as if she had." Dogging her steps, he got the silverware. "As if she was trying to see everything down to what color shorts I was wearing."

With the question raised, she squelched the impulse to ask him for an answer herself. Instead, she wrapped her hands around the salad bowl and went back into the dining room. "She was probably just wondering if I had a new man in my life."

"New man," he echoed, a fork poised in his hand. "As opposed to an old man in your life?"

The half shrug was meant to hide her self-consciousness but only underlined it. "As opposed to no man in my life."

That there was no one in her life made all this a lot easier for him, but still left him wondering. "Why is that?"

A dozen standard answers occurred to her. Because he'd brought her son faux champagne, she told him the truth. "Takes a lot to make a connection. A real connection. I don't believe in casual flirtations."

And he did, he reminded himself. Enjoying his freedom, casual flirtations were, up until now, the only kinds of relationships he did indulge in.

Until now.

The phrase, his own phrase, echoed back at him. He tried not to attach too much significance to any of it. He couldn't afford to.

"Very admirable."

She shrugged that off, too. "Nothing admirable about it. It might even be easier if I did." At least, that would fill the loneliness that crept up on her at times like a deep, black void, threatening to swallow her up. "But I just don't believe in wasting someone's time, or mine, I guess." She gave it a practical spin. "I've got precious little of it as it is, and what I do have, I prefer giving to Jesse. Moving was kind of hard on him."

Okay, they were getting closer to the story. He kept a casual expression on his face. "Why did you?"

To save him. "It seemed the right thing to do" was all she said.

She placed the platter she'd arranged in the center of the dining room table, between the salad and the potatoes. She'd made too much, she thought. Nerves had done that, she hadn't been paying attention.

"Hope you like chicken parmesan."

Looking at the meal, he could feel his mouth watering. Looking at her had the same effect. "Right now, I'd like anything that didn't slide right out of the box into the microwave."

She slipped the serving utensils beside each bowl or plate. The garlic bread she made added its aroma to the mix. "Sounds like you don't get to eat many home-cooked meals."

Ben broke off a piece of the bread and put it on his plate. "Only when I visit my mother."

"How often is that?"

"Not as often as she'd like." He liberally spread margarine on one side of his bread. "Sunday dinners once a month, except now she serves them on Tuesdays because my sister Cindy can't make Sundays. Attendance is mandatory,'' he added with a grin Gina found utterly endearing.

''And you go.''

''I go. But only after she promises not to have someone sitting next to me at the table I don't know.'' He saw Gina raise her brow in a silent question. ''She used to try to fix me up every time I came over.'' In his heart, he knew his mother wouldn't give up subtly trying until he finally had a life partner. Seeing as he wasn't in the market for one, she was going to have a very long wait. ''My sister Erika's getting married, so that turns the heat off the rest of us for a while.''

''How many is 'us'?''

''Three.'' He grinned. ''I've got two more sisters besides Ericka.''

''All single.'' It was a conclusion, not a question.

''All single.'' He paused, then raised his eyes to hers and added, ''Now.''

Gina wasn't quite sure if she interpreted his meaning correctly. ''Now?''

He told himself he was just trying to make small talk, to fill in spaces until she volunteered something he could work with himself, or he could subtly ask her questions. But he knew that he wasn't making small talk, he was sharing. Something he didn't do all that readily, especially not with someone involved in the investigation of a case.

''I was married at eighteen.'' God, could he have been any dumber? Ben thought. His mother, who'd sensed his secret intentions of eloping with Susan, had begged him not to do anything foolish until he knew what direction his life was going in. He'd deliberately ignored her just because she was his mother and couldn't know what it felt like to be in love so badly that her very body ached.

"Straight out of high school, just before college." A self-deprecating smile curved his mouth. "Made a pit stop at a Vegas chapel and married the girl I'd been going with since the tenth grade."

There was a time Gina might have believed in happily ever after. Now she knew better. "What happened?"

He laughed to himself. At the time, no one could have told him anything. He had to learn lessons for himself. He supposed that made the lessons stick better that way.

"I found out you don't make lifetime commitments based on what you know in tenth grade. Things have a tendency of changing." He thought of Susan. There was no malice. No feelings of any kind, really. "We grew up and then grew apart."

"I'm sorry."

He heard the note of genuine sincerity in her voice and was glad that here, at least, he was telling her the truth. "Don't be. It was a great learning experience."

His optimistic view of what a lot of men would have taken as a failure and/or an annoyance, surprised Gina. "Any children?"

He shook his head. "None. Thank God we didn't make that mistake."

But he was so good with Jesse. Was that all an act? "You think kids are a mistake?"

"No, but broken homes are." At the time a part of him had been sad at the break-up, sad that there hadn't been any children, but he'd learned to look at it differently over time. "I want my kid to have a complete set of parents residing on the premises, on call at all times.'' And then he realized who he was talking to. A woman claiming to be a single mother. His words had to sound rather callous. ''Hey, I'm sorry. I didn't mean—''

''I know you didn't. There's nothing to be sorry for. It's a good philosophy.'' Gina thought of the circumstances surrounding Jesse's conception. ''I wish I would have had a chance to implement it.''

Ben backpedaled, striving for damage control. ''Sometimes it's better for the kid if the parents do get a divorce.''

She knew what he was trying to do and appreciated the effort.

''I'm not divorced. And before you guess widowed, I'm not that, either. I was never married.'' One hand on each, she moved the two bowls closer to him. ''Potatoes or salad?''

He looked at her for a moment. The woman knew how to shift gears without missing a beat.

''Both.'' He moved the first bowl closer to him and served himself. When he continued talking, there was only mild interest in his voice. ''You and Jesse's father come to a parting of the ways?''

''You might say that.'' She shrugged carelessly, her eyes growing flat as she thought back to the first time her life had been turned upside down. ''He was just someone I knew fleetingly. This football jock with a million-watt smile who invited me to a fraternity party.'' She recited the details as clinically as she could. ''Somewhere during the night, he slipped something into my drink. I came to in my dorm, my clothes lying in a heap on the floor.''

''Date rape?'' He said the words quietly, so she could

pretend not to hear if she didn't want to tell him. Damn, but he could almost believe her.

The shrug was small, almost vulnerable, though from her expression he guessed she was trying to distance herself from the event.

She hated attaching the word *rape* to something that had given her Jesse. ''Let's say it was the first step of my education in the ways of the world. Jesse came nine months later.''

She told her lies convincingly. So convincingly that Ben was tempted to believe her. He had to keep reminding himself that the child she was talking about was really McNair's. For the sake of argument, he pushed the questions a little further.

''Why did you go through with it? You could have just as easily—''

Her head jerked up, her eyes pinning him. He couldn't have looked away if he'd wanted to.

''Just as easily what? Swept him away? Rubbed him out like an annoying stain on my dress? No, I couldn't have.'' A weary sigh escaped her lips. ''Oh, I'm not a saint. I did think about it. But it didn't matter how Jesse came into being. He was my baby and I had to take care of him. Do anything I could to make sure he had a decent chance at life.''

It took effort to squelch the compassion he felt rising up within him. ''What about Jesse's father?''

She laughed shortly. ''Disappeared out of my life without a trace.''

If the scenario had been true, he would have had no doubt about that. Jerks like that never took responsibility for their actions. ''Did you ever tell him about the consequences of what he did?''

''And have him deny it?'' The very thought angered

her. "What for? I knew what happened, he knew what happened. Jesse happened." She looked up at him. "And Jesse is the very best thing that ever happened to me in my life. I love that little boy more than anything in this world. I've never regretted his being born, not from the moment I first saw him."

If he looked into her eyes, stripped away everything else, the case, his suspicions, McNair, everything, and just looked into her eyes, he would have found himself believing her.

He only wished he could.

Chapter 14

She hardly remembered eating. Oh, she went through the motions, and food met the fork with a fairly rhythmic regularity until her plate was empty, but she didn't remember chewing or swallowing. She just remembered looking up into his eyes and getting lost.

They talked about the pages he'd brought the other night. The pages she'd finally gotten to read after he'd left. She'd told him that she was impressed and he seemed genuinely flattered. She liked the modest way he accepted compliments. She liked a great deal about him. The way he smiled, the way he treated her son like a person, the way he wasn't afraid to read to a group of children he didn't know just because they'd asked him to.

If she'd been Sleeping Beauty, he would have been the prince she'd been waiting for.

But she didn't believe in princes anymore, she told herself. Trouble was, she wasn't listening.

Anticipation hummed through her the entire time they were in the dining room like a tuning fork perpetually sentenced to vibrate.

Maybe she was crazy, she thought, setting everything up this way. Setting herself up this way. But if she were being honest with herself, the first time she saw Ben, she'd felt something. She'd been too busy trying to mask it, trying to ignore it, to admit that it was actually there.

But it had been.

And still was, only now that feeling, that attraction, seemed to be more intensified. So much so that it became almost another entity in the room with them.

She supposed she'd always had a weakness for heroes. And Ben had come to her rescue that first day in the bookstore and wanted nothing in return. That made him a hero in her book. There was no billowing cape, no black mask, no bold *S* emblazoned across his chest, but there didn't have to be. He was still a hero.

And for tonight, maybe he would be hers.

They cleared away the dishes together and she heard herself doing most of the talking. Small talk, amounting to nothing.

Nerves, she supposed. There were no guarantees that the evening would go the way she hoped. Maybe she'd even back out herself, surrendering to the comforting banality of familiarity instead of taking a leap of faith and leading with her feelings.

The last dish safely put away, Ben took her hand. She looked at him. "What are you doing?"

Instead of answering, he placed his finger to his lips. "Shhh." And then he led her to the living room.

The room was the last word in cozy. The first in sensuality.

Gina purposely left the lights off. The fire, which she'd started just before changing for dinner, was still burning brightly in the fireplace. She paused to stoke it before sitting down next to him.

Her body felt tense and she willed it to relax. It didn't listen.

"I could stare into a fireplace for hours," Gina murmured, her voice low and husky.

And he could look at her for hours. At the way the light from the fireplace seemed to lightly graze her skin, darkening the hue just a little. Just looking at her like this, sitting beside him on the sofa, made his gut tighten and his body yearn for things that weren't even scribbled into the margins of the list of rules. Rules he was ignoring.

What he was doing, what he wanted to do, was outside the parameters that he had mentally set down for himself. He didn't believe in using underhanded means to gain information. Not from good people, and Gina was good people.

If there were nagging feelings and glaring facts trying to prove otherwise, he ignored them. Sometimes, you had to lead with your gut.

He didn't want to disrupt her life.

Even though her very existence here tonight was disrupting his.

"Why?"

His voice was as quiet as hers, fading into the darkness that existed just beyond the small space they inhabited. She hadn't turned on any of the lights when they'd entered the living room, preferring the glow of the fireplace to anything artificial.

She took a deep breath. If she wasn't careful, she

could let herself become mesmerized. By the fire and by him.

"If you look into it long enough, everything else disappears. Problems, worries. Inventories that don't tally," she added with a smile as she turned to look at him.

Kiss me, Ben. Please kiss me. I need so badly to be kissed tonight. To be held and made to feel that there's something more to me than just that bit that exists right now.

He liked longer hair, yet he found her short hair very sexy. He tended to gravitate toward blondes, yet the petite brunette next to him made him think of a fiery gypsy. A gypsy who held his fortune, at least for this moment, in the palm of her hand.

He toyed with a strand of her hair, sifting it through his fingers. His eyes were on hers as he drew closer. "What kind of problems?"

She didn't move, didn't breathe. "Just problems," she replied, her mouth scant inches away from his. "Day-to-day, mundane, nothing-special problems."

He could taste her words on his lips, feel the delicate tickle of her breath as it feathered along his face. Better men than he had succumbed to far less.

All the promises he'd silently made, to himself and to her, about keeping things aboveboard and honest faded in a puff of smoke.

In the heat of needs and reality.

Before he could think it through and force himself to stop, he slipped his hands around her face, his fingers tangling in her soft hair, and lowered his mouth to Gina's. The wine she'd had with dinner intoxicated him.

Wine, hell, *she* intoxicated him and he lost his way immediately.

Lost his way and found his soul, the soul he hadn't even realized was missing until this very moment.

The kiss deepened. His hands left her face and he drew her onto his lap and still the kiss went on.

The little she'd drunk at dinner had barely registered at the time. Now she felt her head spinning as if she was experiencing some sort of delayed reaction. Or she'd suddenly found herself on some sort of wild amusement park ride that left her breathless, giddy and wanting more.

Her heart pounding, she threaded her arms around his neck. Focusing, Gina reversed their roles. She became the giver not the receiver, determined not to be swept away before she left her mark on him. Because she was going to be swept away, she knew that. There was no doubt in her mind. He had a way about him, a presence, a mastery. She knew without being told that there were women back where he came from who numbered themselves among his lovers. Women who had given him wild, memorable nights. She was in competition with all of them.

She wanted to make him forget. Forget anyone whom he had made love with before. For the space of an hour, an evening, a night, she wanted him to think and feel and breathe only her. Though she never had before, she needed the validation now.

She needed him.

He felt as if he'd been hit in the solar plexus by a two-by-four. Worse than that. And better. The woman was like some mind-altering drug, opening up all his senses, bringing bright colors and heat in her wake. Making him aware of everything. The hum of the air, the crackle of the flames in the fireplace, the scent of her hair.

But as alive as it made all his senses become, it also closed him off to everything beyond the small perimeter that they had staked out.

And even that shrank down around him until there was nothing else but Gina.

And his craving to have her.

He heard her sharp intake of breath as he cupped her breast in his hand, gently, as if he was afraid that she might break if his touch was too rough, his impatience too quickly unbridled.

Excitement thundered through him like the tide pounding against the beach during a fierce storm. Very slowly, his hand began to move, massaging the soft mound as his mouth roamed over her lips, her face, her throat. He lingered over the pulse he found there. It jumped as he lightly stroked it with his tongue and he felt her hands tighten on his shoulders.

His own body was humming in time with hers, for each caress, each touch, he felt a kindred vibration within his own. In a minute, he wasn't going to be able to think clearly anymore or have even the vague desire to navigate through the clouds around his brain. In a minute, all there would be, would be her.

If he was going to do anything, it had to be now.

Trying to catch his breath, he drew his head back from hers. "Gina, if you want me to stop, tell me now." He couldn't force himself to stop touching her, to stop tracing the outline of her lips with his fingertips. She had to be the one to tell him, to call an end to it. "A minute from now it'll be too late."

"It already is," she whispered, bringing her mouth up to his.

Maybe it didn't make any sense and it certainly wasn't the way she'd always conducted herself, but

Gina didn't care. Ben brought things out of her she hadn't realized were there. Awakened things that, like Sleeping Beauty, slumbered quietly, waiting for the right moment. The right man.

Whether Ben was the right man no longer mattered. He was *the* one, the one who could awaken all these feelings within her, and she needed him to make her feel whole again, even if for only a little while.

He wanted to be noble, he wanted to have a clear conscience. Above all, he didn't want her *on* his conscience.

But none of that mattered at this moment in time. What mattered was making love with her. What mattered was having her.

Damn it, he was supposed to have more control over himself than this.

The war raged inside of him. And nobility was definitely losing.

Ben peered into her eyes, looking for some sort of sign. Looking for absolution. "Are you sure?"

"This is no time to filibuster," she breathed. She didn't remember ever feeling like this before. Itchy. On fire. "Do you want me to sign a permission slip? Give it to me and I'll sign it, but for pity's sake, don't stop now or I'm liable to self-destruct."

He saw the honesty in her eyes.

There was no turning back, no noble intentions large enough that could possibly stand up to what he was feeling right at this moment.

He pulled her back into his arms and kissed her as if all they had left in time was this one moment. Over and over his mouth slanted across hers, arousing her, arousing himself.

Reaching behind her, he felt for a zipper and found

none. He could feel her mouth drawing into a smile against his. With desire licking at him more fiercely than the flames were licking the log in the fireplace, he drew his head back and looked at her.

"I give up. Do I say magic words to get you out of this?"

She shook her head, her amusement lighting up her eyes. "The dress comes up, over my head."

It was he who felt as if he was in over his head. It was a first.

Rising to his feet, he brought Gina with him. Gathering the dress at her waist, he slowly raised it up and then gently tugged it until the material cleared her body. And left him looking at the most enticing creamy white bra and panties he'd ever seen. Only extreme control kept him from swallowing his tongue.

Her dress dropped from his limp fingers.

His eyes swept over her. Devouring her.

She smiled at him. A smile that went straight to Ben's belly and twisted it until his every thought began and ended with her and the warmth he felt right at this moment.

He placed his hands on her hips, his fingers dipping beneath the few strands of material on either side. Gina began to unbutton his shirt. Her eyes never left his as she worked one button free after another. The slower she moved, the faster his heart pounded. When she pulled out the shirttails, he realized he'd stopped breathing. As she splayed her hands over his bare chest, teasing the hair there, he began again. Double time. Gina slid the shirt down off his shoulders, pushing the material down along his arms until it fell to the floor.

Unable to maintain even a small distance between them, he pulled her deep into his arms, kissing the column of her throat, relishing the way her pulse beat just as wildly as hers.

She was having trouble concentrating, trouble not surrendering entirely and just letting herself absorb all the delicious sensations beating against her. But she wanted this to be memorable for both of them, not just her. And for that, she couldn't be passive. Couldn't just let him take the lead without trying to switch their positions. With effort, she undid the buckle of his belt and flipped open the button at his waist.

She felt herself getting giddy again, a hot giddiness that made her head swim. She stilled her hands as she tried to recover.

"Don't stop now," he coaxed against her ear.

Gina shivered just before he closed his lips around her lobe and nibbled on it. She felt blood rushing through her veins, the crescendo of a wild, moving symphony. When she felt him guide her hand to the apex of the zipper, she could barely breathe.

She hardly remembered moving the metallic tongue down. But she heard the groan that escaped Ben's lips, felt the enticing swell form beneath her fingers and it empowered her. This wasn't just a one-way street. She was as much in charge of the trafficking of sensations as he was.

The power was heady. His kiss was even more so.

Her mouth sealed to his, Gina pushed both sides of his jeans down his taut hips. The denim dragged his underwear down with it. He kicked them both aside. She felt the heat of his body as it pressed against hers and lost her hold on the last thin strand of realty.

Everything began to whirl around her as an eagerness took possession of her. And of him.

She felt the clasp at her back open, the bra came

sliding off a beat before she felt her underwear slipping down past her knees. It was all happening in a bright red, blazing inferno.

Somehow, her mouth questing over his, she stepped out of what remained of her undergarments.

She felt the imprint of his body against hers. A rocket went off inside of her, setting all of her ablaze as demands slammed against needs that had been blanketed and denied for so long.

She didn't want to deny them any longer.

Ben couldn't get enough of her.

It was as if he were in some sort of race, needing to get his fill of her before the final buzzer sounded. Before the clock struck twelve and everything around them would return to what it was before, taking the magic, the exhilaration with it. Before he woke up to find that this was just a dream.

He wanted time to stand still.

He wanted this to go on forever. To feel this passion, this need, this anticipation endlessly. Ben lowered her to the floor before the fireplace, eager to explore this new terrain that was suddenly before him. Eager to sample, to taste, to touch. To caress and hold. She was the first undiscovered country and he the first explorer. The past did not exist, the future was too far away. All there was, was now.

And Gina.

She throbbed all over, her body a symphony of desires, of demands begging to be addressed and satisfied. She wanted to feel his body over hers, to join with him so they could search for the final peak together. But he persisted in his exploration, skimming his lips here, teasing her with his tongue there. Reducing her to a pulsating mass as she grasped at him, at the rug beneath her, at anything that could serve as a conduit and let her hang on just a little longer.

Several times, she'd had to struggle to hold back, to keep the explosions that begged for release at bay, because she wanted the excitement to continue. The lovemaking to continue.

And then he was over her, his body poised and wanting, his eyes looking down into hers. There was something there she couldn't read. A sadness that defied definition.

Was it regret?

An apology?

She didn't know, she didn't understand, but she ignored it, afraid that it would intrude and rob her of the last bit of stardust she was reaching for.

Ben framed her face with his hands, looking only at her eyes, her lips.

"You're beautiful," he whispered. *And this is wrong. But, heaven help me, it feels so right.*

He felt her arch her hips against him. He swore silently as the last sliver of decency that he was still husbanding slipped through his fingers.

He was only human and never needier than he was right at this moment.

Parting her legs, he slid into her. Ben groaned as he felt Gina's muscles quickening around him. He began to move and she mimicked him, tempo for tempo, rhythm for rhythm, until he no longer knew where he ended and she began.

Knowing somehow didn't seem all that important.

Moving faster and faster, he rushed with her to the final consummation, the final celebration.

Like the aftermath of a cork launching itself from the

mouth of a bottle of champagne, the resulting shower covered them both at the same time.

Feeling unbelievably contented and drained, Ben sagged against her and felt her arms tighten around him. With effort he tried to balance his weight not to crush her. Euphoria kept him light.

Gina sighed. For one moment in time, she felt as if she finally belonged somewhere.

And that somewhere was here. With him.

Chapter 15

There should be guilt.

The thought slowly penetrated the haze that still swirled around Ben's brain.

He knew there should have been guilt, knew that he should be feeling guilty because of what he'd done and what he'd just allowed to happen.

And there was guilt. But it was to such a small extent he would have missed it entirely if he hadn't been looking for it.

Instead, there was this incredible feeling of all-pervading contentment. Contentment with himself, with life and, most especially, with the woman whose supple body lay tantalizingly just beneath his. A contentment that bore the descriptive label of "afterglow" and bordered on a euphoria the like of which he couldn't remember ever experiencing before. Or, if he had, it was buried so far back in the past, it no longer counted.

With a heartfelt sigh, he let it envelop him. He hadn't the strength left for anything else.

Very slowly, her chest rose and then fell as she released the languid sigh that echoed his own. Gina felt as if a thousand rose petals were caressing her skin. Making her feel soft. Silky.

She struggled to hang on to the feeling a microsecond longer, trying not to think that she'd obtained it under false pretenses.

Where there were roses, there were thorns. For her, the thorns were just a hairbreadth beyond her reach.

But they would draw closer.

She knew that.

She knew that Ben might leave very soon, when he was finished with what he had to do, but that he had made love to a lie. Had joined his body with a woman who didn't exist.

At least, not as he thought he knew her.

Not now, not now, she pleaded with herself silently. It had been so very long since she'd felt like this: hopeful, joyous. At peace.

Gina felt him shifting against her and her eyes fluttered open. Until that moment, she hadn't realized that they were closed. She became aware that her fingers were tangled in his hair. Stroking.

She hadn't realized that, either.

She smiled. Nothing like a good man to turn a woman into a blithering, mindless idiot with a brain the consistency of pudding. But it did feel good. So indescribably good.

He looked at her for a long moment, his eyes holding hers. The guilt grew until it became recognizable. And prickly as it chafed against him. How had he let things get out of hand like this?

He knew damn well how. He'd allowed himself to lead with a part of him that had nothing to do with intellect—and everything to do with feelings. He had feelings for this woman, and that didn't bode well for the case, for him and maybe even for her.

Very carefully, he framed Gina's face with his hands and looked for words he couldn't form.

Still, he had to try. "I didn't mean for this to happen."

The shot was clean and drew blood immediately. Wounded, she shrank back. Hurting.

"I didn't notice anyone holding a gun to your head, Ben." He shifted from her and she drew herself up on one elbow, wishing for all the world she had something to cover herself with besides her shaky dignity. "Are you saying that because you're afraid I'm going to dash into my bedroom and pull out a wedding dress, or because you realize you've temporarily taken leave of your senses and now regret what just happened between us to the soles of your feet?"

Jokes, she thought, she was making jokes to hide the all-pervading hurt that had reared up, large and stinging, out of the well of her happiness. Her eyes stung and she silently threatened herself with bodily harm if so much as a single tear made a hesitant appearance. She was going to carry this off, damn it.

"Regret?" Is that what she thought? Hell, how could she? "As in sorry I held you? Sorry I kissed you? Sorry I spent what just possibly could have been the best half hour of my life? No."

A smile began to form in the center of her being. "Forty-five minutes," Gina corrected him, the smile rising to her lips, "but keep talking. You might just pull this out of the fire after all."

How could she think he regretted making love with her when already he felt himself being aroused again? Regret? Were all the men in her world born stupid?

With honesty nagging at him, he gave her a half truth. "It's just that I sensed this vulnerability about you and I shouldn't have taken advantage of it. And you."

Her mouth curved. In his own way, the man was hopelessly gallant. Maybe white knights did exist. Or at least off-white ones. "As I noticed, no one was holding a gun to my head, either."

"Gina—"

Something tightened in her chest almost instantly. She wished he wouldn't use that name. It just made things that much worse.

"Shh." To forestall anything he was going to say, she pressed her finger to his lips. "No apologies, no explanations. We're two adults, having a very adult time." His brow furrowed and she deliberately smoothed it with the tips of her fingers. Would he think she was crazy if he knew that she wanted to make love with him again? Now, while her body was still warm from his. While the glow still held. "In case you haven't noticed, you're not the Neanderthal type. You didn't—and wouldn't—force me to do anything I didn't want to do."

She sounded far more convinced than he was. The firelight was playing on her skin again, kissing it the way he found himself longing to. "How are you so sure what type I am?"

Her smile broadened. She ran her fingers along his forehead. "For one thing, you don't have the low, protruding brow." Raising her head, she kissed his forehead. "For another, you are a very, very gentle, considerate lover."

The grin began in his eyes as they teased hers before spreading to encompass his face. "Wait until you find the chocolate mint on your pillow."

"I'd rather find your head on my pillow." Her own words surprised her. She was asking him to stay until morning. She'd never done anything like this before. But it felt right. "No strings attached."

"My head doesn't come with strings," he told her wryly before feathering a kiss to her lips, then rising to his knees.

The next thing she knew, she was caught up securely in his arms and he was rising to his feet.

Laughing, she threw her arms around his neck. "What are you doing?"

"It's called playing room service," he replied, stealing another kiss. Carrying her, he began walking toward the stairs. "I'm taking you to your room."

She was completely naked, after having made love to a man she hadn't known two weeks ago. Shouldn't she be feeling the slightest bit awkward or uncomfortable?

The word *no* whispered softly along her mind in reply to her own question.

"Why?"

He took the stairs slowly, looking only at her. Banking down any stray thought that didn't involve this moment and this overwhelming feeling that came rushing back to him. "Because if I'm going to make love with you again, it should be in your bed."

He wanted her as much as she wanted him. The realization was exhilarating. "See, considerate." She wove her arms more tightly around his neck, then laughed as his lips teased the slope of her neck.

* * *

He was stalling and he knew it. Stalling under the guise of telling himself he was just trying to gather more information. To look for a way out for her.

Ben frowned, a general annoyance pervading him as he looked for an outlet.

Until the other night, when they'd made love, he would have never doubted himself. He would have said, with no hesitation whatsoever, that he couldn't be bought off.

But had he been?

Had he been bought off by eyes that seemed to look into his soul, by lips that tasted of all things delectable and tempting, and by a woman who seemed to anticipate his every need while creating needs where he hadn't even been aware any had existed?

Had he been bought off by the promise of what was and what was to be?

He couldn't say and it made him angry. Angry at himself and the quandary that had brought him here to this juncture.

He'd spent all of that night and then most of the next day as well with Gina. She'd taken a personal day because Jesse had no school that day. When she went to pick up Jesse at Kyle's house, he'd come with her. Because it was a holiday, the three of them, much to Jesse's delight, had made a day of it. Ben had taken them to a fast-food restaurant and then to the zoo. Jesse'd had a ball. There was nothing in his manner to suggest that he was a child who'd been recently abducted. Everything about his manner went against every single textbook sign Ben had been taught to look for.

The only time his conscience had actually put in any sort of a tangible appearance was when Jesse had remarked that he was wearing the same clothes he'd had on the day before.

At a loss for an answer, he'd been saved by Jesse himself who'd followed up his own question with another. "Is that your favorite outfit?"

Relieved, he'd nodded and purposely avoided looking at Gina. "Yes, yes it is."

Jesse had nodded knowingly. "I've got one, too, but Mom doesn't let me wear it more than one day at a time. You're lucky."

He exchanged looks with Gina then, and smiled because he knew she'd expect him to. But he hadn't felt lucky. Not where it counted. Because this was all an illusion and he was beginning to dread the moment when he was going to have to put it to rest. The moment the magic would stop and he had to let her know that he wasn't Ben Underwood, hopeful screenplay writer, but Ben Underwood, private investigator. The private investigator who was going to bring her to justice.

One way or another, the moment was coming. And though he intended to help her any way he could, it still didn't put any of this right. In his experience women did not take kindly to being lied to.

He felt stymied everywhere he turned. When he tried to find a reason for why she might have done what she did and brought the conversation around to her past, Gina strayed from it almost immediately.

"There's not much to tell, really. It sounds a little like a boring movie. The kind the critics walk out on and studio executive turn down when they see the script come across their desk."

"Can't be that bad," he'd deliberately teased to put her at ease. "Look how you turned out."

The remark had brought roses to her cheeks and he'd

hated himself for it. Hated, too, the way he responded to seeing the color creep in along her face. He wanted to kiss each cheek. To steal off somewhere and peel away her clothing, inch by inch, layer by layer, until he could let his fingers roam around her body, memorizing every dip, every rise, every nuance of a curve.

Damn, but he wanted her. At the end of a long day, while playing a game of chess with her son on the living room floor, he wanted her. What the hell had come over him?

He was glad that the boy was there as a deterrent. Otherwise he had a feeling his willpower would have been quickly overpowered.

"Maybe I turned out this way despite everything," Gina replied quietly.

When he looked at her oddly, she shrugged away the mood that threatened to overtake her and came over to survey the game board. Ben's king was about to be checkmated. There was no way out of the situation. She smiled at him and wondered if he was just a bad chess player, or if he'd done that on purpose. The latter, she guessed. With affection she ruffled Jesse's hair. He probably wouldn't let her do that much longer, she mused. Little boys were sensitive about looking like a "mama's boy."

"Looks like my little genius beat you again."

Chess had never been Ben's game, though he played it better than this. But his mind hadn't been on the game this evening. It'd been on her.

He put his hand out to Jesse. "Looks like," he agreed. "Good game, my man."

Jesse beamed at the compliment.

"Time to get ready for dinner," Gina informed the

boy. "Help me pick up these chess pieces and then go and wash up for dinner."

"Sure thing, Mom." Nimble fingers began gathering up the pieces and depositing them into the brand-new box.

He wanted to be part of this, Ben thought. The thought had snuck up on him, surprising him. But there was no getting away from it. He wanted this illusion to be his reality.

He found himself hating his job.

Gina's leg brushed against him just as she crouched down to help Jesse with the chess pieces. Her head was bent and Ben found himself staring at the crown of her hair.

He saw the roots that were just hinting at coming in. A faint blush of light color amid the deep, rich darkness of midnight black hair. Everywhere he turned, there was more evidence facing him. Mocking him. He couldn't pretend to fall back on coincidence. There was only so much coincidence to go around and he'd used up his fair share.

Gina raised her head and saw him staring at her. He had the oddest expression on his face, as if there was some sort of internal debate going on. She carefully replaced the last four pieces and slipped the lid back on the box. "What is it?"

Ben shook his head. "Nothing. I was just thinking you work too hard." Getting up, he picked up the box and placed it on the coffee table.

There was something more on his mind than that, she thought as she watched him, but she let it go. Maybe she didn't want to hear.

"Picking up chess pieces is hardly hard work," she quipped, smoothing down his collar. Behind her she heard Jesse running off to the bathroom to wash up. "Stay for dinner?"

More than anything, he wanted to say yes, but he knew he needed a little breathing space to think about things. If he stayed, he'd only make love to her again after the boy was asleep. Not a good idea.

Ben glanced toward the door and told himself he had to be going. For everyone's sake. "I'm going to eat you out of house and home."

"Possibly, but I think I can spring for one more meal."

Not quite out of the room, Jesse turned around to peer up at him from the doorway, adding his silent entreaty to the set.

He was about to turn her down, to make up some excuse and leave. But his feet seemed glued to where they were, as was his resolve. Working together, Gina and Jesse were far too lethal a combination for him to withstand.

So he didn't.

Instead, he stayed, he and his troubled conscience, and he pretended, for the remainder of the evening, that he was who he said he was and there was no case, no evidence and no consequences waiting to face them both.

He left after reading Jesse one bedtime story, feeling progressively worse about himself and what he was doing. And damned troubled about all of it.

When he arrived at the motel, Ben went directly to the telephone and punched out a familiar number. He'd wrestled with his conscience, with bits and pieces of facts that were not coming together, all the way to the motel, and nothing had cleared up, nothing had gotten resolved. Everything remained in a state of confusion.

Maybe once the results of the fingerprint tests were in, he'd feel differently.

The youthful voice that greeted him on the other end only made him feel nostalgic for a time when everything was exactly as it seemed, there had been no need for lies or pretenses and the only crimes he was aware of took place in the movies his mother would allow him to watch once he'd completed his chores to her satisfaction.

But those days were gone and he knew that better than anyone.

"Mom?"

The light note left Maureen Underwood's voice immediately. He could almost see her hand tightening on the receiver. "Benjamin, what's wrong?"

Apart from Eliza, his mother was the closest thing to a psychic he had ever known. He deliberately made his voice sound lighthearted.

"Nothing's wrong, Mom. Can't I call my mother without there being something wrong?"

"You can, but you don't. Not usually."

She had him there, he thought, but he tried to divert her for a second, anyway. It was that same stubborn streak that once had him deliberately breaking curfew, just to be perverse. "I could be calling you about Erika."

"Yes, but you're not."

He laughed softly, shaking his head. If she'd been Caesar's mother, the man would have never ventured out on the Ides of March. "And how do you know that?"

"I'm a mother, I've made a science of listening to

your voices and filling in all the blanks you and your sisters thought you were too clever to tell me. All right, come clean. What's wrong?''

He hadn't called to go over the case, only to hear the sound of her voice. Somehow, there was comfort in listening to her go on and on about things. Even if that ''thing'' turned out to be him.

''Nothing's wrong, ma.'' He smiled to himself as he tucked the telephone between his ear and his shoulder. ''Just working the knots out of a case and I got homesick for the sound of your nagging.''

''I don't nag, I repeat.''

His grin grew larger. ''And repeat and repeat and repeat.''

She pretended to bristle, though he knew she took no offense. ''How else are you and your sisters going to hear me if you insist on tuning me out?''

''How else?'' he echoed with a laugh. Why was there this homesickness pervading him? He never got homesick. ''So, everything's okay on your end?''

Because she instinctively knew, without knowing why, that her son needed this, Maureen played along. ''I'm not complaining. Your sister says she's getting married. I'll believe it when it happens.''

He kicked off his shoes and got comfortable on the sofa. ''You don't believe her?''

He could hear the skepticism in his mother's voice. ''Erika's been in love before.''

That much was true. Erika did fall in and out of love far more than the average person. But he had a feeling it was different this time. ''She never asked me to be best man before.''

''Huh. Well, maybe this time she is serious.'' Never one to stand on protocol, Maureen pushed a little.

"Benjamin, why don't you drop over tonight? We can talk better face-to-face."

He would have liked that, he thought. To sit in the kitchen where he'd spent so much time when he was growing up, letting his mother fuss over him now the way he wouldn't have then. "Can't. I'm not exactly in the neighborhood."

"Whose neighborhood are you in?"

"I'm in San Francisco." He heard her sigh on the other end. He knew that sound and knew what she was thinking. "San Francisco, Ma, not downtown Beirut. You told me you'd stop worrying once I got off the force."

"I lied. Although I'd sleep better at night if I knew you weren't going around wielding a gun."

They'd had this discussion before. In every conceivable fashion. "I don't go around wielding a gun, Ma."

"But you own one."

Suddenly too tired to debate, he searched for an analogy she could relate to. "You own a TV set, but it's not always on."

"No one was ever shot with a TV set, Benjamin."

"Ma—"

"All right, I'll stop." She paused, and he thought she was regrouping for a sneak attack, one parting shot before she retreated, but she surprised him. "I don't want you hanging up, thinking your mother was nagging you again."

He laughed. "Never crossed my mind."

"Ha. You can never lie to your mother, Ben. I see right through you." There was silence for a moment as she debated whether or not to ask. "Are you all right? Really," she pressed, wanting the truth. "Without going into details I know you can't go into, although why it should be privileged from your mother is beyond me. It's not like I'm about to go running off with it and spread it on the Internet. But without going into those kinds of details,'' she continued hurriedly, cutting off a protest she knew was coming, ''can you tell me if you'll be all right, because what I'm hearing right now, between the 'ma's' and the other words, there's something weighing on you. Is it going to be all right for you?''

She'd done her job, and lightened his moment. ''With you as my mother, how could it not be?''

''Flattery isn't going to get you anywhere. I'm immune, remember?''

His lips twitched. The hell she was. Maureen Benvenuti Underwood could melt faster than the wax on a birthday candle when she heard the right words from any of her children. But he let her have the lie.

''I remember.''

''All right then, do what you always do. Get the bad guy and keep safe.''

If it were only that easy this time. ''I'll do my best, Ma.''

''Fine.'' Worried, Maureen added, ''I'm here if you need me.''

''I know, Ma. I know.''

''You're a good man, Benjamin. Trust your instincts to see you through.''

The problem was, he thought as he hung up, he wasn't sure of his instincts. Just as he didn't know who the ''bad guy'' was right now. Was it the woman he called Gina, the woman he'd made love with and wanted, even now? Or was it him?

Ben sighed as he dragged his hand through his hair. He remained where he was, staring at the telephone for a long while.

And not liking what he was thinking.

Chapter 16

Shadows obscured most of the office, robbing it of its lavish appearance, hiding most of the expensive decor.

Anger resided in its place.

He'd dimmed the lights before he'd sat down. It suited his mood.

Everyone else had gone home. Or off to celebrate. The merger he'd predicted, the merger he'd made them all sacrifice their private lives for, had finally gone through. IndieCorp and Mercury Electronics had united. Less than fifty minutes ago. And he was the man of the hour.

As he should be.

Accolades from fawning underlings and jubilant board members had surrounded him, buzzing around his ears like the sound of so many insignificant bees. The words had meant nothing to him.

Closing his hand around the small, chunky glass, he

tossed down the amber liquid and waited for the raw taste to find him. To mellow him.

It failed.

Just as the feeling of triumph failed to find him. His biggest career victory and it was marred. Marred because she wasn't at his side, as she should be. Wasn't there to celebrate him with the others, wasn't there to be with him and form that perfect standard by which others would envy him.

"Bitch."

The word echoed around the empty office, ricocheting off the African carvings that hung on the wall.

He poured another drink and downed it. The anger boiled within him, sizzling like beads of water on a burning hot skillet.

Damn her, damn the bitch, he was going to make her pay for this, too, just as he was going to make her pay for the rest of it. For spurning him. For disappearing with that brat in tow, making him miserable because she wasn't here to see how important he was. How without him, there was nothing.

But she'd see that. Once he had her back, she would see that. And he would enjoy hearing the words come from that ripe mouth of hers.

"I'm sorry." "Forgive me." "I was wrong." She'd say all that, and more. And then she'd beg, beg for mercy.

Before he took his final revenge.

With a guttural shriek that was barely human, he grabbed the bottle from his desk and hurled it across the room. It shattered against the bar, raining bourbon and shards of glass onto the imported carpeting.

The silence absorbed the sound, making it disappear

into the darkness.

He would make her pay.

One hand on the door, Ben was about to leave when he heard the telephone ring. It was the regular line, not his cell phone. Ben debated ignoring it and just continue walking out.

He couldn't have said why, but something made him hesitate picking it up. The same something that told him he wasn't going to like what he heard on the other end of the line.

But there was no use in trying to evade it. Whoever was calling would try his cell phone next. Besides, hadn't he been the one who'd said that nothing was ever solved by running away? He'd preached it to enough runaways during his career. You would have thought the axiom would have sunk in by now.

Crossing back to the bed, he yanked up the receiver and fairly growled his name. "Underwood."

"Ben, it's Rusty."

Hearing the younger man's voice, Ben did something he normally never did. He tried to dodge. "Look, I'm in a hurry right now, so if you—"

"You're going to want to hear this," Rusty assured him.

Ben could hear the pleasure in the other man's voice. Fresh out of college, Rusty still approached everything he did with gusto. He and ChildFinders, Inc. were a marriage made in heaven.

"Go ahead." Hoping for the best, Ben braced himself for the worst.

"I just finished running those fingerprints you sent in. The ones on the book were smudged and I couldn't get a clear print."

"Well, you did your best—"

"Wait, there's more. The ones on the book were smudged because a lot of people must have handled it before you got it, but there was a faint thumb and forefinger on the receipt you sent along. It was the only set of prints on it. Good thinking."

That all depended on which side of the rickety fence you were sitting on, Ben thought, trying to curb an unexpected surge of annoyance.

"And?" He wanted to tell Rusty to cut the flattery and get to it, but jumping down Rusty's throat for doing exactly what he'd asked him to do wasn't going to change the results the other man had gotten. Crossing his fingers mentally, Ben prodded. "Whose are they?"

"The suspect's. Gloria Prescott," Rusty added in case there was any confusion. "You found her, Ben. You found the kidnapper. Is the little boy with her?"

He thought of Jesse, of the bright, eager face with its laughing eyes. How could he be that happy and still be a kidnap victim? How could he call her "Mommy" so soon after the abduction? It didn't add up. "Yeah, the little boy's with her."

"Great, looks like the agency's chalked up another one. Or rather, you did." Rusty paused for a moment as if waiting for him to say something. Ben heard paper being shuffled in the background.

"Looks like."

There was another pause on the line and then Rusty asked in a voice that was somewhat less exuberant, "So why do you sound as if someone just died?"

"Maybe someone did," Ben answered.

There was a knot in the pit of his stomach the size of a boulder. Maybe the woman he thought Gloria, or Gina, was, had just died with the verification of the prints. It certainly felt that way to him.

He wasn't one to grasp at straws, but he was grasping now. "There's no possibility that this is a mistake, is there, Rusty?"

"No. Went over all the tests myself to verify the lab's results. They're Gloria Prescott's prints, all right." Again, he paused, waiting. Listening. "Ben, is there a problem?"

Yeah, there was a problem. A hell of a problem. He'd broken the first cardinal rule of investigative work and let himself fall for a suspect. Suspect, hell, a bona fide kidnapper.

Ben sighed, not knowing if he was angrier at himself for his unprofessionalism, or at Gina for doing the deed. "No, no problem. Thanks, Rusty. I'll be in touch."

He let the receiver slip from his fingers onto the cradle. He wanted to throw it across the room. Cursing, he shoved his hands into his pockets, feeling impotent. Feeling like a fool.

Damn it, he hadn't wanted it to be her. With all the evidence pointing her way, with no other possible explanation as to why there were so many coincidences to deal with, he hadn't wanted it to be her.

Even now, he couldn't reconcile himself to the facts. She didn't seem the type.

Seem. Illusion. It was all just illusion. He'd seen and believed what he wanted to see and believe. What she'd wanted him to see and believe.

Ben reminded himself of the stories he'd read. The ones about perfectly nice people who suddenly went off the deep end and did terrible things no one would have thought them capable of doing. Time bombs, waiting to go off. Was that Gloria's/Gina's story? Had she been a time bomb?

But even time bombs didn't go off by themselves, something set them off.

She'd been thrown over by McNair, he remembered. That could have easily triggered her.

Still, he hesitated. Could his instincts have been so off?

But were they his instincts, or had he been thinking with another part of his anatomy? Had he been reacting to clues, or to the scent of perfume, to the set of a mouth, firm and inviting?

He honestly wasn't sure.

What he did know was that he needed to get his mind back on what he was being paid to do and not on some fairy tale he was spinning for himself. He was supposed to find Gloria and Andrew and he had. Only they answered to Gina and Jesse.

He looked at the telephone.

Ordinarily, he would have called McNair long ago, but there was nothing ordinary about this.

He needed more, Ben decided. The cop in him needed more. He needed some kind of explanation, some kind of clue as to why she'd stolen someone else's child. Try as he might, he just couldn't get himself to buy into McNair's story about revenge. Gina, or Gloria, whatever name she wanted to go by, just wasn't the revenge type. He was willing to bet his life on it.

He might as well, he thought, walking out of the motel room and closing the door behind him. He sure as hell was betting his career.

There were things about being an investigator that the cop in him would have balked at—if he'd been one to follow the rules at all times. But that had been one of the reasons he'd left the force. Rules sometimes got in the way of doing the right thing. The spirit of the law rather than the letter.

Right now, the spirit had him breaking and entering, trying to unearth something that would keep the ''letter'' from locking Gina up.

Careful not to attract any attention, Ben glanced both ways to make sure there was no one looking his way before he picked the lock of Gina's condo door. The lock was embarassingly simple and he thought that she should have invested in something more substantial before moving in.

The woman was a kidnapper and he was thinking of ways to keep her safe, he mocked himself. That would make him the last of the simple-minded Boy Scouts.

A moment later, he let himself in. Ben slipped the lock picks back into his pocket and quietly closed the door behind him. It was a little after eleven o'clock in the morning. Gina was working at the bookstore. He'd deliberately taken the long way to pass by the store on his way to her condo so he could be certain she was gone. Her car had been parked in the lot.

Even so, he took a second to listen for any noises that might warn him that there was someone else in the house.

There were none. He was alone.

Ben reached into his back pocket and took out a pair of surgical gloves. He intended to be painstakingly thorough and he had no intentions of leaving any of his own prints behind just in case they needed to sweep through here later for any reason. There was already enough confusion involved.

He began the process in her bedroom. Ben had no idea what he was looking for, only a vague feeling that he'd know it when he finally found it. ''It'' being something that would absolve her of the crime she appeared to have committed. If he was going to champion her the way he wanted to, he needed something to go on. Unless he found that "something," he had no choice but to call McNair and tell him his son had been found.

As he searched, a frustrated emptiness pervaded him. There was no one to go to with this, no one's advice to ask. He couldn't very well tell Cade about the unorthodox turn the case had taken for him. In all the years he'd always relied on his own instincts, he'd never felt less certain of what he was doing than now.

The closets and drawers were next to empty. Except for the furniture, the small condo was almost spartan in appearance. No knickknacks to draw attention to the accumulation of events and experiences that went into making up a life, no real touches to prove that this was the home of a family that had any intentions of putting down roots. No photo albums of any kind. It was almost like a movie set, made to look real but ultimately make-believe.

Well, what did he expect? It *was* make-believe.

And yet…

Half an hour of methodical sifting and he'd found nothing to help him support his theory that Gina wasn't responsible for what had happened, that there was some different, plausible spin on the events that seemed to have transpired than the one he'd been given.

Instead, in her bathroom, Ben found only things to further give credence to the theory that Gina had gone out of her way to bury the person she'd been a short while ago. He found a box of brunette hair dye in the cabinet beneath the sink and contact lens solution in her medicine cabinet. An extra pair of contacts was stored beside it. When he opened the tiny container, he found that the second pair of lenses were the same shade of cobalt blue as her eyes. Tinted contacts to hide her true eye color.

The same eyes that had looked into his soul when they'd made love.

Ben closed the case and placed it back into the medicine cabinet. He felt disgusted and angry and cheated all at the same time.

Replacing the hair dye beneath the sink exactly the way he'd found it, he went to the nightstand at the side of her bed. He fought against images that insisted on returning to him. Images of the two of them, making love. Images of the way she'd looked, nude and radiant, in his arms just before she'd drifted off to sleep.

Instead he forced himself to go through the drawers. The first one was empty except for a pad and pen. The second drawer contained a book she was obviously reading. The pages seemed to all fan out, as if they'd been somewhere humid, like the beach on a foggy day. When he picked the book up to examine it, he saw that there was a folded eight-by-ten white sheet of paper beneath it. Setting the book aside, he unfolded the paper.

In the middle of the page, in a bold block font, was a single underlined sentence: I'll make you pay for what you did to me.

The words echoed back at him. They were the words McNair had told him she'd shouted at him when he'd told her she was being let go. Had she meant to leave it behind for McNair to find and instead she'd just forgotten?

Swallowing a curse that burned on his tongue, Ben folded the paper and slipped it back under the book, then shut the drawer again.

He was nearing the end of the trail.

As if trying to fabricate hope where none would be sustained, Ben made his way into the kitchen next. The cabinets contained nothing more than dishes and glasses that had obviously been left behind by the man who had sublet the condo to her, and there was nothing out of place in the pantry. There was nothing that could even remotely be construed as something appearing to be in her favor.

He found her driver's license in the refrigerator.

It was in a sealed plastic sandwich bag taped to the bottom of the vegetable crisper. The driver's license that belonged not to dark-haired, blue-eyed Gina Wassel, but to blond, green-eyed Gloria Prescott.

Ben stared at the license feeling as if a knife was twisting into his gut. He couldn't keep denying it, couldn't keep hoping to find something that would clear her. There was nothing that would clear her. She was the kidnapper of Stephen McNair's son.

There was nothing to keep him from making the call he didn't want to make.

He thought of putting the license back where he found it and just walking away. But he knew he couldn't do that. So he carefully folded the plastic bag around the license and slipped it into his pocket.

Leaving, he closed the front door quietly behind him. He hated what he knew he had to do next and was angry at the woman who had put him in this kind of gut-shredding position.

Cold water didn't help.

Her eyes still stung.

Gina leaned against the small, utilitarian sink in the bookstore's bathroom, staring into the mirror. Her eyes looked as bloodshot as if she'd pulled two all-nighters back to back, or at the very least, found her way into the bottom of a bottle of liquid comfort.

More than anything, she was dying to pop out the contact lenses. The trouble was she had a sinking feeling that if she did, there was no way she'd be able to get them back in again. Her eyes would be too irritated to permit it. It'd be like taking shoes off swollen feet. Putting them back on would be self-inflicted torture. Not to mention damn near impossible.

It was the San Francisco smog that was doing it, irritating her eyes so. That and the fact that she just wasn't used to wearing lenses. But she hadn't had the luxury to break herself in slowly. She'd needed to quickly change her appearance, and a different eye color had been one of the fastest ways to go. To match the real Gina Wassel's description.

Taking a tissue, she dabbed at her eyes. Nope, she was stuck. There was no easy way to explain how she'd suddenly gone from being blue-eyed to green without raising suspicions. Especially Ben's if he happened to drop in this afternoon the way she hoped he would. She could, of course, tell him that she had just been adventurous and decided to go with a different eye color, but the truth was far too close to the lie for her to risk it.

Better that she put up with the discomfort and he think she was reacting to the city's smog or having an allergic reaction to something.

She shook her head as she peered more closely at herself. If this got any worse, she was going to be able to pass herself off as a big white rabbit, pink eyes and all.

It was a small-enough price to pay when it came to

Jesse's safety. And in the end, it was all about Jesse, not her.

Walking out of the bathroom, her eyes still damp from the water she'd splashed into them in an effort to make them hurt less, she automatically looked around at the store's clientele. Searching. This time of day, just after the lunch crowd had thinned out, the store was usually rather empty.

The familiar form registered a half beat before the smile rose to her lips. Ben. He must have come in while she'd been in the bathroom, trying to make herself presentable.

The joy she felt at seeing him faded several notches when she saw the look on his face. She crossed to him quickly.

"What's the matter? You look as if you lost your best friend."

The muscles on his arm tightened in response to the touch of her hand. Not his best friend, he thought, but he'd lost a woman he hadn't thought his life incomplete without until now.

Before he could answer her, she formed her own theory about what was responsible for the expression on his face. "Wait, is someone else doing the same story as you are?"

Completely preoccupied by the events of the last couple of hours, Ben could only stare at her uncomprehendingly. "What?"

"The screenplay. Did you just find out that someone else is doing the same story?" Because his expression wasn't changing, she pressed on, hoping that was it. Hoping there was nothing more serious wrong. Something in her belly tightened. "Because even if they are, that doesn't mean that there isn't room for two versions of the same thing, even coming out around the same time.'' She was talking faster and faster, trying to outrace whatever else there might have been on his mind. ''A television version of the last day aboard the *Titanic* was shown on television just before the movie version came out and that made box office history, so—''

He couldn't bear to have her go on like this. ''No, it's not about the screenplay.''

She'd never heard him sound angry before. A nervousness began to take hold, a nervousness she'd almost managed to banish since he had come into her life. ''Well then, what?''

Conscience had made him come. A guilt he couldn't shake, that made no earthly sense to him. Somehow, he felt he owed her fair warning. But he couldn't tell her here, in front of the people she worked with. ''Is there somewhere we can go to talk?''

She automatically glanced over toward Joe at the register. He nodded, making no effort to hide his curiosity. ''All right.''

Ben took her arm, ushering her over to where the periodicals were kept. For the moment, there was no one else around.

''No, in the back,'' she prompted, leading the way to the room they all used to stash their things when they arrived in the morning. The room that doubled as Jon's office and where he took naps on occasion.

She closed the door behind her, nearly bumping into the coatrack where she'd quickly hung her purse this morning, running late. The room was crammed with boxes, books that had yet to be inventoried before they were put on the shelves.

Gina tried to read Ben's expression. The solemnity,

the deadness of his eyes, unnerved her even further. Was he going to tell her it was over between them?

She felt her heart shrink a little in anticipation of the death blow. She'd known when she'd gone to bed with him that this couldn't be permanent. And yet, a part of her had hoped…

"Ben, you're scaring me, what is it?"

There was no way to say this but to say it. The words felt like poison on his tongue. "I know who you are."

Her voice was very still. "What do you mean?"

Did she want him to spell it out for her? All right, he would. "I know your name isn't Gina Wassel, that you're really Gloria Prescott."

Chapter 17

She backed up, bumping against the coatrack again. It hardly registered. Gina stared at Ben as if he'd just sprouted horns and a tail.

"Who are you?" she whispered hoarsely, her mind too numb to form connected thoughts her soul didn't want to admit.

"I'm Ben Underwood."

There was a finality in his voice, as if the name was synonymous with a death knell.

Gina continued to stare at him, hardly daring to breathe, afraid of the answer to her question. Even more afraid not to ask.

"Who *are* you?"

There was a dangerous look in her eyes he didn't know how to interpret. "Stephen McNair hired me to—"

Stephen. It was as if Ben had aimed a nail gun straight at her heart and fired. It took everything she had not to begin to shake with anger and fear. "Did you call him?" He didn't answer. Her voice rose. "Did you tell him where I was?"

"Gina—Gloria," he corrected himself, frustrated at the way his tongue tripped over her name, not knowing what to call her. Knowing only that in his mind, she was still Gina to him. The woman he'd opened up to far more than he had ever intended. "You know that you can't—"

A deadly panic began to take hold of her. *"Did you tell him where I was?"*

"Yes."

He'd gotten off the phone with the man almost two hours ago, then spent the time between then and now wrestling with his conscience. He'd come here to see her because some part of him, the part that wanted to believe she was somehow innocent, had felt she deserved to know what was about to happen. To prepare herself.

Icy needles ran up and down along her body. He'd called Stephen. He'd told Stephen where she was. Where Jesse was. Her breath came in short, shallow pants. "What have you done? Omigod, what have you done?"

Paralyzed, she stood with both hands covering her mouth, trying to think, trying to will a thought, a course of action into her brain.

Jesse.

She had to get to Jesse. Before it was too late. She felt tears forming and damned herself for the weakness even though she knew they were tears of fury.

Ben saw the tears and something twisted inside of him. He reached for her. "Look, I'll help you get through this, I'll—"

She backed away from him again. Out of the corner of her eye, she saw the tower of boxes.

"You'll help me get through this?" Gina cried incredulously, edging toward the boxes. "Don't you understand? You've ruined everything."

He reached for her again, but she managed to shrug him away before he could touch her. Level with the boxes, she suddenly pushed hard against the middle one. The tower toppled, coming at him. Caught off guard, Ben tripped and fell backward.

She didn't stop to look back, even though something within her wanted to make sure that Ben wasn't hurt. *No time, no time.*

Instead, she grabbed her purse from the rack. The sudden yank made it fall onto the pile behind her.

Gina bolted from the room.

His attention drawn to the back office by the loud noise, Joe had rounded the front counter and was on his way to the rear of the store when she flew by him, nearly knocking him over. Joe managed to get out of her way just in time.

"Gina, where are you going?" Joe called after her as she ran out of the store.

She didn't even try to answer him. Every thought was focused on getting to her car and then getting to Jesse. Before it was too late.

Groggy, Ben scrambled to his feet calling her name. He pushed his way through the boxes and made it out of the back room just in time to see Gina rushing out through the electronic doors. She was moving so fast, they barely seemed to open in time to let her pass.

When he ran by the other salesclerk, Joe tried to grab him. "Hey, why are you running after her? What the hell's going on here?"

The shouted demand fell on deaf ears as Ben ran through the doors. He saw Gina pulling out of the parking lot, the tires of her car screeching as she made a sharp turn. She came within inches of colliding with another vehicle. The next second he saw her car fishtailing as she fought to regain control.

Ben pulled his own key out of his pocket as he sprinted across the lot for his car. The next moment, he went tearing out after her in hot pursuit. He knew that the best course of action to follow was to call 911, but there was no time to reach for his telephone. He couldn't afford to take his eyes off the road for even the split second it took to dial the number. He needed to see where she was going, and even a moment's diversion could seriously cost him.

She was pushing sixty in a thirty-five-mile zone. Cars pulled out of her way right and left. He held his breath as he followed.

Where the hell were the police when you needed them, he thought in exasperation.

He knew where she was going. To get Jesse. Andrew, he corrected himself. Either name, he had no idea where the boy went to school. Every casual question he'd tried to pose asking her for the information had been artfully stonewalled. Without knowing where she was going, there was no way of taking another route and getting there first to cut her off.

All he could do was keep her in his sight and pray that they both got there without crashing into another car. People got reckless when they were cornered and she was flying through yellow lights like a bullet.

Watching her, he couldn't help marveling how well she maneuvered in and out of traffic. It was as if she'd taken that defensive driving course Cade had made each of them complete recently. A lot of things came into play when you were dealing with recovering kidnapped children and Cade had wanted each of them to have every advantage possible available to them.

"Damn good thinking, Cade," he muttered under his breath, staying on Gina's tail. Without the course to have sharpened his reflexes, he wasn't sure if he would have been able to keep up.

Gina looked in her rearview mirror, perspiration beading down her back despite the cold and the chill in her heart. She'd run out with her coat, but hadn't been able to put it on.

Damn, he was still following her. She wished there was time to lose him, but she couldn't risk it. There was no time to lead him on a wild-goose chase. Every second she delayed getting to her son was a second more that Stephen had to make it there ahead of her.

She didn't know how much Ben had found out about her, if he'd tailed her when she was bringing Jesse to school and if he'd given that location to Stephen, too. She didn't think Ben had followed her, but she couldn't be sure. Even though she'd begun to grow secure—she upbraided herself for ever being so stupid as to believe she was out of danger—she'd taken precautions, kept alert for any signs that someone was following her.

Her mouth twisted in a cynical, mocking smile. Being stalked did that to you. Heightened your senses until paranoia all but ruled your life.

She felt tears welling up again.

It served her right for slacking off. She'd started to relax, to think that maybe, just maybe, she could lead a normal life. Only to be shown that she was an idiot. That she'd never be able to have what other women had.

Not until Stephen was permanently out of her life.

In her desperation to be free, she'd even thought of killing him, but it wasn't in her. Not even if it meant saving herself.

But if it meant saving Jesse...

The irony struck her even as hysteria grappled for possession of her. She automatically thought of her son by his middle name now. Not Andrew but Jesse, the name she'd made him answer to when they had shed their former identities and fled from everything they knew. To have a life.

A life that was now just a hopeless illusion.

Where did they go this time? She didn't know. All she knew was that it had to be somewhere away from here. Away from Stephen and away from the man she'd fallen in love with.

Taking a corner, she wiped away the tears that refused to stop with the back of her hand. She should have never let her guard down. Never deluded herself into believing that she could fall in love, get married. Be normal.

Forget that. Forget him. Nothing else matters but getting to Jesse.

She had barely cut off the engine and stopped the car before she was leaping out of the driver's side, rounding the hood.

The car was parked askew at the curb. Two beats later, Ben pulled up behind her. She heard rather than saw his car. Desperation had her sprinting up the steps to get to the school's double doors.

Ben raced after her and caught up before she could open them. He grabbed her wrist and spun her around to face him.

"Let go of me," she ordered. Struggling, she tried to yank her wrist out of his iron grip.

He fought against the very real urge to pull her into his arms. To hold on to her until she stopped struggling. Until she would tell him the truth. Instead, he continued to hold tightly on to her wrist. "You can't keep running this way."

"Yes I can. Now, let go of me. Do you hear me? Let *go!*"

"Hey, lady, you need any help?" An older man, walking his dog at the curb, had stopped to look up at them. "Want me to call the cops?"

That was the last thing she wanted. Cops. She already knew they wouldn't take her side.

Ben pulled Gina in close to him, as if to hug her. "Just a family argument," Ben told the man mildly. "Thanks for your concern, but I'd keep walking if I were you—unless you want a lawsuit slapped on you."

Taken aback, the man closed his mouth and put down his head. Tugging on his dog's leash, he quickly walked down the block.

Using the diversion, Gina kicked Ben's shin as hard as she could. Still holding on to her, he lost his footing and nearly went down the stairs, dragging her with him. At the last second, Ben managed to grab the handrail. His hold on her never slackened.

"Dammit, Gina, you're not going to get away with this. Now, stop fighting me."

He dragged her in his wake until they were at the foot of the stairs again. Still holding her he ushered her off to the side, out of the way of casual passersby. He didn't want any more Good Samaritans butting in.

Ben pushed her against the wall, his body blocking any retreat. "I'll do everything I can to help you—"

She curbed the urge to spit in his face. "I don't need your help, I just need you to let me go."

Frantically, her eyes searched his face, looking for a sign that the man she'd made love to had not been a complete fabrication, a complete lie. That he still existed somewhere inside this stranger who threatened to destroy her life and the life of her son.

"Please," she begged. "If there's an ounce of decency somewhere inside of you, let me go."

Despite everything, he felt an inner struggle between what he knew was right and what his instincts told him was right. "*Decency* is a hell of a word for a kidnapper to be throwing around."

Her mouth fell open. "Kidnapper? What are you talking about? Who's a kidnapper?"

He could almost believe her surprise. But he'd lied to her and had carried it off without a hitch. And she had lied to him. Which meant she was still lying.

"You. You kidnapped McNair's son. The son you were supposed to be taking care of." With each word he uttered, Ben saw the bewilderment and horror intensifying as they took hold of her features.

For a moment, she couldn't absorb what Ben was saying to her. It sounded like so much gibberish assaulting her ears.

"Kidnapped? His son?" Reflexively, she shook her head as if she were trying to clear it, trying to make sense out of what he was telling her. She couldn't. "I still don't know what you're talking about."

"Stephen McNair hired my firm to get his son back from you."

"That's not possible." She felt as if she was trapped inside of some macabre nightmare. "Stephen doesn't have a son."

He'd expected her to lie, but not so implausibly. "Then who's Jesse? Andrew, dammit," he corrected himself. The boy had been Andrew on a piece of paper. The boy he'd interacted with, laughed with, read to, was Jesse. It was hard to shake that. "Who the hell is Andrew?"

"Andrew is *my* son." Without realizing it, she gripped his arm as if to drive home her words. "He's always been my son."

There were too many clouded issues, too many things he needed to have cleared up even at this point. "Then why are you calling him Jesse? And why did you assume a dead woman's identity? Why did you change the color of your hair so you could look like her?" With his free hand, he sifted his fingers through her hair. Trying not to remember the last time he'd done that. Instead, he nodded at her eyes, noticing how red they looked. Was she going to cry again? Damn it, he hoped not. He couldn't handle tears. "Why did you change the color of your eyes?"

"Simple." She raised her chin defiantly. "To get away from Stephen. Before he hurt Jesse."

McNair's questions, all centered around his finding Gloria, not the boy, played across Ben's mind like the echo of a haunting refrain. From the very beginning, it hadn't felt right. Still, he continued to grill her. "And why would he do that?"

He wasn't going to believe her, she thought. But all she had left was the truth. And a prayer that Ben had an ounce of mercy within him. "Because I refused to marry him."

His eyes narrowed as he looked at her. She seemed so sincere. But so did actors. That's what they gave out awards for. "He said he rejected you."

To hear it all turned around stunned her. "He—I—oh, God."

Gina closed her eyes to gather herself. She knew she had only one opportunity to convince Ben that she was telling the truth. One opportunity to make him release her to get her child and flee.

When she opened her eyes again, they were directed straight at him. He'd never seen anyone look so earnest in his life.

"Listen to me. Stephen McNair and I met at an art showing about a year ago. I had some pieces on display. He flattered me, told me he had connections, that he could help me. He said that the office building that housed his company was doing some remodeling and he could get me a commission to sell my work to the decorator. He painted a tempting picture, saying that everyone entering the building would see my sculptures. I got carried away with the thought of finally being successful, of making a good living for Jesse and myself."

She'd been so foolish then, so eager to believe that things were finally turning around for her. Looking back, she couldn't believe she'd been that naive.

"At first he was very kind, very attentive, very proper. But he got tired of the role he was playing, tired of waiting for me to come around. He made it very clear that if I wanted him to use his influence, I was going to have to 'trade' something for that help." She looked away, ashamed that she had been taken in the way she had. "He wanted me to become his mistress. When I refused, he upped the ante and asked me to marry him. By then, I knew I had to get away from him."

She couldn't tell if Ben believed her or not. Gina had

no choice but to continue and hope that he'd come around.

"Stephen tried everything he could to get me to change my mind. There were flowers, and gifts, lots and lots of expensive gifts—he thought he'd overwhelm me." She smiled ruefully. "Or maybe just buy me outright, I don't know. But I sent everything back. When I sent back the diamond engagement ring, he became enraged. Said that no one had ever turned him down before and I wasn't going to be the first."

She closed her eyes again, trying to press back the tears. She wasn't going to cry in front of Ben, wasn't going to humiliate herself that way. Tears were for manipulation, and she wasn't about to use that, either.

"He told me that if I didn't give in to him, he'd hurt Jesse."

He watched her face intently, looking for some crack in the veneer. There wasn't any. "Did you go to the police?"

She laughed, but there was no humor there. "And say what? That a multimillionaire—a captain of industry as he liked to refer to himself—was trying to get me to go to bed with him, to marry him, and if I didn't, he threatened to harm my son?" Didn't he realize how ludicrous that sounded? "I was a nobody who dreamed of being a successful sculptor. He could buy and sell his own city. Who would you have believed?"

And then she grew very still, her eyes penetrating his. "Who *do* you believe?"

He wanted to believe her, knew what his heart was telling him to believe, but in all honesty, he still didn't know. "Gina—Gloria—"

"See? You don't know who to believe—the man paying your expenses or me, the woman you slept with to lower her defenses.'' She was never going to forgive him for that, for using her heart against her.

Guilt and anger rose, fighting for his self-respect. ''It wasn't like that.''

Her eyes grew cold. ''Wasn't it? Weren't you just doing your job, trying to get me off my guard?'' And to think that she had thought she was falling in love with him. How could she have been so stupid? ''What I can't understand is why you didn't call Stephen immediately. Was I that good at fooling you? Or did you just want a tumble in the hay before you turned me in?''

His anger was red hot. ''What happened between us had nothing to do with the case.''

''Didn't it?'' she challenged. ''Then why didn't you call him when you found me?''

He told her the truth. What had been bothering him since the beginning. ''You didn't seem like the kidnapping type.''

''Because I'm *not*.'' Oh, why didn't he just let her go? Why was he making her suffer this way?

''Then why was there a copy of a threatening letter in your nightstand?'' he wanted to know. ''I found it under your book. McNair told me that you'd shouted that threat at him.''

''I shouted...'' Her voice trailed off as she tried to think what he was referring to. And then it came to her. ''That was his note to me you found. I kept it to remind myself not to let my guard down.'' She looked at him pointedly. ''Too bad I didn't remember.''

''Gina—''

She threw away her pride. Pride had no place in this when it meant Jesse's safety. ''Please, please, just turn away. Let me get my son and get out of here.''

He couldn't do that. "Don't you understand that if what you say is true, you can't keep running?"

"Oh, but I can," she insisted. She looked toward the stairs. She was so close, so close. If there was just a way to get him to let go for just a minute. But he was holding her fast and standing so close that she couldn't get a good swing in anywhere. "And it *is* true. You have to believe me."

"Keep running and what? Go somewhere else where he'll send someone else to find you?"

She tried her best to convince him. "Maybe they won't this time. I'll hide our trail better." Desperation entered her voice again as it built momentum. "We'll disappear."

He could feel her eyes imploring him. It would be so easy just to open his hand and let her go. But then what? And if what she said wasn't true, then he would be an accessory after the fact. "I can't let you do that. The next person who looks for you might not be willing to listen."

"And you are?" She peered at him. Just what was he saying?

"Gina—" He stopped. It wasn't her name, yet he couldn't think of her any other way. "What the hell do I call you?"

She was losing precious time. "I don't care, just let me go."

"I can't, either way, I can't." She began to pull again, but he held her fast. "Listen to me, Gina—" He pulled her around when she started to look away. "*Listen* to me. The one thing I didn't do when I took this case was investigate McNair. It's not our policy to investigate the client. We assume that the person coming to us is telling the truth. Maybe we shouldn't," he added. “Come back with me and I promise I won’t let him near you or the boy until after I get this all sorted out.”

She didn’t know whether to believe him or not. Even if she didn’t, even if he meant what he said, she knew Stephen. She wasn’t safe anywhere near him. “He’ll find a way to get to me. He’s done it before.”

“If it turns out you’re telling the truth, I swear I’ll protect you.” His eyes held hers. “I can’t do any better than that, Gina.”

“Yes, you can.” She raised her chin, her eyes pleading with him. “You can let me go. You can turn your back now and walk away.”

She curbed the anger bubbling up inside of her, the urge to scream names at him for having deceived her so. For having used her. Instead, she tried to play up to that tiny fragment—if indeed it did actually exist—that had been so tender to her. That had made her feel as if the world was finally in the right place for her.

“If that night we spent together meant anything at all to you, you can just walk back to your car, call Stephen and tell him you made a mistake. That you didn’t find Gloria Prescott or her son. That it was two other people entirely.” Her whole being was pleading with him now. “Please.”

He’d never been so tempted to turn his back on what he’d been schooled to do. But there were reasons why he couldn’t.

Especially if he believed her.

“No.”

Chapter 18

"Where are we going?"

Eager, Jesse strained against his seat belt in the back seat, trying to lean forward. His small hands didn't quite make it to the back of the seat where his mother was sitting.

She twisted around to look at the boy. Ben had insisted on using his car, saying he'd send someone to get hers later. She had no choice but to agree. When they'd left the school, she'd started to get in the back with Jesse, but Ben had stopped her. He'd wanted her sitting in the front where he could keep half an eye on her. He figured if he kept Gina and Jesse separated, she wouldn't do anything foolish like try to leap out of the car with the boy.

Risky or not, there was a look in her eyes that he didn't quite trust.

But if there was an edgy nervousness about her, there was clearly an excited one about Jesse. The idea of being taken out of school before the end of the day purely tickled him.

"Are we going to a park?" Jesse asked hopefully, looking from one adult to the other.

How could McNair have remained indifferent to this kid? Ben just didn't understand it. He'd only known Jesse a few days and had caught himself thinking that when he finally got around to having kids of his own, he'd want them to be just like Jesse. Bright, lively and just all-around neat. That McNair could maintain an emotional distance from the boy didn't speak well of the man.

Did anything? a small voice within him demanded. He couldn't come up with a single thing.

Ben's conscience was chafing him.

"Maybe later, partner," Ben told him. "Right now, we're going to get a few things cleared up." Raising his eyes, he glanced at the small, inquisitive face in the rearview mirror. Though part of him really didn't want to, he knew this had to be asked. "Do you remember your dad, Jesse?"

Confusion creased the small, delicate features. He shook his head. "No."

Gina bit back an oath. What was he trying to do? Hadn't Jesse been through enough? "Of course he doesn't remember his dad. He never knew his dad."

Twisting around again, she looked at Jesse, worried that Ben's question had upset him. Children were sensitive and could easily intuit when something was wrong, when their parents were upset. They were a great deal more tuned in than adults gave them credit for.

She struggled now not to let on that anything was amiss, but it wasn't easy, not with her heart jumping around the way it was. Just as it hadn't been easy going to the school's main office and pretending that there was a family emergency that necessitated her taking Jesse out of class unannounced. With Ben beside her every step of the way, not giving her any space, she'd had to walk a fine line between appearing concerned but in control. The one thing she wasn't right now.

Her mind raced, trying to figure out a way to escape this man who had attached himself to her and her son. It struck her that, unlike Stephen, she wasn't afraid of Ben.

Maybe she should be, she thought, slanting a covert glance in his direction. But somehow, despite everything, despite the deceit, she felt he wouldn't hurt her. Not the way Stephen would.

But what Ben intended to do *would* hurt her. Turn her over to Stephen.

"Is that true, Jesse?" Ben was asking. "You never knew your dad?" He raised his eyes to the rearview mirror again.

Jesse slowly shook his head. "No."

Still, she could have coached the boy, found a way to make him deny knowing McNair. It wasn't your average, run-of-the-mill father-son relationship. "Not even for a little while?"

Why was Ben belaboring the point? Was he trying to talk Jesse into giving him the answer he wanted to hear?

"Now what are you saying to him?" she demanded, forgetting to keep her voice low. "What 'little while'?"

Ben took a corner. There weren't as many cars on the road anymore. He wouldn't have been able to explain why there was this sense of urgency eating away at him. Maybe Gina's edginess was rubbing off.

"McNair said that he hadn't known about Jesse's existence until almost ten months ago."

Which was about the time they'd met, Gina thought. "Well, that fits."

He knew she didn't understand what he meant. "That he received a letter from the boy's late mother, saying he was the father."

Gina's mouth dropped open. For a moment, she was too stunned to say anything.

"Late, like Santa Claus was this year?" Jesse asked. He pulled against his restraint again, wanting to join them in the front. "Mommy said he had a little trouble finding where we were because we had to move so fast."

Gina felt tears forming suddenly. She'd had to postpone Christmas for Jesse until they were settled in at the condo and she had an opportunity to buy him gifts with some of the money Aunt Sugar had given her. Jesse had behaved like a little adult, so brave, so understanding. Just remembering made her want to cry all over again. He didn't deserve to have this happening to him because she'd become the object of one man's obsession.

Neither did she.

"Not that kind of late," Ben explained. He searched for words that would make a six-year-old understand the euphemism.

Gina cut him off before he could find them. "*I* am his mother." She splayed her hand across her chest. "Late or on time," she added, glancing toward Jesse and giving him what she hoped was an encouraging smile.

She knew he had to be thrown off by all this. By being yanked out of class and made to roll up his world again with no warning. Just like the last time. The only difference was they weren't doing it in the dead of night. But Jesse was a trouper and went with the punches no matter what they were. At times, she took her strength from him.

"I've always been his mother," she said with as much pride as she did with veracity.

Ben pretended to be teasing. "This true, Jesse?"

"Uh-huh. My one-and-only Mom." He ended the affirmation with a giggle.

But Gina didn't feel like laughing. "Why are you badgering him like this?" she demanded in hushed anger.

"Because I need to be sure," he answered simply. He floored the gas pedal, just making it through a yellow light that began turning red.

Gina took a deep breath. All right, he wanted proof, she'd tell him where to find it. Maybe then he'd be satisfied and let them go.

"I can give you a whole list of people who could tell you he's my son—starting with the hospital where he was born. Harris Memorial in Bedford, California," she recited. In her mind's eye, she could still see the tall, modern building with its flag flying from the uppermost tower. It had been like an unattainable goal to her that morning. "He was born on a Friday afternoon at 4:10 p.m. after a five-hour labor. It was raining that day and I didn't think I was going to reach the hospital on time."

He picked up her meaning. "You drove yourself?"

"I drove myself," she answered with no fanfare, as if women in the throes of labor made the fifteen-mile journey every day to deliver their children. "Dr. Sheila Pollack was the attending physician. Jesse's pediatrician is, was," she corrected herself, "Dr. Rafe Saldana." She looked at him with an expression that was distant enough to place them on two separate continents. "Would you like their phone numbers?"

She was beginning to convince him. He had to admit that he'd been halfway there to begin with this afternoon. Granted, as his nanny Gina would have had access to some of this information, like the name of his pediatrician, but not the rest of it.

And if that was the case, then that meant he'd been duped. Royally.

For now, he kept that to himself. "No, for the time being, let's just say I believe you."

He'd made her grow leery of him. Gina studied his profile and found no reason to take heart. "Then you'll let me go?"

Duped or not, that was the one thing he couldn't do. "No, because if I can find you, McNair can hire someone else to do it, too." His way impeded by a sudden bottleneck of traffic, Ben cut in front of someone else, crossed through a parking lot and made it to the other street. It was one-way. The time he'd saved was lost again.

"So what's the plan?" For the first time, Gina actually focused on the streets they were driving by. Recognition set in. He was taking her back to her place. Or was he? "We're going back to the condo?"

Ben nodded. "Just to get your things, like you told Jesse." He spared a glance back at the boy, who smiled at him in return. "I'm taking you both back with me."

"Back?" she repeated warily. Had she fled one fire only to be engulfed by another? "Back where?"

He hated the tone in her voice, hated the fact that he

was instrumental in placing it there. But he had no choice.

"You said you were from Bedford, didn't you? Well, so am I. I'm taking you home to my place, Gina. Once we get there, I'll call the police."

"I already told you, the police won't listen to me. It's a matter of my word against his."

"Our word," he corrected her.

There was silence in the car for a long moment. "Then you do believe me?"

He needed to maintain his professional distance, now more than ever. "Let's say I'm getting there. And I intend to investigate this further so that we have proof on our side when we go to the police." It was the best he could do.

Going down the next block, he pulled up in front of the building.

The second Ben turned off the engine, Jesse unbuckled his belt.

"There's Kyle's mother!" He pointed excitedly to the woman carrying groceries. Opening the door, Jesse was halfway out when he stopped to look at Gina. "Can I say goodbye to Kyle and tell him we're going on a trip? Please, Mom? Please? I didn't get to say goodbye to my friends the last time we went away."

She thought of the misery she'd seen in Jesse's eyes when they had left their home, a home she had worked so hard to provide for him. The first real home she had ever had herself. How difficult it had been for him to leave all his friends behind without saying goodbye. She couldn't put him through that again.

Gina got out of the car, aware that Ben had quickly done the same, rounding the hood so that he could stand behind her.

"All right." She took Jesse's hand in hers. "Let me talk to his mom for a minute."

It had been on the tip of her tongue to say no. Ben would have bet his life on it. He could read people that much. And yet, she'd given in to the boy because it had meant so much to him. She'd placed her fear and everything else on hold for the boy. A lot of questions were suddenly answered.

Calling out to Kyle's mother, Gina hurried over. She didn't have to look over her shoulder to know Ben matched her step for step. Until this was resolved, he was going to be her shadow.

Quickly, she fabricated a story for Grace, using the same one she'd given to the principal of Jesse's school. Jesse stood by, not saying a word to contradict or question her. She didn't have time to worry about the example she was setting for him by lying, didn't have time to feel guilty over lying to a woman she had taken a genuine liking to. Her son's life could very well lie in the balance. As well as her own.

Grace smiled warmly at them, curiosity in her eyes as she looked at Ben.

"Sure, Kyle's in the house, playing a video game. You know the one," she said to Jesse. "Earth Conquerors. Can't get him away from it." Shifting the grocery bag to one side, the way a mother did with a small child she carried on her hip, Grace slipped her arm around Jesse's shoulders and began walking with him toward her own condo. "Just stop by when you're about to leave," she called over her shoulder. "I'll have him ready for you."

"Okay, let's go," Ben urged.

Holding on to her arm, Ben ushered Gina up the steps to the condo. "You don't have to hold on so tightly,

I'm not going to run away.'' She looked toward the other condo. Jesse and Grace were just taking the stairs. ''I'm not going anywhere without Jesse.''

''You don't have to run away,'' he told her, stopping at the front door. ''I believe you.''

Gina stopped hunting for her key and looked at him. Was this just another ploy to get her to drop her guard again? ''Without checking out my story?''

''Without checking out your story.''

She found the key and took it out. ''What changed your mind?'' Gina couldn't help the sarcasm that had entered her voice.

''I guess watching the two of you together.'' They couldn't have faked that. Not that well. ''It's not enough that you genuinely care for the boy, it's obvious he cares for you.'' He thought back to the conversations he'd had with McNair. Even the last one. He'd never had the feeling that the boy was anything more than an ornamental prop in all this. ''And McNair didn't seem as interested in getting his son back as he was in my finding you.'' Ben took the key from her and inserted it in the lock. ''When I brought it up to him, he said it was because you had something that belonged to him.''

That didn't surprise her. ''Yes, his pride. I stole it from him,'' she said simply as Ben opened the door. She stepped through first. ''As I said, he doesn't like to be turned down.''

''I still don't.''

Gina froze in the doorway.

Like the key figure in a hostile takeover, Stephen McNair was sitting on the sofa in the center of the small living room.

She struggled to stifle the scream that rose in her throat. She'd hoped, prayed, never to have to see him again. Had Ben known he was going to be here, waiting like this? Had he been just talking at her door to distract her?

Not knowing what to believe, staring at McNair, she backed away from Ben.

"How did you get in here?" she asked, her voice deceptively calm as she ground out the question.

McNair rose to his feet. "That's neither here nor there." He looked at Ben contemptuously. A smirk curled his thin lips. "I take it she's already told you her side of the story." He waved aristocratically long fingers in the air, as if conjuring magic. "Some fantastic fabrication about the boy really being hers."

"Maybe not so fantastic," Ben corrected him. "I tend to believe her."

McNair laughed shortly, being magnanimous for the moment. "Don't feel bad, she has that kind of effect on men. I assure you, it's damn near hypnotic." He drew closer and Gina stepped back, maintaining the same distance. McNair's brow clouded. "Certainly managed to hypnotize me. But she's a con artist, through and through, and she'll do anything to get what she wants."

Ben kept an eye on Gina, not wanting her to do anything stupid. "Funny, she said the same thing about you."

Her heart lurched in her chest. Ben *was* siding with Stephen. "Ben—" she began, but he held up his hand to silence her.

But it was McNair who interrupted. "Surely you're not going to believe her."

Ben had just about had his fill of this pompous ass. Everything Gina had said about McNair played itself through his brain at once. "Why? Because you're rich and she's not?"

Ben could see McNair struggling with patience as he drew himself up. "No, because she's lying and I'm not."

"Well, we'll have to see about that, won't we?" Ben began to reach for Gina.

The next moment, Ben found himself looking down the barrel of a weapon that fit so neatly into McNair's hand, it looked as if it had been made expressly for that purpose. Ben didn't doubt that it probably had.

"Sorry, but I don't have time to play games, Underwood." McNair held out one hand, fingers beckoning, indicating Gina. "Send the lady over to me and we'll call the case closed."

Ben's own gun was tucked into the holster strapped to his ankle. There was no way he could get to it without McNair getting off a clear shot. Ben stalled for time. "What? Before you see your son? Or aren't you concerned about him anymore?"

Anger began taking over, dissolving the last remnants of patience. "No theatrics, Mr. Underwood. They're beneath you. We both know what I want. And you've delivered it. Admirably, I might add." The smirk looked almost evil. "You've earned every penny of the fee."

It killed Ben that ethics had caused him to lead the man to Gina's door. "You know you can't get away with this."

"On the contrary." McNair's voice was deliberately singsong, deliberately mocking. "I can get away with anything I want. Or haven't you heard? Rich people can buy almost anything or anyone." His eyes became malevolent slits as he turned them on Gina. "Now, get over here," he ordered.

Trapped, with nowhere to run, Gina remained exactly where she was. Defiant, she fisted her hands at her sides. She wasn't about to stroke Stephen's ego. "No."

The mocking smile disappeared instantly, burned away in the heat of McNair's rage.

"I said get over here. Get over here or I'll shoot you where you stand, you bitch!" And then a strange look came into his eyes as he shifted them toward Ben. "Did she sleep with you? Is that it?" His voice rose, growing high. Growing hysterical. "That is it, isn't it? You slept with him when you wouldn't sleep with me, you whore."

Fury contorted his face until he looked almost demoniac. Screaming obscenities at her, McNair raised his gun a fraction of an inch.

Ben read murder in his eyes and knew he meant to kill Gina. He hurled himself against her, pushing Gina out of the way as the gun discharged. The shot missed her and sank into his shoulder.

He'd felt this pain before. Red-hot waves exploded in his arm, burning him.

Forcing himself to block out the pain, Ben didn't stop to see if Gina was all right. Dropping to the ground, he rolled into McNair. The gun went off again, firing wild as McNair fell backward.

Scrambling to his feet, Ben grabbed Gina's hand. He was running for the front door before he fully regained his balance. Behind him, McNair was shooting at them again. Ben could have sworn he felt a bullet whizzing by his head, missing him by inches.

He'd always been pretty lucky.

The air still knocked out of her, Gina realized they

were running for the car. Terror sliced through her as she tried to twist and get away.

"I have to get Jesse," she cried. "I can't just leave him here."

She tried to pull free, but he held on to her hand. The ache in his other arm was growing prodigiously. "Jesse'll be safer where he is. McNair doesn't know where we left him. Besides, it's you he wants. And I don't intend for him to get you."

Biting off a curse at the pain, he pulled open the passenger door and pushed her inside, then slid over the hood to his side and got in.

He jammed the key into the ignition and gunned the engine. Gina's eyes widened as she looked at him. There was a thick, red ooze soaking through the sleeve of his jacket.

"You're bleeding. You've been hit."

"Tell me something I don't know." Turning the wheel, he peeled away from the curb. As he did, he automatically looked down at the gas gauge. It was below the quarter-full mark. Way below. "God, I wish I'd remembered to fill up the tank."

She looked at the gas gauge. They had enough to hopefully lose Stephen before they had to stop at a gas station. Maybe.

"So do I." Gina twisted around in her seat and saw that Stephen was already out of the building and running toward a car.

Her stomach contracted in a knot.

"What I can't figure out," Ben said, "was how he got here so fast. I only called him a couple of hours ago."

When Ben had come to her in the bookstore, she'd thought he'd just made the call to Stephen. Had she known otherwise, she would have never let him take her back to the condo.

"He has a corporate jet at his disposal, and his own helicopter on standby," Gina said. He'd taken her on a ride in the latter once, preening like a peacock over his "toys." She'd begun to sense then that he was a man she needed to distance herself from. But she'd never dreamed at the time how dangerous he could become. "A couple of phone calls would be all it'd take to arrange things."

There was a catch in her voice. He knew what she was thinking. She was worried about Jesse. Ben spared a glance in her direction as he wove his way in and out of traffic. His head was beginning to spin.

"Don't worry, Jesse'll be all right. There's no way McNair could know about Kyle." He saw her reaching for the cell phone in her purse. "Don't."

Ignoring him, she began to dial. "But I have to call Grace and give her some sort of an excuse. She has to keep Jesse overnight—and not let him go outside to play with Kyle."

"Kyle's glued to the video game, remember? He's not going anywhere and neither is Jesse." Ben put his hand over the cell phone. The movement cost him dearly. Fresh flames traveled up and down his arm. "Wait until we get to a pay phone. Cell phone calls are incredibly easy to intercept and I've no doubt that Mr. Technology back there can pick up every word you say. We want to keep Jesse safe."

"Yes," she said softly, grateful that he'd just kept her from making a fatal mistake. She slipped the phone back into her purse. "We do."

Ben didn't answer. He was struggling to keep the road in focus as he took another sharp turn. The pain in his arm was getting worse.

The tanker truck seemed to appear out of nowhere.

Chapter 19

His head felt as if it was going to explode.

Ben jammed down on the brakes. Gina's scream melded with the shriek of tires and the crunch of metal meeting metal as the front of his car made contact with the tanker truck's cab.

Clipping just the edge, his car spun around drunkenly in almost a complete circle.

Breathing hard, Ben managed to regain control over the car. Gina had ceased screaming. Maybe a whole two seconds had passed, no more. Two seconds that felt like a lifetime.

His heart pounding, his body weakened and aching, Ben pressed the gas pedal as far as it would go and flew down the street. The tanker truck in his wake was turned askew, its cab and body forming a shaky letter *L*.

More important, in its present state, the vehicle blocked the intersection.

He tore through the next intersection, leaving the

near-accident far behind him. "How do you feel about driving?"

"Ask me when my heart stops racing." Peeling her fingers away from the dashboard, Gina looked at him and realized Ben wasn't just making a wisecrack. His face looked too pale even for the fading light. She immediately looked at the soaked jacket sleeve. He was losing too much blood. They had to do something fast. "Pull over," she ordered.

Turning his head in her direction took effort. The world insisted on tilting at a dangerous angle when he took his eyes off the road. "Why?"

He looked as if he was going to lose consciousness at any minute. "Because I think I should drive."

The wry smile was feeble at best as it inched across his lips. "Are you criticizing my driving?"

He'd forgotten he'd just asked her how she felt about taking the wheel, she realized. Fresh panic came in the wake of fear.

"I wouldn't dream of it," she said softly. "You drive like a pro." They were coming to a strip mall. "Now, pull over."

Ben guided the car to the curb. It was all he could manage. "Yes ma'am," he muttered, raising his hand to his forehead. The salute was never completed. Ben slumped in his seat.

Bolting out of the car as if she'd been ejected, Gina ran to the driver's side. She could feel the draft of cars whizzing by her as she pulled open Ben's door. She pushed him over to the seat she'd just vacated.

Thank God they weren't bucket seats, she thought, getting in behind the wheel. There was no way she could have managed to slide him over to the opposite end if they had been.

Taking the wheel, she glanced at the gas gauge. Stunt driving took a toll. The car needed gas badly. Impatient, she waited for a break in the stream of cars. When it finally came, she pressed down hard on the gas. "Hang on, Ben, I'll get us through this."

His eyes fluttered as the words came to him through a haze as thick as New England clam chowder. He managed a ghost of a smile. "My hero."

"Shut up and save your strength," she retorted, valiantly blocking out the salvo of fear that shot through her again. "I haven't forgiven you for this yet." She would have meant it, too, if she hadn't been so worried about him. She fought against panic taking hold of her. It wouldn't do either of them any good if she fell apart now. "I've got to get the car to a gas station and you to a doctor."

"Better than the other way around," he mumbled, and then her words penetrated. He tried to sit up straight and couldn't. But he could still voice a protest. "No, no doctor."

"I'm not having you bleed to death in the car. Red doesn't go with the upholstery."

"You do it," he rasped, his hand clutching her arm. "You bandage it. Can't risk hospital." It hurt to talk now. Ben pushed the rest of the words out. "McNair'll be checking. Looking for you."

He was right.

There was a near-empty gas station at the corner. Gina brushed away tears with the back of her hand as she pulled up in front of one of the pumps. She'd risked going as far as she could. The gas gauge needle was beyond Empty and was now hugging the extreme end of the gauge. They'd driven the last block on fumes.

Getting out, she looked at Ben. He was unconscious but breathing.

Telling herself that he'd brought all this down on himself didn't change the fact that she was afraid for his life. Afraid that the bullet Stephen had fired had hit something vital and that it was just a matter of time before she lost him.

How could you lose something you never had? she mocked herself. He'd just been pretending all this time. The words, the actions, the lovemaking, all pretense.

She shoved her credit card into the slot, then pulled it out quickly. A message to begin pumping traveled across a tiny screen above the slot. Gina flipped up the retainer and pushed the nozzle far into the gas tank. Using the card was risky. It left a trail for Stephen to follow, but she couldn't afford to waste the time it would take to run into the small convenience store where the cashier was ensconced and pay for the gas in cash. Every second counted.

Nervously, she looked around her as she waited for the tank to fill up. Her heart was pounding so hard, she could feel it slamming against her rib cage. Every lengthening shadow represented a potential danger.

Slowly, the world began to come back into focus. Ben realized that he'd been fading in and out of consciousness for a while now. It took a minute for him to become aware of Gina. She was taking his arm and draping it around her shoulders as she half dragged him out of the car. The heavy breathing belonged to her. One hand was wrapped around his waist.

"C'mon, dammit, Ben, I can't do this alone. One step at a time," he heard her telling him. "You can do this, Ben. Walk for me."

He was trying. God knew he was trying his best to hold up his weight. But it wasn't easy.

Frustration ripped at him, punching its way through the haze surrounding him and breaking it up. "This is bull," he growled more to himself than to her. "I'm supposed to...be...taking care of...you, not the...other way...around."

"We'll take turns," she panted, leaning him as best she could against a wall. She used her shoulder to brace him as she inserted the key the smirking clerk in the dismally dark front motel office had given her. "Yours'll be coming up soon, I promise."

Ben realized that he was being brought inside somewhere. Into a dingy, oppressive-looking room. Stale air surrounded him, refusing to move. The scent of cheap perfume clung to the peeling wallpaper and to the faded drapes that sagged against window frames made crooked by a succession of earthquakes, large and small.

The next thing he knew, he was sagging himself, falling backward onto a bed. The mattress embraced him, taking on his shape. Sliding Gina into him. He realized that she was still holding on to him. He managed to turn his head toward her.

Disengaging herself, Gina got back up to her feet. Ben found himself staring up at a sprackled ceiling that had captured more than its share of dirt and hapless insects. "Where are we?"

Gina brushed herself off automatically. The room gave new meaning to the phrase "two-bit dive."

"In a motel," she told him. "I'm not even sure of the name. Most of the letters in the sign in front of the lot were out."

By the sound of it, she was moving around the room.

He heard running water. Her voice was even farther away. "I hid the car in back," she said, raising her voice above the water. "I think we're safe. Stephen probably expects us to be driving straight through to Bedford."

She was beside him again, and he felt her tugging on his jacket. Pain shooting through him, Ben did what he could to raise himself up on his elbow and help her. It wasn't much, but at least he didn't feel as if he was going to pass out again. That was something.

Gina tore the remainder of his shirtsleeve away from his arm. Ben winced and tried to cover the onslaught of pain he felt with banter. "I had no idea you were so eager. You're going to have to give me a minute or two to collect myself."

She'd found a cracked plastic basin in the bathroom and had filled it up with water as far as she was able. Dabbing gently at his wound with the edge of a towel, Gina could almost feel the pain traveling through his arm. "Shut up, Ben."

A deep chuckle struggled to the surface. "You keep saying that."

"Because you keep not listening. Now, lie back and be still." She washed away some more of the blood and he winced again, though not a single sound escaped his lips. It made her feel awful. "I'm sorry. I've never cleaned a gunshot wound before."

"You're doing fine." Clenching his fists, he exhaled the words.

"No, not fine." Exasperation colored each syllable as she continued bathing the wound, trying to see how extensive the damage was. She was way out of her league here. "Fine would be if I could take you to an emergency room."

He couldn't allow her to do that. "Gunshot wounds have to be reported."

She rinsed out the cloth and began again. The wound looked better than she'd first thought.

"So, the hospital'll report it and we'll get the police." Gina tried to remember the first aid course she'd taken when Jesse was born. They hadn't covered gunshot wounds. "Maybe they'll listen this time."

And maybe, as she'd pointed out before, they wouldn't. He didn't want to waste the time. "I'd rather do it on my home territory where we don't have to prove we're the good guys." There was a question in her eyes. He put his own meaning to it. "I used to be a cop."

She smiled wryly, suddenly tired and drained. "And I used to not look over my shoulder all the time."

He could see the strain on her face, hear it in her voice. She shouldn't have had to be put through something like this. And he hadn't helped, Ben reminded himself. He'd been part of it.

"We'll get through this, Gina. I promise. And then you won't have to look over your shoulder anymore."

She made no comment. Ben was making promises she didn't know if he could keep. If anyone could keep. Stephen had gone completely out of control, throwing caution away and behaving like a madman. It was as if he no longer cared about his precious position in the scheme of things. She no longer felt safe in predicting anything about Stephen's behavior or taking another moment for granted.

"Not your fight," she told Ben quietly.

The fact that she really believed that stung, but he knew he had it coming. "The hell it's not."

She wasn't about to let herself get carried away by

hopes that had no basis. It was Ben's fault that Stephen knew where she was, but in an absolute sense, Ben owed her nothing. They were strangers. She didn't even know if Ben was his real name. Gina hadn't been hers.

She changed the subject. "I'm no expert, but I think the bullet went clear through." Ever so lightly, she dabbed disinfectant on the small, round exit wound. "There's another hole in the back of your arm." She forced a smile to her lips as she dabbed more peroxide on the small gauze pad, then pressed it lightly against his wound. "You got lucky."

"Yeah, I did." She realized that he was looking at her.

"What's this scar next to the wound?"

"I was shot in the same arm before."

"Maybe you're not as lucky as I thought." Gina got up and crossed to the card table to get the white bag with a local pharmacy's logo on it she'd dropped there when they'd come in.

"How long was I out?"

"Long enough for me to get to a drugstore and buy these." She emptied the bag on the bed. Gauze pads, bandages and tape fell out. "Then drive us to this hole in the wall."

"Holes in the wall can be good." He didn't think that McNair would look for them here. He watched her lay out what she was going to use. He liked the fact that she didn't seem to rattle easily. With a madman pursuing them, she hadn't folded like a house of cards, the way a great many other women might have. "Did you call Kyle's mother?"

Ripping a length of tape to use once she'd finished bandaging him, Gina stopped and stared at Ben. She was surprised that he would think to ask. Now that he believed that Jesse was her son, he no longer had any vested interest in the boy. Jesse was no longer the kidnapping victim he'd been sent out to find.

"Yes. The minute I got to the drugstore." She stuck one end of the tape on the edge of the bed. "I told her the truth because I didn't want to take a chance that Stephen would get to Jesse." She expected some sort of protest from Ben, but he made none. "Grace promised to look after Jesse until I could come to get him." Moving the basin with its discolored water aside, she picked up the package of gauze and opened it. "If I get back."

He lifted her chin with his good hand until her eyes met his. "You'll get back. Nothing's going to happen to you, I swear it."

She was so tired, so very tired. She wanted to believe him, wanted to have someone to lean on. But there was no earthly reason to trust him. "You're in no condition to enforce any promises you make."

"I've been in worse condition than this."

He felt her cool fingers against his skin as she quickly wound the bandage around his arm, keeping it just tight enough to curtail any more flow of blood. The contact made his stomach muscles tighten.

Ben smiled to himself. It was a good sign. He had to be coming around.

"Is that a container of orange juice over there?" He nodded toward the rickety card table where she had deposited all her hasty purchases. He tried to remember when she could have done that. The last few minutes had run together, bleeding into the time he'd spent being unconscious.

But he was conscious now.

Gina glanced over her shoulder at the card table even though she knew what he was looking at. "Yes."

With effort, he raised himself up so that he was half sitting against the headboard, the flattened pillows propped up against his back. "You think of everything, don't you?"

She didn't take it as a compliment, only an observation. Gina bit off another length of tape, securing the bandage in place. "I have to. I'm a single parent on the lam. There's no time for any second-guessing or do-overs."

His strength was returning. Maybe all he'd needed was that short time out to gather himself together. He'd always been fortunate that way. Gina had stopped fussing around him.

Utilizing the opportunity, Ben combed one hand through her hair, cupping the side of her face. "You won't be 'on the lam' for long. This'll all end very shortly. I promise."

More promises.

For a moment, because she needed it, she allowed herself to linger, to absorb the feel of his hand against her skin. To let herself drift and pretend.

But that had gotten her in trouble with him in the first place. Pretending that everything could be normal for her. That she could have a normal life despite Stephen's existence.

A normal life with Ben.

Fool me once, shame on you. Fool me twice, shame on me.

Gina drew her head back, away from him. "So you say. But you don't know Stephen." She rose to her feet as briskly as she could, pretending now to be indifferent to his promises and walked back into the bathroom with the basin.

Ben heard her emptying it, then putting it away. It sounded as if she was opening and closing doors. The next minute, she was back in the room. She stopped to pick up the carton of orange juice before crossing to the bed.

"There's no cup of any kind in the bathroom and I didn't think to get one. You're going to have to drink the orange juice from the container."

"Won't be the first time." As he took the container from her with his good hand, he grinned and laughed softly under his breath.

She didn't see anything particularly humorous about a carton of orange juice. Maybe his wound was making him light-headed again. "What?"

He opened the carton's lip. "Will you write a note to my mother? She was always after me not to do things like that when I was growing up. Said it was the sign of someone who'd been raised in a barn." Tipping the carton back, he drank deep. It made him feel better.

So did having her sit here with him like this.

Gina took the carton from him and set it aside on the floor, then sat down beside him again. "So all that wasn't just made up? You actually do have a mother?"

"It's practically mandatory for every living creature to have one at conception—as well as a father."

Gina shook her head. The image still didn't really compute. "I'm sorry, I just didn't picture you with anything as normal as parents."

It was an interesting choice of words. "Who says my parents are normal? My mother's sixty, going on sixteen." At times, he could swear she acted younger than any of his sisters. "And my father—" Without realizing it, his expression changed. "Hell, I'm not sure what he's up to these days. If the past is anything to go by, he's probably on his twentieth cheerleader by now. Maybe literally." He shrugged and instantly regretted it.

"They're not married anymore?" Even as she asked, she wondered if any of this was actually the truth. Or if he was lying again for reasons that weren't evident to her.

He shook his head slowly. "Not for a very long time." It had taken him years to reconcile himself to that fact. He wondered how long it had taken his mother. She'd never let any of them witness one ounce of bitterness. "My father left her for someone half his age. I've got a half brother named Jason somewhere. My mother raised the four of us on her own."

It was hard not to hear the affection that came into his voice when he spoke of her. Somehow, she found comfort in that. A man who loved his mother couldn't be all bad, right?

"She's a hell of a lady." He laced his fingers together with hers. "In a way, you kind of remind me of her."

Warning signals went up. "Don't try flattering me now. I'm still angry at you." Her actions warred with her words. She made no move to draw her hand away.

"Doesn't change the fact that you are. A hell of a lady," he clarified when she raised an eyebrow.

Because she was so close and he couldn't resist, Ben slid his hand up to her face and cupped the back of her head. The next moment, he brought her mouth to his. The kiss sizzled between them, evaporating what little air there was in the room.

"I'm feeling better now," he murmured against her mouth.

"I can tell."

Against all common sense, Gina brought her mouth back to his.

Chapter 20

This was crazy.

She knew that. But she needed this, needed to feel this wild feeling surging through her veins that only Ben seemed to be able to generate within her. Needed to forget the terror that hovered over her, the threat of consequences, needed to forget everything but this isolated moment in time she found herself in.

Needed Ben.

She didn't want to think, only feel, only respond. And she did so respond to Ben.

Her lips raced tiny, quick butterfly kisses over his face and neck, nullifying his ability to make rational decisions. Numbing his resolve.

"Hey, slow down," he told her softly, drawing his head back. A smile played on his lips. Ben stroked her hair, tucking a stray strand behind her ear. Feeling things he'd never felt before, even about the woman he'd married. Gina drew out emotions from him he hadn't thought himself capable of. ''In case you hadn't noticed, I'm a little handicapped here at the moment.''

''Didn't think that would stop you.'' Feeling foolish, she started to get up.

He caught her by the hand. ''Who said anything about stopping?'' Gina sat down on the bed again. ''It'll just slow me down some.'' His eyes grew serious as he searched her face, worried. With everything that had happened, he hadn't taken the time to find out how she was. ''Are you all right?''

The question struck her as almost funny. She pressed her lips together to hold back the sudden surge of hysterical laughter.

''The man who's been stalking me for the last six months, who caused me to uproot and leave behind the best life I'd ever known, has just appeared in my house with murder in his eyes and wielding a gun. No, I am not all right. I am very far from all right.'' She took a deep breath and then let it out again. When she did, she felt marginally calmer. Letting the situation get to her wasn't going to help her deal with it. ''But right now, I don't want to think about anything. Not about him, not about what could happen—''

''Shh,'' Ben soothed, kissing her lips lightly, once, twice, three times, melting her a little more each time. ''Nothing's going to happen, remember? It's going to be all right.''

She smiled against his mouth. ''You promised.''

''I promised.''

Kissing her slowly, deeply, Ben began to undo the buttons on her blouse. The edges sighed apart. Very gently, he slipped his hand in between the material and, ever so softly, caressed her breast. He heard her shuddering breath escape, felt her melt against him as the urgency of her response built.

He made love to her slowly, gently, as if she were made of spun sugar, too sweet to be devoured all at once, too fragile to feel the intensity of his desire. The passion that increased with each movement, each passing second, was not a wild thing. Instead, it was a stable force whose base continued to widen.

Gina felt it welcoming her, absorbing her.

His goal, beyond making love with her, beyond creating pleasure for her, was to make Gina feel safe because he was there with her. Having robbed her of the safety net that was beneath the tightrope she was making her way across, he could at least do that for her. Could make her feel that she wasn't alone. That she wasn't going to be harmed. Because he would never allow anyone to hurt her or her son. Ever.

He was doing just what she wanted, spinning a web so tightly around her that her mind was restricted to the moment, unable to touch the past, the future. Living only within each stroke of the clock.

They undressed each other, shedding clothes as they shed barriers until they were divested of everything except the overwhelming need they felt for each other.

Gina skimmed her hands along his flat, tight belly, her excitement feeding on the feel of hard muscles beneath her fingertips, glorying in the embodiment of power she felt radiating from him. Each kiss built in momentum, taking her closer and closer to the place she wanted to be. She could feel the frenzy growing within her.

She was making him crazy.

Nipping at his skin with her teeth, anointing it with her tongue. Covering his torso with wild, inflaming imprints of her mouth. He could hardly keep up with her and the sensations she generated within him.

Looking at her, he would have never guessed about the tigress who resided within. Gina gave every indication of being a proper lady, one who made you remember your manners even if they had been abandoned at the threshold of youth years ago. Yet now she clawed at him with the wild desperation that was the hallmark of someone who was fleeing something.

She set fire to his very soul.

Catching her wrists with his good hand, he held them above her head. When she looked at him in dazed, wide-eyed wonder, rising to the surface after bathing in a sea of deep, wet, openmouthed kisses, he merely smiled at her.

He could almost read the question in her mind. If he'd let her, she would have easily straddled him, initiating the last leg of the journey. In her present state, it would be over with too soon.

"Let me make a first move on my own," he whispered against her cheek.

Moving his body over hers, he began to do to her what Gina had just done to him. Over and over, he kissed her, her face, her neck, the hollow of her throat, the swell of each breast until she was reduced to a mass of quivering, undulating delectable flesh. And when he could hold himself in check no longer, Ben moved her legs apart with his knee. Gently, watching her eyes, he slid into her, careful not to make the final maneuver anything but the rightful joining of two kindred souls.

He had no details of the fraternity party violation that had resulted in Jesse's conception, but instinct showed him the path to take with her. Gentleness until she began to lead the way toward something else.

And when she did, they began the ever-increasing, frantic pace that would bring them to where they both wanted to be.

The explosion rocked them both. Even as the euphoria that had engulfed them slid back into the shadows, he could still taste her cry in his mouth. She'd called out his name, and that, more than anything else, was responsible for the wild, thundering excitement he'd felt in his veins. He'd been uppermost in her mind even in the throes of her climax.

Slowly, he moved off her, taking care not to crush her beneath his weight. As he fell away, he sucked in his breath. The pain radiated through the right side of his body, traveling in both directions. He struggled to even out his breathing.

She was instantly concerned. Guilt pushed forward. She shouldn't have let this get out of hand. He was hurt. "Your shoulder?"

"Yeah." A half shrug accompanied the acknowledgment. "I kind of forgot about it for a while."

Gina was exquisitely drained and reveling in the feeling, hugging it to her. "I noticed."

She turned her head toward him and discovered that there was no space between them. His face was touching hers. She moved back, but not before absorbing the sensation and taking comfort in it. If she let herself, she could get so accustomed to this. Accustomed to having someone to turn to. Someone beside her for the good moments and bad.

All illusion, a little voice warned silently. But the warm feeling persisted, hanging on.

Feeling her pulse grow steadier, she forced herself to concentrate on something beyond his nearness. "So, what's the plan now?"

He'd already thought this out. It had come to him the instant he saw the gun in McNair's hand. Ben pressed a kiss to her forehead, having no idea how much that small gesture meant to her.

"After I catch my breath, I'm going to make a call to the agency and have one of my partners set wheels in motion to swear out a warrant for McNair." He saw the dubious look on Gina's face. "He drew a gun on you in front of a witness. A witness he wounded." For emphasis, he nodded toward his bandaged shoulder.

Gina worried her lower lip. "Do you think it'll stick?"

"Oh, it'll stick all right." He had no doubts of that. "There's no turning back for him now. He made a fatal mistake and we've got him."

Gina looked toward the window. A single neon light, orange and obtrusive, radiated through the dust-laden drapes. She'd learned not to count her chickens. "Not yet," she whispered.

"But we will." Ben knew the only way she was going to have any peace was when they actually brought McNair in. He sat up, a fresh wave of pain rising up with him. Ben looked around to see where his clothes had ultimately landed. "They have a pay phone in the front office?"

Sitting up, Gina thought a minute. "Yes. Well, not exactly in the front office, but just outside on the side closest to the rooms. I drove past it when I parked the car. You're still not going to use the cell phone?"

He shook his head as he reached for his pants and underwear. Shrugging into the latter, he turned to look at her. Desire slammed into him with the force of an out-of-control freight train. Even the muted light from the dim lamps made her look like a goddess. He wanted to make love with her all over again. But there wasn't time. They had to get going.

"No sense in taking unnecessary chances. McNair has to be pretty desperate by now and he's going to use anything he can to stop us." Stepping into his pants, he rose to his feet and pulled them up over his hips. "Want to come with me?" He didn't like leaving her, not even for a few minutes.

Gina got off the bed and began getting dressed herself. Slipping on her jeans, she closed the snap at her waist and looked over her shoulder at him. She wanted a few minutes alone to sort out her feelings. An hour ago, she'd hated him. Now her life seemed to be in his hands, as well as a few other things as well.

"No, I'll just stay in the room and wait for you." She saw his brow furrow. Was he really worried about her? Or was it just his guilty conscience that prompted his concern? She wished she knew. "It's only a few feet away. I'll be all right."

Zipping up his jacket over his torn shirt, Ben looked dubiously at the lock on the door. Flimsy, it represented the bare minimum as far as protection went. He supposed that it could offer some resistance. Certainly long enough for him to get back to her in the eventuality that something went wrong.

Ben ran his hand along the back of his neck, wishing he could shake this uneasy feeling that was dogging him. There was no reason to think that McNair would actually track them to the motel. It wasn't as if this was the only one in the area. Gina wouldn't have been careless enough to have used a credit card to pay for the room and neither one of them had used the cell phone.

He knew that, like Gina, he wasn't going to relax until McNair was in custody. Although, the last half hour they had come pretty close, he thought with a smile. ‘‘All right, but lock the door after I leave.’’

He *was* worried about her. She still wasn’t sure if it was because he felt guilty about leading McNair to her or because there was something stronger at play.

Gina masked her thoughts with a show of amusement. ‘‘Should we decide on a secret code? Two short raps and one long one?’’

He laughed shortly, relieved that she was taking things well.

‘‘I think my yelling ‘Open up, Gina, it’s me’ should be enough of a clue.’’ About to go out the door, Ben suddenly stopped and doubled back as she looked at him in surprise.

Her surprise melted into pleasure as he caught her by the waist with one hand and pulled her to him, then kissed her on the mouth. Hard.

It took her a second to orient herself and catch her breath. He’d all but made the room fade away. ‘‘What was that for?’’

A slow, sexy smile curved his mouth. ‘‘If you have to ask, then we’re going to have to do the last half hour over when I get back. I obviously didn’t do it right.’’ He looked into her eyes. No, he thought, he couldn’t leave it at that, at a flippant remark. Not when he felt the way he did. She deserved more. ‘‘I’m sorry, Gina.’’

She didn’t have to ask him about what. She understood and nodded. ‘‘I know.’’

He crossed to the door again and opened it. ‘‘I’ll be right back,’’ he promised, stepping over the threshold. ‘‘Don’t open the door to anyone.’’

Following him, she put her hand on the doorknob, ready to close it. This time, her eyes sparkled as she looked at him. "Not even if they huff and they puff and they threaten to blow the room down."

He heard the nerves in her voice and squeezed her hand. "Not even then." He watched her close the door. "I don't hear the lock," he called out to her.

She twisted the metal latch and the tumbler echoed as it caught. "There. Happy?"

"Happy."

Hurrying to the front office, he saw the pay phone on the wall, just as Gina had described. Fishing through his pockets, Ben came up with a handful of change. He laid the coins out on the tiny counter just beneath the phone. Telephone numbers in different handwriting and different-colored ink and pencils surrounded the telephone like a surreal halo.

He glanced at a few as he tapped out the numbers on the keypad that would connect him to the agency. More than a couple promised the caller a good time.

Ben shook his head and wondered how many lonely people were out there. He'd been in their number, he realized, despite his active dating life. Until he'd met Gina.

Gloria, he corrected himself. Her name was Gloria. He wondered if he could get used to calling her that. Then wondered if she'd give him the opportunity to try.

Ben waited as a disembodied voice told him how much money to feed the phone in order to get his call to go through.

Slipping the correct amount into the slot one coin at a time, he listened impatiently to the melodic tones as they registered. Just as he put in the last one, he thought he heard a noise behind him. Gina.

"I thought you said you were going to stay in the room," he began, turning from the phone.

It was the last thing he remembered. Something hard came crashing down on his head.

They were going to have to get something to eat, Gina thought. Maybe they could stop at a fast-food place on their way. Picking up her purse, she rummaged through it, counting her change and the few bills that were there. It was going to have to be a really cheap fast-food place. She was running out of cash.

Gina whirled around at the sound of the glass breaking behind her. Her breath stopped in her throat, clogging the scream.

Stephen was in the room. She turned to run.

Shards of glass crunched beneath his feet as he ran to catch her. Grabbing her by the hair, he yanked her back before she could reach the door.

"Surprised?" he breathed against her.

Tears from the pain radiating from her scalp sprang to her eyes. She clutched the purse against her as if it were protective armor. "How did you...?"

The laugh made her skin crawl.

"I won't bore you with details. Suffice it to say I have ways." Releasing his hold on her hair, he backed away a step. "I've told you that before. You'll never get away from me, Gloria. I've told you that before, too. If I can't have you, no one can."

The look in his eyes left her no doubt about the state of his mind. The gun in his hand was aimed directly at her.

Stall, she had to stall. "Are you going to kill me?"

"Very good," he mocked her. "Yes, but not here." His mouth twisted in a condescending sneer as his eyes swept over the room. "Not in a cheap motel room. If we're to go out in a blaze of glory, I have something a little more dramatic in mind."

She heard only one word. "We?" Was he planning on killing himself as well? *Dammit, Ben, where are you? How long does it take to make a lousy phone call?*

"Of course, 'we.' Surely you don't think I'm going to wait around for some stumbling policeman to make an arrest. And I'm not about to sit in prison, cooling my heels while some overpriced lawyer keeps making appeals that get rejected." He ran the barrel of his pistol against her cheek. "Smile, darling. Your fifteen minutes of fame is about to come up." He saw her eyes dart toward the door. McNair's expression turned malevolent. "He won't be coming to your rescue this time. I've taken care of him."

Anger scissored into her fear. "What did you do to Ben? Did you hurt him?" she demanded, yelling at him.

"I gutted him like a fish."

Shrieking, Gina swung around, her nails extended. She tried to gouge out his eye, but McNair was faster than she was and pulled back. Her nails raked across his face instead.

"You bitch. Turn me down for that two-bit nobody? I'll show you who's the better man." Grabbing her arm, he twisted it behind her back until she almost fell to her knees. Jamming the gun into her back, he pushed her to the door. "Now, we're getting out of here and into my car."

She tried to dig in, but he dragged her with him. "Move, damn you."

"If you kill me now or later, what does it matter?"

"Oh, it matters, Gloria, it matters very much. Trust me, being gut-shot is a particularly painful way to die. Now, move!"

Twisting her arm even harder, he pushed her out the door.

"Mister, hey mister, you all right?"

The reedy voice came out in a burst of stale cigarette breath and beer, forcing Ben into consciousness. The overwhelming pressure on his brow transformed into a headache the moment he opened his eyes. Someone was shaking his shoulder. His bad shoulder.

Pain assaulted him on all fronts.

A thin man with a three-day-old stubble, wearing clothes that looked as if they had been slept in for a week, was bending over him, curiosity more than concern written across his face. Ben realized that he was lying sprawled out on the cracked asphalt just beneath the pay phone.

He touched the top of his head and came in contact with a hell of a bump. The wince was automatic. "What happened?"

Extending a bony hand, the motel clerk helped him to his feet. "I dunno, I was coming out to get some ice and found you lying here."

McNair.

Gina.

Panic seized him instantly. Ben swung around to look toward the motel room where he'd left Gina. The door was hanging open. He cursed roundly at his own stupidity. He should have never left her alone.

Ben turned on the clerk. "Did you see anyone driving off?"

The man jerked his thumb toward the office. "There's a pay-for-view wrestling match on. I shelled out forty bucks to get it. Coulda been the circus passing through here with a whole bunch of damn marching elephants and I wouldn't have noticed.''

''Great, just great,'' Ben spat out in disgust. He hurried back to the room.

''Hey, you ain't gonna sue anybody, are you?'' the clerk called after him. '''Cause it ain't my fault!''

Ben didn't bother answering. Running into the room, he saw the shattered window and the glass on the floor. ''Gina!''

But even as he called her name, he knew she was gone. He swore again as he looked around. It looked as if she'd put up a struggle, he thought. She hadn't gone peacefully, but she had gone. He felt his heart sinking.

Coming up behind him, the clerk peered into the room. ''Damn, but you people sure know how to party.'' He frowned as he saw the glass by the broken window. ''Maybe I should be suing you.''

There had to be a clue, some sort of indication where they were going, Ben thought in desperation. Gina would have tried to leave him a sign of some kind.

If she knew where she was going, he thought angrily. Damn it, what did he do now…?

His cell phone rang in his pocket.

He realized his hands were trembling as he pulled the cell phone out. Ben flipped it open, praying it was Gina. Or even McNair, threatening, gloating. Anything. All he needed to work with was a transmission signal. There was a tracking device in his car, courtesy of Megan.

''Hello?'' No one answered him. ''Hello?'' he repeated. A faint noise crackled in the phone.

''Anybody there…?'' the clerk asked, nosy.

Ben waved him into silence, listening intently. He could make out Gina's voice. She was talking to

McNair. She must have found a way to secretly dial his number on her cell phone and keep the channel open.

A hell of a woman, he thought, racing out to the back of the lot.

The car was there, just as she said it would be.

"Hey, who's going to pay for all that damage in there?" the clerk yelled after him.

Turning on the ignition, Ben spun the car around one hundred and eighty degrees and headed for the street. "I'll mail you a check," he called out.

But first, I've got to find Gina, he added silently, praying that neither her battery nor his gave out before he got to her.

Chapter 21

"Figured it out yet?"

Stephen's face was devoid of any sanity. His mouth was distorted as it twisted into a smile that made Gina's blood run cold. Adrenaline raced through her with no outlet, no course of action open to her. She prayed that Stephen had lied to her, that he hadn't killed Ben.

If he had—

She couldn't think about that now. She had to think of a way to save herself. She couldn't let Jesse become an orphan.

In a voice that was far steadier than she felt, she said, "I've figured out that you're crazy."

Headlights from cars passing in the opposite direction shone into the car, contributing to the dangerous, edgy atmosphere as they played along his face.

"Yes, maybe I am at that. Crazy to let a whore like you become an obsession. But all that's water under the bridge." He spared her a malevolent look. "And very shortly, we will be, too."

Gina contemplated jumping from the car, but Stephen was going too fast. She needed to get him to slow down, to get him so angry that he swerved off the road.

"The reason I became such an obsession to you is because I *wouldn't* become your whore."

McNair flung his fist at her, hitting her across the face with the back of it. Caught by surprise, Gina didn't have time to jerk away. The diamond ring he wore ripped into her cheek. A trickle of blood began to ooze from the gash. Gina pressed her lips together to hold back the cry of pain.

"You became his fast enough, didn't you?" Stephen demanded. "Didn't you?" The accusation echoed inside the car.

"That's because he's twice the man you'll ever be." Stephen grabbed the gun he'd tucked beneath his thigh for easy access and aimed it at her. Bravado pushed words out of her mouth. She wanted to make him blind with rage, it was her only chance. "Go ahead, get it over with. Shoot me," she taunted him. "But that'll spoil your little plan, won't it?"

Dammit, Gina, shut up, Ben ordered silently, listening to the byplay on the cell phone that lay open on the passenger seat next to him. If only there was some way to will his thoughts to her. He wasn't sure how much of a head start McNair had and he was afraid he wouldn't be able to reach them in time to stop whatever it was the man had in mind.

Frustration ate away at him. He couldn't call 911 because he didn't dare break the connection between the two phones. It was the only way he had to track down the other vehicle.

McNair's comment about being underwater soon gave Ben a sickening clue where they were heading. The Golden Gate Bridge. A bridge that had figured so prominently into the suicides of so many people who felt they had come to the end of the line.

The road the other car was following led directly to the bridge. McNair intended to either jump off or somehow drive off the bridge with Gina.

Dammit, he should have killed McNair when he'd had a chance. All he would have needed to do was get to his gun instead of grabbing Gina and running. That was two mistakes he'd made.

Three, he corrected himself. He'd taken the case in the first place.

Sweating profusely, Ben pushed down on the accelerator as far as it would go. The speedometer needle jumped even higher.

Twisting down another street, he passed a police car. Less than two beats later, he'd gained an entourage. Red-and-blue dancing lights flashed demandingly in his rearview mirror.

Now they come, he thought in disgust.

He couldn't stop to talk and explain what was happening. That would eat up too much precious time and they might not believe him without first checking his story out.

Here's hoping San Francisco's finest is an understanding bunch.

The speedometer needle passed eighty.

She could see the Golden Gate Bridge coming up in the distance, ablaze in lights. At night, it was a magnificent sight, like a regal, bejeweled woman going out for an evening on the town. Gina could remember looking out of her dorm window at night and just staring at it. Seeing it there, night after night, had created a peaceful, reassuring feeling.

Now the sight of it sharpened the fear that was carving away at her.

She looked at Stephen's rigid profile. She had to find a way to stall for time. This would all resolve itself well if she could just stall long enough, she thought frantically, praying that for once her optimism wasn't unwarranted.

"Why don't you pull over?"

The look McNair gave her was demeaning. "So you can offer yourself to me in hopes that I'll forget about all this?" Stephen sneered. "Too late, Gloria, you should have thought about that sooner. Much sooner." His voice took on ranting tones. "I could have made you a queen. You and that brat of yours would have never wanted for anything. But you had to throw it all away, make a laughingstock out of me."

They'd reached the foot of the bridge. Gina's heart sank. At this time of the evening, the rush-hour traffic had all but disappeared. Traffic itself had thinned out. There was no one blocking their way, no one to slow his progress.

It was all up to her.

"No one was laughing at you, Stephen. No one even knew about me." Her mind was blank. She had nothing to draw on. "You need help, Stephen. You need to see a doctor."

"See a doctor? How dare you? How *dare* you?" He grabbed her arm, holding her in place in case she had any thoughts about jumping out of the car. He wasn't going to allow her to ruin this, too. "What I need is to see you dead."

A faint buzz in the distance transformed into something discernible as it drew closer. He stopped talking and listened.

Sirens.

The air turned ripe with his curses. Gunning the engine, McNair swerved around two vehicles and headed for the center of the bridge. The sirens grew in volume, in number. Coming to a screeching halt, the car fishtailed. He ignored it, ignored everything but the urgency to carry out his plan.

One hand holding his weapon, Stephen grabbed Gina's arm again and yanked her over the hand brake, dragging her into the driver's side.

"C'mon, c'mon," he said, pulling on her arm, "there isn't much time."

She tried to grab on to something to keep from being pulled out, but Stephen was too strong for her. He dragged her out of the car. No sooner was she out than he released her arm and grabbed hold of her waist. He half carried, half dragged her with him as he backed up to the side of the bridge, holding the gun to her all the while.

He indicated the railing. There was nothing on the other side but a tiny ledge. Beyond that was the ocean, its surface a choppy black.

"Climb, damn you, climb."

"No!" she screamed, bracing her hands against the railing to keep him from forcing her over it. "If you're going to do it, do it here! I'm not going to go through this charade with you! You're a self-centered, deluded, pathetic excuse for a human being."

"Shut up! Shut that foul mouth of yours!" Beside himself with rage, sputtering like a rabid dog, McNair raised the gun to her temple.

The sound of a gun discharging resounded in the night air, a macabre sound echoing over and over.

Braced for the shattering pain, Gina was numbed when it didn't overtake her. Instead, she felt McNair's hand loosen from around her waist, felt the friction as he began to slide down against her back.

A silent scream ricocheted in her throat as she stumbled away from him.

"God dammit, you've killed me." The accusation gurgled out of Stephen's mouth even as blood trickled from the corners. He sank down the rest of the way, a nonthreatening heap at Gina's feet.

Colors, voices, people were all coming at her at once, blending in eerily with the sound of sirens in the background.

Someone was holding her.

The scent of the cologne peeled away the numbness that had clamped its jaws around her.

Ben.

"Ben!" She sobbed his name before she could even focus.

"It's me, baby, it's me." Covering her face with kisses, he picked her up in his arms, cradling her against him.

Which was a good thing, because her legs had suddenly gotten too weak to support her. "Your arm," she protested feebly.

He'd shifted most of her weight toward his good arm. "Shh, it's my turn to play nurse."

"He told me he killed you," she sobbed.

He kissed the top of her head. "No, he just gave me one king-size headache."

It was only then that she began to make out people,

words. There were squad cars and police patrolmen all around them.

He'd come in to save her just like the cavalry, she thought giddily. No, like a white knight. "How did you...?"

He didn't want her to talk. He wanted her to save her strength. When he'd seen McNair holding the gun to her head, the whole world had frozen. He hardly remembered pulling out his own weapon and firing. He just remembered the prayer that had crossed his mind. The one that had guided his aim.

"Ran every light from there to here. The police just kind of came along for the ride." He looked at her face as one of the patrolmen moved past him to examine McNair. He'd never seen another living person look as pale as Gina. Except for the welt on her cheek. McNair had done that. Ben struggled to hold on to the threads of his temper. "Are you all right?"

She sighed and leaned her face against his shoulder. "I am now."

A stocky policeman made his way to the center of all the activity. It was clear that he was in charge. "Someone want to tell me what the hell's going on here?" he demanded.

"Well, one thing's for damn sure. It ain't going to be him." The policeman examining McNair rose to his feet, dusting off his hands. "He's ready for a body bag and a date with the coroner."

The stocky policeman turned to Ben. "Then I guess it's going to have to be you."

"With pleasure," Ben replied. He looked at Gina and smiled at her. It was over. Her ordeal was finally over. "As soon as you get a paramedic to take a look at the lady."

* * *

"I can't believe it's all finally over," Gina murmured three hours later.

Leaning her head against the car headrest, she sighed. It felt as if she'd lived an entire lifetime in the last few hours. After the paramedics had seen to the cut on her face and assured Ben that she was all right, she and Ben had given their statements at length several times over to a parade of police personnel, beginning with the patrolmen at the scene and ending with two detectives at the precinct where they were taken. Once Ben's identity and former connection to the Bedford police, as well as his present position with ChildFinders, Inc. were verified, things went a great deal more smoothly.

The detectives had told them it appeared to be an open-and-shut case. Gina had clung to the word *shut.*

They were going back to Kyle's house to pick up Jesse. She and Ben were going to have to be available to the police for at least the next few days in case there were any further questions. But after that, she was free.

Free.

Ben looked at her as he came to a light. He wouldn't have exactly phrased it that way. It wasn't over, at least not yet. "This is going to be all over the front page of the newspaper and the lead story on the six o'clock news for weeks to come, you know that, don't you? A man like Stephen McNair doesn't go quietly."

She thought of the way the man had died, the way he had intended to end it if Ben hadn't arrived in the nick of time.

"No, he certainly saw to that," she answered wryly.

He was still thinking of the news media. He knew how relentless they could be in their quest for a story.

There was no reason for her to have to go through that. He didn't want her to.

"I could find somewhere for you to stay for a while, until it blows over."

"That sounds like heaven. But I'm through hiding. Through putting my life on hold. It's about time I got back to living."

After everything that had happened, he'd been afraid that she would turn into a recluse, afraid to venture out. He'd seen it happen.

"Where?"

She didn't even have to stop to think. "Back in Bedford." That was where home was for her. In Bedford where her career looked as if it was finally going to take wing. Where her friends lived. Where Ben lived.

He hadn't realized he'd been holding his breath until she said that. Relief flooded over him. "As Gloria Prescott?"

"That's my name." Although she'd gotten accustomed to hearing him call her Gina.

He was trying to read between the lines and not give off any unintentional signals that would have her backing away. "So it'll be business as usual?"

Gina laughed softly, surprised she had enough energy for that. "As usual as it can be, given the circumstances."

He felt his way around cautiously. "You might need someone to run interference for you, at least in the beginning."

She picked up something in his tone. Something that heartened her. Not everything about the last several hours had been bad.

"That sounds like a good idea." Gina turned in her

seat to look at him. The seat belt dug into her shoulder. "Do you have anyone in mind?"

"I might." There was a diner just up ahead on the corner. He didn't want to keep glancing at her in small snatches. He wanted to look into her face, her eyes, as they talked. "Want to pull over for some coffee? We could discuss this."

"That sounds good to me."

The diner had seen better days, but everything within it had been scrubbed clean and it was neat. There was a faint scent of disinfectant mixing with the aroma of rich coffee and freshly baked apple pie. Gina had said yes to the coffee and passed on the pie. The knot in her stomach had yet to come undone.

She waited until the waitress's shoes were no longer audible, then set down the coffee cup she'd been nursing. Her eyes met Ben's.

"So, what is it you wanted to talk about?"

He felt like a singer about to kick off a baseball game by singing the national anthem only to realize that he'd forgotten the words. Ben searched for a way to begin.

All he had to do was think of the last few hours and how they could have turned out differently and he knew what to say. "I'm sorry, Gina. So sorry that I put you all through this."

They were sitting in a booth. She glanced at their reflection in the window. They made some pair, he with his shoulder wound, she with the bandage on her face. She covered his hand with hers, making a silent covenant. "You saved my life, so we're even."

Ben shook his head. That wasn't the way he saw it. "No, no, we're not. Because you saved mine, so we're back to being uneven."

"And you don't like that." She could tell by the way he phrased it.

Turning his hand up, he took her hand in his. "I don't like being beholden, no."

Something inside her began to shrink away. Was he trying to give her some kind of message, put her on notice? "Is that all it would be, a payment of a debt? Erasing a balance on some nebulous balance sheet of debits and credits?"

Where had she gotten that from? "No. You know better than that."

"Do I? Maybe you should tell me. Tell me exactly what there was between us."

Was. He didn't like the word. It made it sound as if it was all over. The passion, the desire, everything, over. In the past.

Well, wasn't it? McNair was dead, she didn't need him to protect her from the man any longer. Protect her from the man he'd led to her door in the first place, Ben reminded himself ruefully.

"It was wonderful" he said quietly, taking her hand again. "At least it was for me."

She bit her lower lip as she looked at him. "It was for me, too."

Then maybe, just maybe, it didn't have to be relegated to the past. Maybe it could be in the present as well. And the future. "Then there's no reason that it couldn't continue to be, is there?"

Gina looked at him for a long moment. No, she wasn't going to allow herself to read things into his words, wasn't going to take a single thing for granted. She wanted him to spell it all out for her.

"My head's been rattled around tonight, Ben. You're

going to have to be clearer than that for me. What are you saying?''

"I'm saying that I don't want this to end when I bring you and Jesse—Andrew—finally back to Bedford.'' He realized he was taking things for granted, that he would be the one to help them with the transition, but he pushed on, anyway. "That I don't want it to end because your name's not Gina anymore.''

She cocked her head slightly, like a bird listening to the wind whisper a love song through the leaves. ''So you want to what, start dating?''

The question made him laugh. It was a deep, rich sound that surrounded her. That made her feel safe. ''I think we're past that point.''

Without saying she agreed, she put another question to him. ''What point haven't we passed?''

Okay, this was where he went for broke, he decided. He'd thought about it and it felt right. The moment he'd thought about it, he knew it was what he wanted to do. ''The point where I get down on one knee and ask you to marry me.''

Her mouth dropped open. She'd expected him to haltingly suggest living together. She would have settled for that. ''What?''

Instead of answering, Ben slid out of the booth, still holding her hand, and got down on one knee. ''I love you and I want you to marry me. I want to give you and your son a new last name, so that no matter what first names you decide to go by, I'll always know how to find you.''

''You already know how to find me.'' The tears were making it hard to see. She blinked them back, wishing she wasn't so emotional. She didn't want him to think she cried over everything. ''I'll be the woman right beside you. Always.''

He rose to his feet, bringing her up with him. ''So what do I call you?''

She hadn't realized, until this very moment, just how much she loved this man that deception had brought into her life. She supposed, in a way, she had Stephen to thank for that. ''How does 'darling' sound?''

''Darling,'' Ben repeated, grinning. ''Has a nice ring to it.''

The grin disappeared as he kissed her.

* * * * *

Look for A HERO IN HER EYES,
Marie Ferrarella's next book in the exciting
CHILDFINDERS, INC. *series,*
available in February 2001 from
Silhouette Intimate Moments.

#1 *New York Times* bestselling author

NORA ROBERTS

brings you more of the loyal and loving, tempestuous and tantalizing Stanislaski family.

Coming in February 2001

The Stanislaski Sisters

Natasha and Rachel

Though raised in the Old World traditions of their family, fiery Natasha Stanislaski and cool, classy Rachel Stanislaski are ready for a *new* world of love....

And also available in February 2001 from Silhouette Special Edition, the newest book in the heartwarming Stanislaski saga

CONSIDERING KATE

Natasha and Spencer Kimball's daughter Kate turns her back on old dreams and returns to her hometown, where she finds the *man* of her dreams.

Available at your favorite retail outlet.

Silhouette®

Where love comes alive™

Visit Silhouette at www.eHarlequin.com

PSSTANSIS

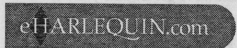

Silhouette® —

where love comes alive—online...

eHARLEQUIN.com

your romantic escapes

Indulgences

- Monthly guides to indulging yourself, such as:
  - ★ Tub Time: A guide for bathing beauties
  - ★ Magic Massages: A treat for tired feet

Horoscopes

- Find your daily Passionscope, weekly Lovescopes and Erotiscopes
- Try our compatibility game

Reel Love

- Read all the latest romantic movie reviews

Royal Romance

- Get the latest scoop on your favorite royal romances

Romantic Travel

- For the most romantic destinations, hotels and travel activities

SINTE1